THE EDGE

With the Executioner, there were no such things as half measures or limitations. He went head to head with the enemy each time he stepped into the killing grounds, asking no quarter and giving none, taking the slim odds of survival as nothing more than business as usual.

A brush with death was more the rule than the exception for Bolan, and he wouldn't have it any other way. The Man from Blood thrived on the challenges that came when one chose the hard course, chose to push life to the edge, to ride that adrenaline-charged rush of combat for all it was worth.

Once a warrior had experienced the Edge, he could never be the same. To know that frenzied uncertainty, the realization that every move counted, was something that clung to a man no matter how much he removed himself from the war front. For Bolan, his missions amounted to more than doing good and playing a high-stakes game of Beat the Reaper.

The fact that there were men out there who escaped justice every day troubled him greatly. He made allowances for flaws in the system, but kept an eye on those who would slip through the cracks. And pursuing such a life, Bolan knew, would always keep him at the Edge.

DON PENDLETON's

MACK BOLAN®

FIREPOWER

A GOLD EAGLE BOOK FROM

WORLDWIDE®

TORONTO • NEW YORK • LONDON • PARIS
AMSTERDAM • STOCKHOLM • HAMBURG
ATHENS • MILAN • TOKYO • SYDNEY

First edition March 1992

ISBN 0-373-61426-8

Special thanks and acknowledgment to
Ron Renauld for his contribution to this work.

FIREPOWER

Printed in U.S.A.

However formidable a given foe, they can be met with the hope of victory so long as one's own force is loyal and committed to its cause. So fear not the enemy without, but be ever wary of the more perilous adversary... the enemy within.
—General Kent Rembo, *Strategies of War*

I am as committed to my cause as the enemy is to his. Only time will choose the victor.
—Mack Bolan

CHAPTER ONE

A semitruck rolled through the dark countryside outside Tucson. The vehicle was headed westbound on a long, grueling backroads course federally mandated to keep it and its five sealed drums of radioactive wastes away from major population centers during its long trek from the Reed-Blackpoint Enterprises plant in Tucson to southern California.

The wastes were by-products of Blackpoint's computer-console-manufacturing operations and constituted only a small part of the truck's load. The drums would be unloaded at the Federal Radioactive Waste facility in La Paz County, after which the semi would continue to San Diego with the rest of its cargo, seventeen massive crates of computerized radar-tracking equipment earmarked for export to clients in Saudi Arabia.

Originally designed as components in missile-guidance systems for the Air Force, the gear had been stripped of all military applications and modified for use in flight monitoring at commercial airports. The project was but one of several similar enterprises initiated by Reed-Blackpoint, which was fast gaining a reputation as a role model for defense-oriented manufacturers working to manage the transition from Cold

War military output to peacetime production without a significant disruption of either the corporation's work force or profit margin.

There was little activity on the road at this late hour. It had been more than ten minutes since the truck had encountered another vehicle traveling in either direction. As it rolled past groves of trees and wide stretches of rolling farmland, the truck's headlights occasionally bounced off billboards or the wide eyes of possums roaming the road's shoulder.

Inside the cab, driver Billy Ruff battled fatigue by swilling hot coffee from a thermos and singing along with country music blaring on a dashboard radio. Ruff's cheek was padded with a chaw of tobacco, and every few miles he'd lean to his left and spit a brown stream out the open window.

"Will ya plant yer two lips on my lips?" he howled with romantic longing after ridding himself of another bitter mouthful. "Will ya dig to the roots of my soul?"

Shortly after crossing the Maricopa County line, Ruff rounded a bend and suddenly stopped singing. "Whoa, Nellie," he muttered as he put on the brakes.

Up ahead, a dark blue Trans Am and a black Buick blocked the intersection, their mangled front ends still entwined from an apparent collision. The pavement was littered with shards of glass and broken plastic from shattered headlights, but there was no sign of blood and both windshields were still intact. Ruff doubted there'd been any fatalities.

A bronze-skinned man in a flannel shirt stepped clear of the wrecked vehicles and waved as he approached the semi, limping slightly. He squinted against the glare of headlights. Behind him, a woman sat on the ground next to the Buick, her head resting against her bent knees.

Ruff slowed to a stop and left the engine running as he opened the cab door. "Everyone all right?" he called.

The man on the asphalt nodded. "Yeah, just a fender bender."

Ruff took a closer look at the man. He looked to be in his midthirties, with thick eyebrows that seemed to run together when he frowned. The trucker guessed the man was Indian, either Natchapo or Hopi, and he thought the guy looked familiar. "Hey, don't I know you?"

"No, I don't think so."

"Are you sure?" Ruff persisted. "Do you work for Reed-Blackpoint back in Tucson?"

The other man shook his head.

Ruff glanced past the man, eyeing the woman on the ground. "What about her? Is she hurt?"

"Just a little shook up, that's all."

"I got my CB," Ruff volunteered. "How about I call the—"

"No, no, please," the other man said hastily. "No cops. We want to square this away without dragging in the insurance people."

"Well, all right," Ruff replied warily. "Gonna have to do something about these cars, though."

The man nodded. Gesturing back at the cars, he said, "If you could just help me unlock our front ends, we can get out of your way."

Ruff could see that there was no way for him to get his rig past the cars as long as they were clogging the intersection. Climbing down to the asphalt, he spit tobacco juice to one side and rolled up his sleeves. "Okay, let's see what we can do."

The woman stood as the men approached the cars. "Thanks for helping," she told Ruff.

"Used to be a Boy Scout," the trucker drawled modestly. "This is my good deed for the day."

Introductions were quickly exchanged. The Indian's name was Ellis, and the woman called herself Michaelea. Both of their cars had sustained considerable damage, but the woman's Buick looked the worse for wear. Its front hood was jammed half-open, and fluid ripped from either a puncture in the radiator or a dislodged water hose.

"I was thinking she should get in her car while you and I rock the front end," Ellis told Ruff. "We might be able to bounce her bumper out from under mine."

The trucker bobbed his head. "Yeah, that might work. Let's give it a shot."

The woman got in behind the wheel of her Buick as the two men began applying their weight to the front fenders. The bumpers shrieked and squealed from the chafing of raw metal against metal. When Michaelea turned the key in the ignition, her engine groaned dully and refused to turn over.

"Damn!" Ellis swore.

"I was afraid of that," Ruff said, shaking his head. He pushed down on the car's shocks again. "I think we can still work her loose, though. It'll just take a little longer than we thought."

Ruff told the woman to put the car in neutral and then get out of the car. As she did so, the men resumed rocking the Buick's front end.

Preoccupied with his mission of mercy, Ruff had his back turned to his rig and didn't notice when a lone figure slipped out from behind a row of hedges lining the road and circled to the back of the trailer.

Cal Ovitz was a tall, athletic man dressed in black. A navy blue ski mask was pulled down over his face. Climbing onto the ICC bumper, he leaned his weight against the trailer doors and removed a lock pick from his sweats. Placing a penflash between his teeth, he directed a thin beam of light onto the padlock securing the doors and went to work. In a matter of seconds the tumblers clicked, and the lock parted in the man's hands. He pulled it off the hasp and carefully opened the door.

"Bingo."

Holding one hand out into the night, the man snapped his fingers twice. Moments later another figure emerged from the shadows. Marlowe Tompkins had a heavier build than Ovitz but was similarly dressed. He was carrying a box, which he passed up to Ovitz, who dragged it inside the trailer.

"Okay, let's move it—quick!" Ovitz ordered as Tompkins climbed aboard.

There were a row of small lights providing faint illumination inside the trailer. Leaving the doors slightly ajar, the two men carried the box past the waste drums, which were anchored to floor mounts with thick steel cables. They paused momentarily as Tompkins removed something from his pocket and pressed it against one of the middle drums. Then they proceeded to the front, where the crates with the radar gear were stacked on wooden skids.

The men put down the box they'd brought aboard. Ovitz shone his penflash on one of the crates while Tompkins pulled a small crowbar from his pant pocket and pried the lid off, revealing thick wads of a foam-like packing material blanketing the equipment. The men removed several pieces of the padding to make room for the smaller box.

"Perfect," Ovitz said as they fitted the box inside the crate, then began to put the lid back on.

"Not quite," said a voice to their rear.

The men turned, startled.

Mack Bolan stepped out from behind two of the loaded skids, holding his Beretta 93-R in one hand and a high-powered flashlight in the other. "Step back," he advised as he moved forward, shining the light in their faces. "Reach for your guns and I drop you both."

The newcomer clearly meant it. Dark-haired and leather-jacketed, his intense blue eyes drilled into the masked men, who slowly moved away from the opened crate.

"Look," Ovitz began to explain, "we can—"

"Forget it," Bolan interrupted.

Keeping his Beretta trained on the men, the Executioner propped his flashlight on one of the crates, directing its beam at the box that had been brought aboard. Raising the lid, he confirmed his suspicions. The box contained circuit boards and an assortment of other electronic components.

"Let me guess," Bolan said, glancing back at Ovitz and Tompkins. "Plug these into the radar equipment, and you're back to having missile-guidance systems, right?"

"I don't know what you're talking about," Tompkins protested.

"Oh, I think you do." Raising a walkie-talkie to his mouth, Bolan said, "Ground to Skeeter. Come in."

"Skeeter to Ground," came the tinny reply over the communicator's small speakers.

"Bring the gift wrap," the warrior instructed. "We got 'em."

"I wouldn't be so sure about that," the taller man said as Bolan lowered the walkie-talkie.

"Oh?"

"Apparently you didn't notice," Ovitz announced matter-of-factly, "but we slapped a plastic explosive on one of the waste drums behind us."

"Sure you did." Bolan sounded skeptical, but a glimmer of concern flashed in his eyes as he glanced past the men. In the dim glow of the overhead lights it was difficult to make out the drums, but he thought he could detect a slight protuberance near the base of the middle receptacle.

"It's rigged to a remote detonator," Ovitz explained. "We're wired, so our driver knows there's been a little problem. If it isn't solved, he's going to push a button and we'll all end up in the next county."

Bolan thought there was still a chance Ovitz was lying. He'd dealt with his share of self-destructive enemies, and his gut feeling was that neither of his prisoners harbored a kamikaze's death wish. But given the potential threat of a radioactive-waste explosion, he knew he couldn't call their bluff. Still, he kept his Beretta trained on the men. "So what are you saying?" he asked, trying to buy time. "You were expecting to be caught?"

"Not exactly," Tompkins replied, "but we always like to leave ourselves an out."

"Sounds like a pretty final out."

Ovitz shrugged. "We all gotta go sometime. It's your call."

Tompkins put it more clearly. "Hand the gun over."

Ovitz sensed Bolan's hesitation. "So what's it gonna be?" he asked with a twisted grin. "You gonna put that popgun aside and let us go, or does our man push a button and turn us all into radioactive toast?"

BILLY RUFF GAVE one last push on the front end of Michaelea's vehicle, finally disengaging it from the other car. He and Ellis rolled the Buick clear, then called out for the woman to get back in and steer so that they could guide the disabled vehicle off the road. As they did so, Ruff heard the drone of an approaching helicopter in the distance. Because there'd been suspicions that Ruff might be involved in the plot to tamper with the radar shipment, he hadn't been advised of Bolan's presence in the back of his truck or any other additional security measures, and this latest development caught him by surprise.

"Hmm," he wondered aloud. "Who could that be?"

The chopper's lights came into view above the tree-tops a few hundred yards away. Ellis realized it was headed for the intersection, which wasn't a good sign. He broke away from the Buick and reached into his coat, withdrawing with a .357 Magnum. Pointing it at the trucker's face, he bellowed, "Hands up!"

"Huh?"

When he found himself staring down a gun barrel, Ruff inadvertently swallowed his tobacco chaw. It lodged in his throat, and he suddenly doubled over, coughing the wad up. Ellis thought the trucker was going for a gun. He pulled the trigger, pumping two shots into the man's chest.

Ruff righted himself and stared at Ellis in disbelief. His hand went to his chest, coming away with blood. When he opened his mouth to speak, more blood bubbled up with tobacco juice and trickled out between his lips. Ruff's last words died in his throat as Ellis rushed forward and propped him up, crying out to Michaelea, "Get in the other car!"

By now the chopper was closing in on the intersection, raking the roadway with a bright swath of light from its nose-mounted spot. Ellis continued to hold up the trucker, pressing his gun to Ruff's head as if he were still alive and therefore a visible hostage. With considerable difficulty he jockeyed the corpse toward the Trans Am as Michaelea got behind the wheel and keyed the ignition. When they'd staged their collision, Ellis had taken care to make sure the Pontiac remained operable. The engine roared to life. As soon as Ellis dragged Ruff into the back seat, the woman floored the accelerator and they sped off.

"Skeeter to Ground," Jack Grimaldi's voice crackled over Bolan's walkie-talkie inside the truck. "Got a couple of runaways with a hostage. We're in pursuit."

Bolan heard the chopper trailing away from the intersection. He considered keying the microphone and reporting a problem in the truck, but decided against it. There wasn't much Grimaldi could do, anyway.

"Make up your mind, pal," Tompkins pressed. "You gonna play hero and get us all killed, or are you gonna be smart?"

Slowly Bolan set his gun on the nearest crate, along with the walkie-talkie.

"Smart man," Tompkins said, taking the warrior's gun.

Ovitz moved forward and took the walkie-talkie, snapping off its antenna and ripping out its battery pack. He opened his coat and glanced down for a moment, directing his voice at the small microphone concealed inside his sweats. "Get your wheels over here, quick!"

Bolan noted the tension in Ovitz's voice and took hope. There was nothing like frustration and impatience to cloud a man's judgment. Now if only the other man would become rattled, as well.

"You really didn't have to bother with the masks," he said calmly, trying to hit a nerve. "We know who you are and who you're working for."

"That so?" Tompkins said with a casual smirk. "I doubt it."

"Suit yourself."

"You know what, pal?" Ovitz rasped. He pulled out a Browning automatic and pointed it at Bolan's chest. "You talk too much."

Ovitz pulled the trigger. The Browning had no silencer, and the shot thundered loudly in the close confines of the van. Bolan reeled with the impact of a 9 mm parabellum, spinning sideways and crumpling like a puppet whose strings had just been severed. His head struck the edge of one of the crates, opening a gash that spilled blood down his face as he sprawled limply to the floor. The flashlight had been knocked loose by the fall, and it shattered when it hit the floor, plunging the interior into relative darkness.

"What did you do that for?" Tompkins cried at Ovitz as he fished for his penflash.

"He was asking for it. Let's get out of here."

"What about the explosives?"

"Leave 'em," Ovitz said as they scrambled past the waste drums for the exit. "We'll set 'em off once we're clear."

The chopper was barely visible in the distance as the two men rushed out of the truck and jumped to the ground. Twin beams of light shone around the bend, then a pair of headlights came into view as a 1969 Mustang took the corner wide, nearly spinning out of control before the rear wheels found traction and pulled the car back on course.

Behind the wheel was Al Blyford, like Ellis Hayes a full-blooded Natchapo Indian with long black hair and bronze skin. He was wearing a tan suede jacket with tasseled fringe. A well-worn .38-caliber pistol rested on his lap. As he braked the Mustang alongside the truck and waited for the masked men to pile in, he flicked a cigarette out the window and eyed the disabled Buick.

"Nice wreck," he murmured.

"Get us out of here," Tompkins ordered, yanking off his ski mask as he slid into the back seat and slammed the door. Ovitz crawled into the front.

Blyford floored the Mustang. The souped-up V-8 engine responded with a fierce jolt, and with a screech of tortured rubber the car lunged off into the night, leaving Bolan and the abandoned semi behind.

Ovitz shed his mask and helped himself to one of his driver's cigarettes. After drawing his lungs full of smoke, he exhaled and glanced back, meeting his partner's baleful gaze. "Come on, you know he had it coming."

"You lost your cool. That's all I know."

"Hey, you didn't believe him, did you? About knowing us?"

Tompkins shook his head. "No. If they had anything on us, they wouldn't have bothered setting a trap."

"That's what I figure, too," Blyford interjected, pointing at the transceiver mounted under his dashboard. "From what I heard he was bluffing all the way."

"I hope so," Ovitz muttered, taking another drag on his cigarette.

Tompkins changed the subject. "What about Ellis and Michaelea?" he asked Blyford. "Did you see which way they went?"

"North," Blyford replied. "Trying for the interstate, no doubt. Had a chopper on their ass."

"We heard," Tompkins said. "Let's hope they get away."

Ovitz opened the glove compartment and took out a remote detonating device. He stubbed out his cigarette, then pried off the safety. "In the meantime let's give the authorities something else besides us to worry about."

"Good idea," Tompkins agreed.

Blyford frowned. "Wait," he said. "Are you sure we're far enough away?"

"Positive." Blowing a thin cloud of smoke, Ovitz slowly pressed the button.

CHAPTER TWO

Riding beside Jack Grimaldi in the lightweight two-seat chopper was John "Cowboy" Kissinger, Stony Man Farm's armament expert. A pair of binoculars dangled from a strap around his neck, and cradled in his hands was a high-powered Ruger rifle with a mounted infrared scope.

Grimaldi keyed the transceiver mike. "Skeeter to Ground. Do you read?"

Still there was no answer. The Stony Man flyer put the microphone back, worry etching his hard face.

"Must have his hands full," Kissinger ventured.

"Yeah," Grimaldi said with little conviction. He didn't like the way this mission had gone down, but there wasn't a hell of a lot he could do about it. His task was to stick with the getaway car. Like it or not, Bolan was on his own.

"Are we going to be able to keep up with them?" Kissinger asked, watching the Trans Am race along the two-lane tarmac below.

"Piece of cake. With that hostage, though, I want to hang back a little. Rattle 'em too much and they might get trigger-happy."

"Maybe I'm wrong," Kissinger said, "but it looked to me like they'd already shot the guy before they dragged him into the car."

"Oh, yeah? Maybe we better take a closer look."

Using his free hand, Grimaldi shifted the spotlight's bright beam on the vehicle below them. Kissinger raised the binoculars and focused on the back windshield.

"Too much glare," he said. "Kill the spot and pull alongside. I'll try the scope."

Grimaldi switched off the beam and accelerated the chopper as Kissinger swung open the side door. He aimed the rifle at the Pontiac and peered through the ocular lens of the gun's sights.

"Still can't quite make 'em out. How about if—"

Kissinger's voice was drowned out by a sudden explosion back near the intersection. Reverberating shock waves jostled the chopper slightly. Glancing back, Kissinger saw a bright flash of light rising above the treetops.

"What the hell?" Grimaldi exclaimed, cutting speed as he concentrated on stabilizing the aircraft. "Was that the truck?"

Kissinger went to his binoculars again and tried to pinpoint the location of the blast. "I can't make it out. It's on the other side of the tree line."

"Should we double back?"

There was no need for Kissinger to answer, and both men fell grimly silent. They knew there was nothing to be gained by retreating at this point. It was a safe bet the semi had taken some kind of hit, and given the size of the explosion, it was equally likely that Bolan had been caught in the middle of it. What was more, if the blast had taken place inside the truck, the site would be contaminated with radioactive waste. One thing was certain—there was nothing they could do for Bolan now...except stick with the Trans Am. With any luck they could at least exact some retribution on the big guy's behalf.

"They'll pay," Grimaldi vowed, breaking the silence as he resumed chasing the Pontiac.

"Damn right," Kissinger seconded, forsaking the binoculars once more in favor of the rifle.

They were still flying over open country, but up ahead the two men could see a ribbon of lights marking the interstate. The last thing they wanted was to have the chase drag out into a highway full of innocent bystanders. By the same token, however, they didn't want their thirst for vengeance to come at the expense of the man being held hostage.

"I can try taking out a tire," Kissinger suggested as Grimaldi gained on the Trans Am.

"Too risky. They're going at least eighty miles an hour. A blowout would somersault them into the rocks."

"Well, we have to do something."

Less than a mile later the fleeing suspects tipped off Grimaldi and Kissinger as to the condition of hostage Billy Ruff. As the Trans Am rounded a curve leading to the interstate, the trucker's body was shoved out of the moving vehicle, leaving streaks of blood as it bounced and cartwheeled along the pavement. It finally came to rest amid sand and cinders on the road's shoulder.

"That does it," Grimaldi snarled. "Let's get them!"

As he closed the gap between the chopper and the Trans Am, a window opened inside the vehicle and Ellis leaned out, taking aim with his .357. Grimaldi banked sharply as the gun fired, a round cutting dangerously close to the bird's main rotor. Kissinger had the rifle ready but knew that in all the commotion he'd just be wasting ammunition if he fired at this point.

"Let's try heading them off," Cowboy suggested.

"Gotcha." Grimaldi pushed the chopper's turbines for all they were worth. When he'd pulled a hundred yards ahead of the Trans Am, he suddenly brought the chopper to within ten feet of the roadway and swung the craft around so that it was facing the oncoming Pontiac. Sand and gravel flew in all directions under the force of the chopper's rotor wash.

"Give me another half turn so I can get a crack at them," Kissinger said, raising the Ruger to firing position.

"First let me try to take them alive. They've got some talking to do."

"Leave it to you to be reasonable," Kissinger grumbled, lowering his rifle.

Grimaldi waited until the Pontiac had halved the distance between them, then abruptly toggled the spotlight and aimed its harsh glare at the Trans Am's windshield.

Inside the car, Michaelea raised one hand to ward off the light, but her reaction was too late. Blinded by the spot, she let out a scream and lost control of the vehicle. Ellis leaned over, clawing at the steering wheel, but he couldn't prevent the Trans Am from swerving wildly across the dividing line. When Michaelea panicked further and put her foot on the brakes, the Pontiac spun off the road and slammed sideways into a guard-rail.

The car vaulted into the air, flipping onto its side before smashing, rear end first, into a ditch strewed with boulders. The car's momentum carried it across the rocky surface with a shattering of glass and the dull crunch of yielding metal. By the time the Pontiac finally came to a rest, one of the headlights was shattered. The other shone into the night like a Hollywood spotlight at a movie premiere.

Grimaldi quickly landed the chopper in a flat clearing on the other side of the road. He left the rotors running as he bounded out with Kissinger, pulling a Government Model .45 from his shoulder holster. It didn't seem likely that anyone in the car would be capable of making a run for it, but they weren't going to take any chances.

As they crossed the road, Grimaldi slowed down and held an arm out to warn his comrade back. "Gas leak," he said, sniffing the air.

The two men stopped near an intact section of guardrail and peered down into the ditch. The Trans Am's engine had stalled during the crash, but the starter was still on, and both men could hear the battery sparking beneath the hood. One twisted wiper was swishing eerily back and forth across the windshield at an angle that forced the metal arm to scrape against the glass. Upon closer inspection, Grimaldi saw Ellis slumped against Michaelea inside the vehicle, pinning her against the driver's door. He looked dead, but the woman was conscious and frantically reaching around him, trying to turn the engine off. However, the steering column had apparently collapsed in such a way that she couldn't move the key.

Grimaldi rose and swung a leg over the guardrail. "I'm going to—"

"No way!" Kissinger intervened, grabbing the pilot. Pulled off balance, the pilot toppled backward, landing on Cowboy at virtually the same instant one of the sparks ignited gas fumes in the engine compartment of the Trans Am. A loud blast rocked the night, followed quickly by a second, even louder discharge from the ruptured gas tank.

Bits of metal, flesh and fabric flew up past the guardrail and landed on the road, some of it still in flames. As they slowly rose to their feet, Kissinger and Grimaldi could hear the crack and sizzle of fire devouring the Pontiac.

"You all right?" Kissinger asked.

"A lot better than if you hadn't tackled me. So much for getting some answers out of them."

Downhill, the Pontiac had been reduced to a charred and twisted hulk of metal. There was no way its occupants would ever answer a question again. In fact, it would be nothing short of miraculous if forensic specialists could piece together enough body parts for any kind of identification.

Sirens howled to life in the distance. Glancing out at the interstate, Grimaldi saw a patrol car picking up speed as it weaved through traffic and took the nearest exit. He holstered his weapon as Kissinger retrieved the Ruger from the side of the road.

"Let me put this back in the chopper before anyone jumps to the wrong conclusion," Cowboy said.

A Highway Patrol cruiser pulled up less than a minute later, and two officers piled out. Grimaldi flashed credentials identifying him as a special government agent. The photostat made no reference to Stony Man Farm and, as was common practice in situations such as this, Grimaldi refrained from linking himself with that top-secret enterprise.

When Kissinger joined the group, they related what they could about the incident, saying they'd been working security following a tip that the Reed-Blackpoint shipment was going to be sabotaged somewhere en route to San Diego. No mention was made of the reason they'd been assigned the job rather than the FBI or some other outfit falling under the proper ju-

risdiction. Their story was close enough to the truth to
wash.

As they flew back across the isolated terrain, both
men felt a sudden weariness wash over them. Kissinger took the transceiver microphone and dutifully
passed along an update to Hal Brognola, director of
operations for Stony Man Farm, who was overseeing
this operation from a hotel suite back in Tucson.
Brognola suspected the worst even before Kissinger got
around to spelling it out.

"And Striker?" the big Fed asked. "He pulled
through?"

"I don't think so," Kissinger reported. "Those folks
in the Pontiac were blown to bits, and that explosion
was nothing compared to what Mack took. No..."

There was a pause before Brognola spoke, a slight
crack in his voice. "I can't believe it."

"I wish to hell you didn't have to. We're going back
to see how close we can get, but it just doesn't look
good."

"Well, keep me posted."

"Will do."

Kissinger hung up the mike and checked the reading
on a Geiger counter resting near his feet. It was a cus-
tom-crafted piece of equipment, wired to a wandlike
probe mounted under the spotlight in front of the
chopper. Infinitely more sensitive than similar devices
used by hobbyists, the counter was capable of detecting radioactivity from a range of up to six hundred
yards.

"Still no reading, Jack."

"I'll bring us a little lower." He eased the joystick as they neared the intersection.

Kissinger went back to the binoculars and stared down at the open countryside, focusing on a thick cloud of smoke rising up just past the tree line.

"Wait a second," Cowboy suddenly called out.

"What?"

"Get a little closer. Just past the trees."

Grimaldi obliged, periodically checking the Geiger counter. "So far so good."

"There's a fire by the intersection, all right," Kissinger said, a spark of hope in his voice. "But it's not the truck."

They drew closer and Grimaldi could see, as well. "A grass fire."

Kissinger shifted the binoculars, bringing the semi into view. "I don't believe it! It's still in one piece!"

"Cross your fingers," Grimaldi said, leaning on the controls. "We're going in."

He brought the chopper closer, but despite the counter's readings, it wasn't until he'd circled the truck several times without seeing any signs of structural damage that he felt assured that somehow the radioactive cargo had remained intact and sealed despite the explosion, which had apparently taken place some fifty yards away in a vacant field. Flames had spread out from a crater formed in the earth and were continuing to devour dry grass and weeds in its path.

As Grimaldi brought the chopper lower, Kissinger peered over the top of the binoculars, raking the land with his naked eye. A slow smile began to creep across his face as he grabbed for the transceiver mike and put a call out to Brognola.

"Skeeter to Chief."

"Chief here," Brognola answered, apprehension in his voice. "What did you find out?"

Kissinger's face erupted into a full-fledged grin. "I found out that you just can't keep a good man down."

CHAPTER THREE

Alisha Witt had five gold poker chips in front of her. She sighed as she gathered them in her long, slender fingers and placed them amid the other bets in the middle of the table.

"And I'll raise five thousand," she announced, sitting back and calmly fitting a pencil-thin cigarillo into an onyx-and-pearl holder.

"That's the last raise...and I'm out," said the dealer, Herbert Nipree, a harried-looking man in a rumpled leisure suit seated to the woman's left. Worth millions after years of working his way up the ranks in the munitions trade, he prided himself in his blue-collar roots and made few behavioral concessions to his wealthy status. After he set aside his cards, he pulled out the kitchen match he'd been chewing on and dragged his thumb along its tip. It lit with a pop, and he held its flame to Witt's cigarillo.

"Thank you, Herbert."

"If you want to thank me, don't drive me out of the bidding next time." Herbert winked good-naturedly as he discarded the burned match and fetched a fresh one from the pocket of his suit.

Witt blew a cloud of smoke across the room, a lavish hotel suite done up in shades of pastel green and

peach, and adorned with lithographs by Warhol and
Stella. The curtains were half-drawn but still afforded
a view of the gleaming lights of downtown Monte
Carlo, where tourists streamed through the night en
route to late-night dinners and games of chance in the
posh casinos.

Alisha Witt had learned long ago to avoid the house-
run gaming halls, not only here but in Las Vegas and
Atlantic City. It was a matter of knowing the odds. She
knew the smart players avoided the public glamour
spots in favor of private games. For her, too, there was
the fact that these smaller, smoke-filled gatherings were
less an end in themselves than a means to achieving
other goals. She considered such gatherings as reconnaissance missions, valued opportunities to scout for
new talent and size up potential allies and opponents.
Despite all the folklore about poker faces and playing
it close to one's vest, Alisha found that there were few
better ways to glimpse into a man's soul than to get him
caught up in a high-stakes game of five-card draw.

In addition to Witt and Nipree, there were three
other players in the room, each of them well-suited to
Witt's needs in a different way. She knew she'd made
a favorable impression on them, mixing her play with
calculated displays of wit, charm and sensuality, but
she hadn't yet made up her mind which of them was the
likeliest prospect for exploitation. Not that she felt
forced to make a decision. In situations like this she
usually allowed herself a few days to play the field and
let the would-be suitors come to her with proposi-

tions. That way, when it came down to the more delicate negotiations, she could deal from a position of strength.

To Nipree's left was Khadir Edan, an olive-skinned Saudi with short, glistening black hair, dressed in a dark brown Armani suit. With a casual shrug he tossed in his hand and reached over to a silver serving tray beside him for a wedge-shaped cracker piled high with beluga caviar. As he bit into it, he saw Alisha watching him and offered a sly, ingratiating smile. A gold filling sparkled in the man's mouth as he suggestively licked the caviar away from his teeth.

Alisha smiled back and casually averted her gaze. Although his association with the OPEC oil cartel made Edan easily the wealthiest man in the group and in the position to offer her more than any of the others, Alisha suspected that he'd be her last choice to strike a liaison with. There was something about his vanity and smug self-assurance that put her off. He was the type to toss crumbs to the needy and expect undying gratitude from whomever's feet they happened to land at. Too, there was Alisha's loathing of the Middle Eastern chauvinism, which made it likely she'd reject the oil merchant just on basic principle.

Beside the Arab was General Melvin Puckzer, a squat bullnecked Englishman whose ample girth strained at the material of his NATO uniform. What he lacked in personal wealth he made up for in position. He had valuable military and political contacts both within NATO and without. Early in the game Witt had figured on Puckzer as the easiest mark. Between his steady drinking and his lame attempts to brush his leg "accidentally" against hers under the table, she had him pegged as a pushover, not to mention a lousy poker player. Rather than place a bid, he handed his cards to Nipree and stared wistfully at the pot, which had swollen to more than ten thousand dollars.

"Guess you can't win 'em all," he grumbled.

"In your case," Nipree said, "you can't win any, eh?"

"Bloody well right," the Briton said as he poured himself another gin.

That left the man in the tuxedo seated directly across from Witt. Tomi Leitchen was Puerto Rican, with a shaven head and thin black mustache. He remained expressionless as he calmly counted out five ten-high stacks of hundred-dollar chips and slowly slid them into the middle of the table.

"I'll call." He took his snifter of cognac and gently sloshed the amber fluid back and forth to rouse its vapors. Staring back at Witt, he betrayed the slightest smirk. "What does the lady have?"

"I think it's what you gentlemen call a full boat," she purred, her voice layered with a convincing French accent that she'd mastered during her years as a high-priced call girl in Paris. She laid her cards faceup. "Aces over sevens."

"Whoa," Nipree said admiringly, turning to the Puerto Rican. "How you gonna top that, Tomi?"

The man shrugged and displayed his hand. "I guess my four deuces will have to do."

"It would appear I've been outfoxed." Witt let smoke trail from her flared nostrils, and her violet eyes sparkled with amusement. "Well done, Tomi."

"Luck of the draw," the Puerto Rican replied modestly.

"Bloody hot little fingers you have there tonight," Puckzer said, shuffling the cards as the Puerto Rican drew in his winnings.

"Everyone meets up with Lady Luck sooner or later."

"I suppose you're right." Witt stubbed out her cigarillo and rose from the table. "But I don't think she's going to tap my shoulder tonight, so if you'll excuse me, gentlemen, I think I'll call it a night."

"So soon?" Nipree protested. "Your credit's good."

"Yes," she said, "and it'll stay that way if I keep to my rules. Play only what you bring to the table."

"You bring a lot, Alisha," the general said, letting his gaze take in the beaded sequins of the woman's tight-fitting dress.

She chuckled lightly. "Well, I hate to disappoint you, General, but I'm not about to play strip poker, thank you very much."

Puckzer's pallid face flushed as he shrugged his meaty shoulders. "Can't blame a guy for trying."

"I'll have to think about that."

Nipree stood. "Can I walk you to your room?"

Witt had no intention of playing favorites at this point. She shook her head, letting her golden hair brush back and forth along her bare shoulders. "I know the way. Good night again, everyone."

The others murmured farewells as the woman took her purse and stepped out of the smoky room. So far so good, she thought to herself as she paused to light another cigarillo.

The hallway, like the room, was opulent, lined with oak panels and pedestals holding lavish floral displays set in antique Oriental vases. There was a picture window halfway down the corridor, facing a different direction than the window in Herbert's suite. She paused to stare out at the rapturous view of moonlight glimmering on the soft waves of the Mediterranean. Although she preferred other hotels in terms of accommodations or closer proximity to her chalet in the French Alps, whenever she came down from the mountains, she chose to spend her first day and night here at the Azure Waters because she'd yet to find a more breathtaking view of the Riviera, day or night.

It was after midnight in France, and over the past three hours Witt had lost more than thirty-four thousand dollars to the men in Herbert's suite. For her, though, the loss was petty cash, a minor business expense that would more than pay for itself down the line, just as the slit skirt and low neckline of her five-thousand-dollar designer dress had already paid off, fueling the men's desires and anticipation. Whichever of them she ultimately decided to go with, they'd be eager for more of her. She was sure of that.

The four men knew of Alisha Witt only as a hip Parisian socialite with a taste for the arts, and she'd long mastered the role to the point where it was second nature for her. To them and anyone else who cared to inquire, she attributed her wealth to an unerring grasp of the international art market, claiming that a few timely acquisitions and sales every year were all she needed to maintain a life of idle luxury. Behind this public facade, however, lurked another Alisha Witt, a shrewd businesswoman every bit as ruthless and unrelenting in the pursuit of wealth and power as any number of more visible moguls and corporate raiders who regaled in their own publicity.

There were several reasons for Witt cloaking her business dealings behind the veneer of a carefree social life. Gamesmanship was part of it, without question. Beyond the intrigue of poker games and reading between the lines of cocktail conversations, there was the challenge of setting one's sights on a target and then closing in for the kill. Nothing gave her greater pleasure than setting up her victims without their being aware that she was the agent of their demise.

Her training as a call girl had bestowed upon her a casual charm and flair for supposedly innocent curiosity that allowed her to beguile men and get them to divulge professional secrets they'd never reveal to an acknowledged adversary. And, of course, when it took more than party banter or dinner chat to gain the information she sought, Witt was adept at using the bedroom to break through a man's reticence. As Madame Disen had taught her time and again, God gave men a leash between their legs so that women could have something to lead them by.

But, however much the thrill of the hunt accounted for Alisha Witt's modus operandi, there was another, more essential reason she couldn't step forward and claim credit for her machinations in the realm of finance. That reason would be her secret relationship with the notorious American billionaire T. S. Meyler, the mysterious recluse best described by the *Wall Street Journal* as a cross between King Midas and Attila the Hun.

Rarely seen in public and constantly going about his business behind a screen of faceless emissaries and shadow entities, Meyler had made his initial fortune as an inventor with a knack for weapons development. But in recent years the man had shifted focus and was almost universally reviled as the Corporate Cannibal for his specialty of clandestinely manipulating volatile takeovers in such a way that he'd walk away with multimillion-dollar profits without having had to create any product or provide any service to the marketplace.

Whenever Witt was in the company of some victim bemoaning the ways Meyler had caught them in his treacherous web, she'd feign sympathy but smile inwardly, and for good reason. Only she and a handful of others knew that the eccentric figure the world knew as T. S. Meyler was in reality no more than a monumental puppet in the hands of Alisha Witt. She kept Meyler, a half-mad drunkard and heroin addict, under lock and key at a fifteen-million-dollar safe house in the wilds of Arizona, trotting him out for periodic display under controlled circumstances so that the press could keep his presence alive with yet another anecdote of this, the wackiest billionaire since Howard Hughes.

To ensure control over Meyler's financial empire, Witt had secured power of attorney under a variety of aliases, but the deadly charade didn't end there. There were myriad other strings to be pulled, countless other pretenses to be kept up. In the years since she'd become Meyler's guardian, she'd resourcefully lined up a network of acquaintances from all fields of the business world, and she prided herself in being able to secure a favor here, a favor there, in such a way that her pawns often operated without ever meeting one another... or even realizing they were mere chess pieces on her global game board.

Her stay in Monte Carlo was but another round in the unending game. If all worked well, this week she'd size up the four men she'd been playing poker with, then focus on the one who she could best use in lining up yet another coup for her alter ego, the mysterious Mr. Meyler.

From the corridor, Witt descended a marble staircase to the cavernous lobby. There was a huge fountain with sculpted dolphins spouting water toward a massive, two-story-high crystal chandelier that dominated the gigantic atrium around which the hotel rooms had been built. There were two clerks at the front desk. One was tending to an argumentative woman wrapped in furs and banging her purse on the counter as she railed in nonstop Italian. She sought out the second clerk, a young man in his midtwenties, who seemed relieved that he now had an excuse to avoid the altercation.

"Bon soir, Mademoiselle Witt."

"Bon soir, Jean." In fluent French Alisha asked if there were any messages for her. The clerk nodded and reached into an alcove behind him for a folded sheet of hotel stationery.

"Merci," she said with a smile, tipping the man a twenty-franc note. She was barely listening as he offered his profoundest thanks. Unfolding the slip of paper, she turned from the desk and read a short, cryptic message: "Send sunshine to us poor souls in the cold country."

With a weary sigh she circled the fountain and cloistered herself in one of the international phone booths.

"I need to make a call to the United States," she told the operator. "Arizona," she added before giving the number.

It took a few minutes to make the overseas connection, but finally the call went through. The voice on the other line was that of a man with a faint Southwestern drawl.

"Hello..."

"Cal? It's Alisha, darling."

"Ahhhh."

"I got your message," she purred seductively. "Is everything going according to plan?"

"Well, actually, we've run into a little snag."

"Oh?" The woman's countenance darkened, and she felt her patience dwindling as she listened to Cal Ovitz's report on the incident with the semi outside of Tucson. Finally she crushed out her cigarillo and interrupted. "I don't understand, Cal. There wasn't supposed to be any tip-off to the authorities until after you'd planted the conversion kits."

"I know that," Ovitz said. "We all know that."

"Well, obviously someone tipped them off ahead of time," Witt deduced. "They probably inspected the shipment at the warehouse and found everything in order, then figured there'd be some tampering en route to San Diego."

"Looks that way."

"What about this man you supposedly killed? Did he get a good look at you?"

"No," Ovitz told her. "Our tracks are covered."

"I wouldn't be so sure."

"We're looking into it. I'm sorry about this screw-up, but we'll fix it. I've got everything under control."

"You're sure?"

"You have my word, Ali. We're checking all our people and—"

"Spare me the details. Remember, it only takes one loose thread to unravel the best-knit sweater."

"I understand. You know me. I'm not going to let you down."

Witt could sense the tension in Ovitz's voice and felt the need to soothe him. He was too valuable, at least at this point, and he knew too much to be discarded for the incompetent he was.

"I have total faith in you, darling," she cooed into the receiver as she fondled the telephone cord, trying to picture the man on the other end, hungry for reassurance. "I'm sure you can handle this. As well as you handle me, yes?"

There was an uneasy laugh on the other line. "Yeah, that's right, Ali."

"Then you'll take care of this quickly? So we don't fall behind schedule?"

"Of course."

"Good," she told him. "I miss you. I'd hate for you not to be out here when I want you."

"I'm counting the days, Ali." Already there was a renewed sense of purpose in Ovitz's voice.

"Good, good." She blew a kiss into the receiver. "That's to tide you over, my love. Good night."

"It's still daytime here," the man told her.

"I know, silly boy, but it's night here, and I have to go to bed." Witt forced another sigh. "Alone. I'll dream of you, though."

"You do that, sweetheart."

"Yes, darling," she said, blowing a final kiss, then gently setting down the receiver. But as she rose from the chair to leave the booth, she muttered angrily, "Stupid bungling fool! Do I have to do everything?"

From the phone booth the woman stormed to the elevators, raiding her purse for yet another cigarillo. The NATO officer was waiting for her. Witt quickly reined in her emotions. "General?"

"Afraid I lost my stake, too," Puckzer remarked, taking out a packet of matches and striking one to light Alisha's cigarillo. "That makes us kindred spirits."

"I suppose it does," she said, trying to get a read on the Englishman. He was drunk; she knew that much.

"I'll have to insist you stop calling me general," he told her. "My name's Melvin."

"Melvin?" Alisha laughed. "Not a very British name, is it?"

"Ah, if you'd only been around to tell that to my parents." Puckzer chuckled, reaching out to hold open the nearest elevator door. "Come, let's go to my room and drown our sorrows."

"Drown? But, General, it was only a game."

Easing past Puckzer into the elevator, Witt could smell the liquor on his breath. The general stepped back, letting the doors close. As he pressed the fifth-floor button, he said, "Only a game. Perhaps you're right."

"Of course I am." She winked at him, adding, "Melvin."

She resented being pressured by Puckzer's advances, but she figured she might as well make the best of the situation. It wouldn't be too hard to find out how much the man would allow himself to be used, and in his condition there was always a chance he'd black out and not even remember whatever questions she might put to him. Even if he did and the answers proved unsatisfactory, it was likely he'd have enough of a drunkard's shame come morning to hold himself responsible for her rejection.

There was a moment's silence as the elevator began to ascend. Then the general slowly turned to Alisha and grinned with a hint of sudden malevolence that caught her off guard. "In all fairness, since I've let you call me by my first name, I should be allowed the same indulgence, yes?"

Witt offered a puzzled frown. "I don't understand. You know my name is—"

"Michelle," the general interjected. "Or at least that's the name you used when you were turning tricks for Brigadier General Tramlac in Paris a few years back."

"No, you're mistaken," she protested as an icy chill trailed down her spine.

"But not to worry, love. That's not the name I'm interested in, anyway," the general assured her. "No . . . how about if I call you T.S.?"

"T.S.?"

"Or perhaps Ms. Meyler . . ."

Witt feigned ignorance again, taking a half step backward until her bared arms were brushing against the carpeted walls of the elevator. "I don't know what on earth you're talking about."

"Oh, you don't have to worry. I haven't told anyone else." The general took a step closer to her. "It can be our little secret."

Her mind raced as she tried to fathom the import of this unexpected development. Brigadier General Tramlac had been a regular customer during her Paris days, when she was known as Michelle the Dominatrix and specialized in sadomasochism for the whips-and-chains crowd. But that was a lifetime ago, when she was just beginning to learn her craft. Why was her past catching up with her now, especially at this crucial juncture?

She remembered reading about Tramlac, Britain's longtime ranking NATO official, dying of cancer recently. Had there been some deathbed exchange between him and Puckzer? Something about how Tramlac sometimes came to Paris for his weekend benders with T. S. Meyler, then a struggling, unknown inventor with a secret penchant for bondage? That had to be it. How else could this idiot general have pieced things together? But how he'd figured it out wasn't important. He knew, that was enough. No, it was too much. Too many threads were unraveling. Witt had to take action.

She looked at the general, now less than a foot away, leering at her with even less restraint than in the hotel suite. "Very well," she whispered seductively as she moved into the man's drunken embrace, letting her hand drift down and brush against his groin. "Do you want to know another secret?"

"Perhaps."

She gave him a sudden squeeze, then pushed him away and stared at him defiantly as she reached out for a switch to stop the elevator. "I like a man who plays rough," she taunted.

"I know," the general said. "Tramlac told me."

"What are you going to do about it?"

"What do you think, bitch?"

Puckzer strode forward, clawing at her dress with his thick, callused hands. The glittery material tore in his fierce grasp. She lashed out, slapping him across the face. "Bastard!"

"Whore!" the general roared, striking out with the back of his hand. "Bitchy little whore!"

The woman reeled backward, slamming into the wall. She could feel a throbbing across her cheekbones where a welt was already forming. Good, she thought to herself as she staggered close to the control switches. Her dress had been ripped down the front, exposing the dark lace of her low-cut bra. She could see the general's eyes on the round curve of her breasts and breathed harder, making them swell even more.

"You're not man enough for me!" she grated.

"No? I'll show you a man!"

The general grabbed the woman's arm and held her against her feisty resistance. With his other hand he yanked at the straps of her bra until they gave way. As he groped for her soft flesh, Witt turned, wriggling one hand free long enough to start the elevator again. Then, running her fingers through the man's coarse hair, she pulled him close, burying his face in her cleavage, feeling his hand slip down the contour of her waist and begin tearing at the seamed slit in her skirt.

As the general started to work his fingers inside the elastic band of Witt's panty hose, the elevator stopped and the doors swung open. She suddenly brought her knee crashing up hard into the general's groin. Caught off guard, he groaned and loosened his grip. With cold precision she took hold of the man's thumb and bent it backward at the same time as she straightened his arm.

Disoriented and overwhelmed by pain, the general stumbled clumsily as Witt forcefully led him out of the elevator. As she'd hoped, there was no one in the corridor. Gaining momentum, she continued to shove the man toward the railing overlooking the hotel atrium.

"You bitch!" the general howled in agony.

She gave him one last hard push and let go. Puckzer let out a scream of shock and horror as he felt himself toppling over the railing. He reflexively reached out for something to hold on to, but Alisha sprang back from the railing and stared as the general vanished from view. Even as she was moving back to the railing, she could hear the crashing of the man's deadweight against the crystal of the chandelier, which began to sway by its thick chain mounts.

As a door opened behind her, Witt slumped to the floor, forcing tears into her eyes as she tried to cover her breasts with the torn remnants of her dress. A man in a housecoat came charging out of one of the nearby rooms, followed by a woman in a flannel robe and hair curlers.

"He tried to rape me," Witt cried out like a lost soul in the grips of hysteria. "Oh, God, he tried to rape me!"

CHAPTER FOUR

"So I peeled it off the drum and dived out of the truck," Mack Bolan explained. "As soon as I hit the ground, I wound up and let it fly."

"And not a moment too soon," Hal Brognola said. "From what I gather, a second's difference and that whole truck would have gone up, and you along with it."

"That's what they had in mind."

Bolan grimaced as he got up from the hospital bed. A bandage covered the gash on his forehead, and his ribs were still sore from absorbing the point-blank impact of Cal Ovitz's Browning automatic, but he managed to grin through the pain. "Lucky he didn't plug me in the head, or it would have been a different story."

"Oh, you mean you don't have a bulletproof face?"

"Only when I haven't shaved."

Brognola had brought along a change of clothes, and as Bolan changed into them, the warrior asked, "Any luck getting an ID on anyone?"

The big Fed shook his head. "They're trying to get some prints off that couple in the Pontiac, but it doesn't look good. And it'll take a couple of weeks to get anywhere with dental readings."

"What about the cars?"

"All stolen a couple of hours before it went down." Brognola frowned. "Whoever they are, they're pros."

"That's good to know," Bolan said sardonically as he slapped his feet into a pair of shoes. "I'd hate to think that after all these years I nearly had my clock punched by an amateur."

"Leave it to you to worry about something like that."

Bolan buttoned his shirt and headed for the door. "Come on, let's get out of here. We've got things to do."

They were at Tucson Methodist Hospital, where Bolan had been brought the previous night for X rays and observation after suffering a concussion from his fall inside the semi. There were a few other bruises, and he had a slight ringing in his left ear from the explosion, but the Executioner was no stranger to pain and it would take a lot more than what last night had dished out to keep him out of commission.

It took Brognola less than ten minutes to pull the necessary strings to secure Bolan's release, but even he was unable to override the standard hospital dictate that Bolan be confined to a wheelchair until he was outside the building. The Executioner fumed at the pampering and was quickly on his feet the moment they cleared the front exit and the doors had swung shut behind them. Brognola returned the wheelchair to the nurse and joined Bolan at the curb, where a Lincoln Continental was waiting for them, as was a man in his fifties with short-cropped black hair, wearing a light gray suit with a turquoise-and-silver bolo in place of a tie.

"Mr. Bolan," Daniel Blackpoint said, extending a hand to the Executioner. "It's a relief to see you on your feet."

"Easier to do my job that way," Bolan said as he shook the other man's hand. A full-blooded Natchapo who'd enlisted in the military as a teenager looking for an escape from the drudgery of reservation life, Blackpoint had served in Korea with Hal Brognola, establishing a battle-forged friendship that had endured through the years, during which Blackpoint had parlayed college degrees in engineering and business administration into his present position as co-owner and chief executive officer of Reed-Blackpoint Enterprises. When Blackpoint had become concerned in recent weeks that someone was waging an all-out campaign to sabotage his business, a call to Brognola had initiated the sting operation that had nearly cost Bolan his life.

Once the three men were in the Continental and heading out into afternoon traffic, Blackpoint said, "I owe you an apology, Mack. Believe me, I had no idea these people would resort to planting bombs and—"

"Hey, it goes with the territory. No need to apologize."

"Still, I feel responsible for having brought you into this," Blackpoint protested. "After all, this is business, not national security or anything."

"Don't be so sure," Brognola told his longtime friend. "Maybe whoever planted those conversion kits was just out to blacken your name, but who's to say they aren't following through on similar schemes elsewhere?"

"What do you mean?" Blackpoint asked as he sped up the interstate ramp on his way out of the city.

"I mean, they wanted to make sure your shipment was intercepted at customs, but maybe they've tampered with some other cargo being sent overseas by other firms," Brognola explained. "It happens too often for comfort, trust me. A load of air-conditioning equipment gets the green light for export to Syria, and when it gets there they open up the crates and they're filled with components for nuclear warheads."

"I remember reading about that," Blackpoint conceded. "But they caught those people."

"Some of them," Bolan said. "But there's a whole network out there. You take a few players out, there's always somebody else ready to step in and pick up the slack."

"That's right," Brognola agreed. "And our feeling is that whoever was behind this incident last night is probably plugged into this network somehow."

"That's not good." Blackpoint drove silently for a while in the light traffic. After crossing the Agua Fria River, he turned on his blinkers and changed lanes. Nearing the Dysart Road exit, he said, "All this time I was just thinking in terms of a dog-eat-dog business problem. I can't believe I didn't see the big picture."

"Don't worry about it," Brognola told him. "That's our department."

Once off the highway, Blackpoint headed south on Dysart toward Avondale. Halfway there he turned off on a side street leading to an eleven-acre industrial park, all of it fenced in and bearing the Reed-Blackpoint logo. There was a checkpoint just inside the main gate, and even though the Lincoln was easily recognizable, a guard detained the vehicle long enough to get a clear view of Blackpoint and exchange a few words with the Natchapo before waving him through.

"Well, seems like security's tight enough," Brognola observed. "At least on this end."

"We take as many precautions as possible," Blackpoint said as he drove past rows of parked cars to the administration building, a three-story, mirror-surfaced structure that reflected the surrounding desert skyline. As he pulled into his parking spot beside the building, Blackpoint frowned at the empty space beside his. A sign above the space said that it was reserved for Blackpoint's partner, Clark Reed.

"Looks like Clark's not back from lunch yet," Blackpoint said as they got out of the Lincoln. "I was hoping you'd get a chance to meet him."

"We're apt to be here at least a couple of hours," Brognola said. "We'll catch him on the way out."

Brognola and Bolan could feel eyes on them as they followed Blackpoint through the main lobby. The rumor mill had been working overtime since the previous night's altercation. Several people approached

Blackpoint for the inside story, but he waved them off, not wishing to discuss it at that moment. They passed through a set of double doors and started down a long corridor lined with executive office suites.

"Staff looked a little spooked," Bolan observed.

"Can't say that I blame them," Blackpoint said. "I'm sure word's gotten around that we've got a traitor in our midst. I just hope we can get to the bottom of this as soon as possible."

"With any luck," Brognola offered, "Kissinger's made some headway with Randy Walker, a private investigator called in to help."

They were halfway down the corridor when they came to a door marked Security. Inside the office, Kissinger and Grimaldi were going over records with a thin, boyish-faced man in his early thirties.

"Randy, this is Mike Belasko," Brognola said, using one of Bolan's cover names. "He'll be helping us on this case. And this is Daniel Blackpoint."

Randy grinned as he shook Bolan's hand. "A pleasure, Mike. We can use all the extra hands we can get on this one." Then he turned to the CEO and smiled. "Mr. Blackpoint."

As handshakes were exchanged, Brognola said, "I called Randy this morning and asked if he'd help take a look around here."

"I see," Blackpoint said, but it was clear from his expression that he didn't.

"I work for Pat Inston's PI outfit up in Mesa," Walker explained. "I've been down here helping Air

Force Intelligence look into sabotage at a few of the air bases. When Hal told me what happened last night, there just seemed to be too many connections with some of the things we've been working on, so I juggled my schedule and plugged in here for the afternoon."

"Guy's a real wiz, too," Kissinger put in, glancing up from a ledger. "Helped us narrow things down in a hurry."

"Then you've found something?" Brognola asked.

"Well, it's what you expected us to find, I guess," Walker explained, reaching for a trail of paper feeding out from a nearby printer. He tore off a sheet along its perforations and handed it to Brognola. "Stock inventory. All those checked items are missing from stock. Add 'em up and you've got seventeen conversion kits for the radar shipment."

"This is terrible," Blackpoint said, slumping into the nearest chair and shaking his head. "Just terrible."

Brognola eyed Walker and Kissinger. "Do you have some kind of list of who had access to inventory?"

"Yeah, but I'm not sure how much good it's going to do." Walker showed Brognola and Bolan another computer readout with nearly three hundred names. "Everybody from maintenance on up through security and administration. There's another list with login times, but even if you narrow it down to just the past couple days, you still have forty-two suspects."

"Well, I guess that's where we'll have to start, then," Brognola said.

"Sounds like a lot of legwork," Bolan said.

"Then it's a good thing we're bringing in more legs," Brognola said.

"More legs?"

Pulling Bolan out of earshot, Brognola said, "Grimaldi's already on his way back to Virginia. He'll round up reinforcements and fly back tomorrow. You don't mind, do you?"

Bolan shrugged, taking the news in stride. It was usually his prerogative to work alone, bringing in backup only as a last resort. But he could already tell that this assignment was different from most. The target wasn't clear yet, and they couldn't afford to waste time on a lot of hit-and-miss efforts to get to the bottom of things. No, as usual, the big Fed was right to bring in more bodies, and Bolan was equally sure that the reinforcements wouldn't be from the Bureau, the CIA or some other above-the-counter agency. He'd call in the cream of Stony Man Farm, and since Phoenix Force was presently on assignment overseas, that left only three other men besides Grimaldi.

"Able Team?"

Brognola nodded. "You got it."

CHAPTER FIVE

Clark Reed was losing it.

Outwardly he looked calm as he stared out the window of his den and watched the gardener tend to his prized collection of cacti and succulents. But on the inside the frail, white-haired partner of Daniel Blackpoint was a storm of torment and anxiety, all but immobilized by the quandary he'd placed himself in.

How could he have allowed himself to be led along so easily? Greed? Without question that had been a motivation, but there had to be more to it than that. Envy? Of course. It was a classic syndrome, one he should have seen coming from the outset. How many times had a mentor watched with content the meteoric rise of his protégé, only to be slowly but inevitably consumed by jealousy at the newcomer's continued success and a sense that soon the master would be eclipsed by the student?

From the time he'd first opened his electronics firm in the late fifties, Clark Reed had tapped into Arizona's Indian reservations as a source of cheap labor, and nearly twenty years ago he'd taken Daniel Blackpoint under his wing, seeing in the scrappy Natchapo a fiery spirit and drive that merited opportunity, a chance to succeed beyond the assembly line. Reed had taught

Blackpoint all he knew, nurtured the man the way Henry Higgins had nurtured Eliza Doolittle, molding him in his own image until it became clear that Blackpoint was capable of taking the helm on his own. When the company had gone public five years ago, Reed had stepped aside gratefully, matching Daniel's thirty percent share of Reed-Blackpoint stock while opting for the title of chairman of the board and the anticipated leisure of semiretirement.

But when Reed-Blackpoint Enterprises had not only carried on without his primary input but had prospered beyond his wildest imaginings, Reed felt the sting of resentment. Blackpoint was always willing to assign credit to his senior partner, but Reed felt it was a show of false modesty, part of the Natchapo's unerring knack for public relations. Reed felt increasingly patronized whenever his former disciple approached him for advice, and while he'd managed all along to keep his feelings to himself, he couldn't dismiss them or prevent them from festering.

And finally he'd gotten it into his head that he needed to bring Blackpoint down, to put him in his place and resume control of the company that bore his name. That had been the plan: arrange for a scandal to tarnish the Indian's reputation, then work behind the scenes to push for his ouster. Once that had been accomplished, Reed would step forward, humbly and with all due regret, and proceed to reclaim his rightful place as head of the corporation. And then he'd continue the spiraling rise of profits, perhaps even surpass the growth Blackpoint had realized. The world would take notice and grudgingly admit that the old man hadn't lost his touch.

It had been Reed who'd contacted Cal Ovitz about tampering with the shipment of radar equipment bound for Iraq. Ovitz had designed the security system at the Tucson plant, and during their contact Reed had sensed that Ovitz could be trusted to carry out the job in such a way that the ultimate suspicion would be shifted to Blackpoint, thereby planting the seeds of the Natchapo's ruin.

But at the last minute Reed had gotten cold feet...or a case of conscience, as he preferred to think. In any event, even before the shipment of radar equipment had begun its westward trek the day before, Reed had made the anonymous phone call, prompting the sting operation that had led to three deaths and a near-ecological disaster.

Reed knew he wasn't under suspicion for what had happened, at least not yet. If he could somehow put this all behind him, he could write the whole incident off as a case of poor judgment, the sad whim of an old fool. He could back Blackpoint all the more, perhaps even surrender his stake in the business as an act of public generosity and private contrition that would hopefully cleanse him of this brooding sense of wrong.

The first step to his redemption would require dealing with Ovitz. Reed would have to buy the man's silence, as well as that of anyone else involved in the conspiracy. And then, of course, they'd have to find a scapegoat to pin the sabotage on. That would be easy enough, though. The key was to make Ovitz listen to reason.

Reed had three million dollars salted away in the Cayman Islands, undocumented corporate profits gleaned before his retirement and set aside for just such a situation. He figured he'd offer Ovitz two million and negotiate upward if need be.

The old man checked his watch. It was nearly two. Ovitz was supposed to have come more than a half hour ago. Reed wanted to get this over with and return to the plant as soon as possible. Blackpoint had mentioned that some outsiders were coming in to investigate the incident with the semi, and he wanted to be on hand as much as possible to throw up smoke screens and buy some time until he'd extricated himself from this unholy mess.

The phone rang, startling him. He was about to pick it up when he thought better and let it ring. He'd told his secretary he was out having a long lunch with some old business associates and was going to drop by for his biweekly visit to the office later than usual, so he didn't want to blow the cover. The phone was hooked up to an answering machine, allowing Reed to screen the call. It turned out to be a reporter from the *Tucson Reader*, asking for a reaction to last night's incident with the Reed-Blackpoint semi. Reed let the man leave a message without picking up the receiver. Glancing back out the window, he saw the gardener get into his pickup and drive off.

Once the reporter was off the phone, Reed paced the room for a few minutes, then settled in at his desk, turning on his computer. He usually put in a few hours a week at home, tending to what amounted to little more than corporate busywork. He wrote a monthly column in the company magazine, drafted speeches for what seemed a never-ending series of dinner banquets, wrangled with items for upcoming board meetings— just enough of an input to maintain the illusion he was still a vital cog in the machine. He felt it was partly this dreary routine that had spawned his misguided plan to return to power, but Reed vowed that if he came out of the present crisis unscathed, he'd embrace his figure-head status without complaint for however many years he had left.

As it turned out, however, Clark Reed had only seconds left.

As the computer whirred through its diagnostic start-up, Reed leaned back in his chair and let out a loud, nervous sigh, then stopped in midexhalation, hearing a faint sound behind him. As he started to turn around, he felt the cold touch of metal against his right temple. It was the last thing he'd ever consciously feel, just as the gunshot was the last sound he'd ever hear. A .22-caliber bullet ripped through his skull with enough force to swing him around in the swivel chair. Blood and brains splattered the computer screen as he slumped from the chair, slamming his wrist hard against the edge of the desk before landing in a twisted heap on the carpet.

Cal Ovitz stepped back from the body and lowered the gun. He'd been in the house for the better part of an hour, waiting for the gardener to leave so that he and Reed would be alone. He was wearing latex gloves, and as he crouched over the dead man, Ovitz grabbed the man's right hand and placed the weapon in his limp fingers.

"Sleep tight," Ovitz whispered, straightening. As he turned to leave, he caught himself and straddled Reed's body, staring at the computer. A smile crept across his face as his gloved hands hovered above the keyboard. He reflected briefly, then began to type, filling the computer monitor with a chain of luminescent words. A message he figured the world would come to think of as Clark Reed's deathbed confession.

"I'm not sure if anyone suspects me," Ovitz typed, "but it doesn't matter, because I know I'm guilty and I can't live with it any longer...."

It was late in Monte Carlo, almost twenty-four hours since the death of NATO General Melvin Puckzer. Alisha Witt sat quietly in the small dining area of her suite at the Azure Waters. As she nibbled at a slice of toast and sipped freshly squeezed orange juice, she kept an ice pack pressed against her bruised face. The swelling was down and she suspected the marks left by Puckzer would be gone in another day. They were a small price to pay, considering how they'd helped to substantiate her initial description of what had happened between her and the general prior to his untimely death.

She'd had the evening paper sent up along with the food. There was a front-page story with a photo showing local authorities hauling Puckzer's drenched body from the hotel-lobby fountain. As the woman had hoped, the media had bought her version of events and was having a field day with the idea that Britain's top-ranking NATO officer was a sex-crazed rapist who had received his just deserts when one of his victims had fought back in self-defense. She was being portrayed as a poor, defenseless socialite whom the general had stalked after a cocktail party in the suite of U.S. industrialist Herbert Nipree. Beyond that, details were sketchy.

The press wasn't the only force that had been hovering around Witt's apartment all day, anxious for more information. The local police had been by several times, as had men in trench coats from NATO and Interpol. In each instance she'd begged off, claiming to be too devastated by the attempted rape to endure further questioning. She'd put on a convincing performance and Jean, the hotel clerk she'd been tipping so heavily during her stay, had returned the favor and come to her rescue, securing a sympathetic team of doctors and counselors to run interference with the media and investigators alike, telling everyone that the woman needed time before she'd be ready for a full-scale interrogation. Of course, what she really needed time for was to shore up her alibis, beginning with

Herbert Nipree, whom she'd called immediately after her first interview with the police.

Nipree had agreed to corroborate her cover story about the cocktail party. They both knew that any mention of Puckzer and Witt having been involved in a high-stakes poker game wouldn't serve any useful purpose, and Nipree had further promised to speak to Khadir Edan, the Saudi financier, and see to it that he'd stick by the story, too. Tomi Leitchen had already left Monaco earlier in the day, reportedly bound for Nice to catch a flight back to Puerto Rico. Witt hadn't mentioned him to the police, and Nipree had suggested it stay that way, since neither he nor Edan cared to be linked to someone with Leitchen's reputation. It was assumed that the Puerto Rican's silence could be counted on, since dealing arms outside the law required maximum discretion, and Leitchen would have no interest in publicizing that he'd even been to Monte Carlo recently.

After securing Nipree's aid, she had spent much of the rest of the day on the phone, making the necessary calls to ensure that any background checks run by NATO intelligence or Interpol wouldn't lead to Madame Disen's "establishment" or unearth any other links between Alisha and T. S. Meyler. She'd had to call in a few markers and put herself in the debt of a few others, but by nightfall it seemed as if she'd covered all the bases.

And yet she was still uneasy, not sure what her next move should be. General Puckzer may have been silenced, but his death created as many problems as it had solved.

Puckzer had been the primary officer in charge of NATO munitions rollbacks, and with steady calls for increased demilitarization within the European community, the general figured to have his hands full dispensing with surplus weaponry. It had been Witt's hope to persuade him to subcontract a firm run by an acquaintance of hers that specialized in disarmament procedures and long-term weapons storage. That acquaintance, of course, was but another subsidiary of the T. S. Meyler financial empire. If secured, the contract would have been worth more than a hundred million dollars, which Witt was sure could have been structured in such a way as to provide at least twenty-three million in up-front cash. And that money, in turn, would have been earmarked to support an unfriendly takeover bid she planned to launch against Reed-Blackpoint Enterprises, provided that company became vulnerable in the wake of the equipment-tampering scandal that was supposed to have unfolded the night before.

She'd spent months getting all the pieces of this particular puzzle into place, but given the circumstances of Puckzer's death, there was no way she could proceed on the NATO front without rousing suspicions. She'd blocked out similar grand scenarios involving Nipree and Khadir Edan, but any attempts to initiate them at this point seemed ill-advised now, as well. She'd only draw suspicion on herself, not only from

Nipree and Edan, but also with the authorities and the press. It somehow didn't strike her as appropriate for a rape victim to be hustling business on behalf of some "mere acquaintances" so soon after an assault, particularly one that had ended with her attacker plummeting to a grisly death.

And, as if these complications weren't enough, with Ovitz having problems back in Arizona, it was conceivable that the Reed-Blackpoint takeover would fall through even if she could round up the necessary cash flow.

She continued to mull over her predicament as she showered. Without question, the trip to Monte Carlo had backfired. What next, then? Logic called for her to return to her chalet in the Alps and play the role of rape-victim-on-the-mend. But the authorities would be expecting that, and they'd be hovering around her like flies, pressing for an inevitable interrogation that might very well undermine everything she'd been working for all these years. What was more, cloistering herself away would leave her dependent on her connections to keep the T. S. Meyler empire afloat, and with a plum takeover like Reed-Blackpoint dangling before her, the last thing she wanted to do was take herself out of the action.

The doorbell rang as she was toweling off from the shower. It was the first intrusion in over an hour, and her first impulse was to ignore it. Come morning she could apologize to whoever it was and claim she'd gone to sleep early, feeling drained after a day of weeping.

When the bell rang again, however, she wrapped herself in a thick white robe and padded silently to the door. Peering through the peephole, she was stunned.

Standing outside her door was Tomi Leitchen.

"Alisha, are you there?" he called. "I heard about what happened and switched planes in Marseilles. I just got back."

The woman wasn't sure what to make of it. Was this some kind of trap? Or, thinking fast, she wondered if she might have snared herself a new Romeo, the one man from last night's poker party she could still feasibly do business with.

There was only one way to find out.

"Just a minute, please."

Standing before the door, she composed herself, drawing in a deep breath and summoning more tears. She eyed herself in the hall mirror and fingered her hair to make it more disheveled. Reaching down, she slightly loosened the sash on her bathrobe, just enough to allow a glimpse of flesh when she leaned forward or turned too much to one side. True, they were crude ploys, but Witt suspected that in the world of seduction such simple tricks had endured for centuries for the even simpler reason that they worked.

Drawing back the dead bolt, she blinked the tears from her eyes, letting them fall down her face as she opened the door. "I'm sorry," she apologized. "It's just been so—"

"You don't have to explain," Leitchen said. "May I come in?"

Witt hesitated, as if she were about to say no, then stepped back and gestured the Puerto Rican into the room. "Yes, please..."

"Thank you." Leitchen entered the suite, which was roughly the same size as Herbert Nipree's and similarly decorated, although the lithos here were all Georgia O'Keeffe landscapes.

She went to the wet bar, letting her voice crack slightly as she asked, "Can I get you anything?"

The Puerto Rican shook his head. "No."

"I...I can't believe you just turned around and flew back here. We hardly know each other."

"I wanted to," Leitchen told her. "I guess maybe in a way I feel responsible for what happened."

"What?"

The Puerto Rican nodded. "If I hadn't won the last of your chips, you might have stayed longer last night and the general wouldn't have cornered you like he did."

Witt shook her head, smiling sadly. "That's sweet of you to say, but, no, he was determined. No matter how long I might have stayed, he'd have still..."

Her tears flowed freely now, and she leaned against the archway separating the dining room from the kitchen. She drew a hand to her face and turned slightly away from Leitchen, sniffing. "I'm sorry."

"Shh, hey, now." Leitchen stepped closer, removing a handkerchief from his coat and holding it out to her. She took it and dabbed her eyes.

"It's just that…it was so, so…degrading." She broke down and began to sob disconsolately. "I hurt so much…so much."

"How can I help?" Leitchen asked.

She looked up at him, coaxing vulnerability into her gaze. As she leaned into him, seeking out his shoulder, she moaned, "Hold me. Please, just hold me."

Leitchen obliged, wrapping his powerful arms around her. As she continued to wail, Witt felt the Puerto Rican's lips kissing the top of her head.

"It's okay," he told her quietly. "It's going to be okay."

She held him tighter until her thigh was rubbing up against him and she could feel his arousal. Yes, she told herself, tilting her head back and seeking out Leitchen's lips. It was definitely going to be okay.

CHAPTER SIX

It was dusk on the East Coast. As he guided his six-seat Cessna toward the heart of Shenandoah National Park, Grimaldi marveled at the serene majesty of the Blue Ridge Mountains, where nature still seemed to hold a ruling hand and the pace of life harkened back to another, less hectic era. Lights sparked to life in some of the country homes scattered around the rugged Virginia terrain and a sparse flow of traffic wound its way along Skyline Drive, but otherwise there was little sign of activity. Grimaldi had lost track of the number of times he'd made this trek, and yet each time he was struck anew by the area's beauty, the sense of permanence in the jagged, sprawling range and the lush coat of evergreens it wore like a cloak of royalty. It was, for him, a source of strength and peace, the perfect retreat for a warrior.

Once he'd flown past the stoic rock visage of Stony Man Mountain, a patterned winking became visible in a remote clearing. Grimaldi began his descent and lined the Cessna up with the lights, which marked a landing field laid out within the walls of Stony Man Farm.

"Grimaldi Airline Flight 17 coming in for a landing," he cracked to the ground crew as he brought the plane in. The Farm looked tranquil enough to the undiscriminating eye, but Grimaldi could pick out a few telltale hints as to the compound's real purpose. Besides the private airfield, there was the training ground and obstacle course only half-hidden by towering hardwoods, several huge satellite dishes on a knoll near the two-story gymnasium and, of course, the high-security fence enclosing the Farm and patrolled by roving security crews determined to avoid a repeat of the assault, years ago, that had nearly proved the undoing of the entire Stony Man operation.

Just as he was coming level with the treetops, Grimaldi glimpsed a car passing through the main gates. That would be Able Team, just back from Baltimore and a well-deserved day off watching the Orioles slug it out with the Detroit Tigers. He wondered if they'd heard the news yet.

After touchdown Grimaldi jockeyed his plane to a small hangar nestled beneath tall trees at the end of the runway. The ground crew was already in position. He left the aircraft to their care and strolled casually across the grounds, passing the gymnasium on his way to the farmhouse. The car he'd seen earlier was just coming to a stop in front of the structure, and Grimaldi caught up with Able Team.

"Hey, who won?"

"The hot dog vendors. Who else?" Rosario "Politician" Blancanales joked, stifling a belch as he bounded up the porch steps. Raised in the impoverished, crime-ridden barrios of East Los Angeles and San Diego, Pol was more compact than any of the other men of Stony Man Farm but easily made up for in agility and street smarts what he might have lacked in terms of brute strength.

Beside him was Hermann Schwarz, dark-haired and bespectacled, quick of hand and possessing a technological know-how that years ago had earned him the moniker of Gadgets. He eyed Grimaldi curiously. "I thought you were in Arizona with Cowboy and the chief."

"I was. The weather was so nice they sent me back to fetch you guys so you can work on your tans."

"Right," muttered Carl "Ironman" Lyons, the team's unofficial leader. The blond-haired, blue-eyed California native might have looked like an archetypal surf bum, but he'd spent his life as an LAPD cop riding crime waves far more dangerous than any sheet of watery foam rolling in from the Pacific. "Something's happened," Lyons guessed as he followed Grimaldi and the others inside. "Is Bolan all right?"

"Yeah, he's fine. Cowboy, too," Grimaldi said.

"Then what's the deal?"

Glancing through the house, Grimaldi saw a man and woman seated in the den. "Barbara will spell it out."

The men piled into the den, where Barbara Price, Stony Man's mission controller, and Aaron "The Bear" Kurtzman, were nursing cups of coffee in the den as they huddled over a computer readout. Barbara looked at home in a khaki jumpsuit and leather boots, her ash-blond hair pulled back in a ponytail.

Kurtzman, a broad-shouldered hulk of a man restricted to a wheelchair in the wake of the notorious assault on Stony Man Farm, handled communications for the outfit, a task that had turned him into one of the nation's most versatile computer wizards.

"Hello, gents," he said as the group settled onto the sofa and several chairs set around the den. "I hear the Birds pulled it out in the ninth."

"Yep," Blancanales said. "Puts 'em just a game out of first."

"Let's cut to the chase," Lyons said, eyeing Barbara. "Grimaldi says the chief wants us in Arizona."

"That's right." With Grimaldi's help she went on to brief the men about the Reed-Blackpoint situation. She tried to maintain her composure as she related Bolan's close call, but the men were all aware of her relationship with the Executioner and sensed her concern. None of them were surprised when she said she'd be accompanying them when they headed west in the morning.

Once they'd dispensed with background, talk turned to the matter of battle plans, with Barbara and the Bear focusing on the possible global implications of the sabotage. The men listened intently, formulating possible scenarios for their involvement.

"There's been a lot of concern in recent months about sabotage and foul play in the defense industry," Barbara explained. "It's reached epidemic proportions in the past year."

Spread before the team on the coffee table was a map of the American Southwest. Circles were scrawled along the Rio Grande high-tech corridor in New Mexico as well as several areas marked off in Arizona.

Lyons guessed they signified military installations or other enterprises linked to the Pentagon. He eyed Price and asked, "Assuming there has been a big outbreak of foul play, is there any idea why?"

"Well, the theory is that most of the incidents are acts of desperation," the woman explained. "With all the slashes in the defense budget, it's a more competitive market businesswise than it was a few years ago. A lot of contractors who used to be able to practically write their own checks are finding themselves under a lot more scrutiny."

"Nothing wrong with that," Blancanales said. "Hopefully that'll cut down on those four-hundred-dollar toilets and sixty-dollar screwdrivers."

"Yes, that's a definite plus to all this," Price confessed, "and even the Pentagon has to admit there's been a lot of extravagance in the past when it came to handling funds. Most people are saying that in a lot of areas the budget cuts will actually improve defense, because there'll be a greater focus on efficiency and accountability."

"But..." Lyons prompted.

"But," Price said, picking up the cue, "there's also a downside, and it's not just happening to Reed-Blackpoint. Some of the bigger contractors have also been claiming sabotage, not only in terms of product but in research and development.''

Kurtzman went on to explain. ''The feeling is that there are some smaller, renegade outfits waging all-out campaigns to ruin the reputations of Reed-Blackpoint and the bigger contractors. Some of it might be spite, but there's also talk that dirty tricks are becoming part of financial strategy in cases where there's a corporate takeover in the making.''

''Interesting,'' Grimaldi muttered. ''I didn't think of it that way.''

''Well, in this day and age,'' Price said, ''something like that can wind up being a decisive factor. If somebody spends a few thousand dollars throwing a monkey wrench into the right place, it can be worth millions down the line when the lawyers move in looking to cut a deal.''

''Makes sense,'' Lyons said. ''Isn't there some law that if a contractor gets its hands dirty a certain number of times it'll get blackballed from any further government contracts?''

''Exactly,'' Kurtzman replied. ''And when that happens, the renegades are in a position to move in and bid to take over the contracts.''

''And,'' Price added, ''the 'wounded' company winds up being a prime target for a takeover, especially from some of these corporate raiders who like to come in, skim off the pension-fund surplus, sell off loss leaders and divert cash from development and research.''

"Whoa, whoa," Blancanales said, waving his hands in the air. "Takeover, loss leaders, diverting pension-fund surpluses. When did we turn into the Harvard Business School?"

"I'm with Pol," Lyons said. "Sure, maybe there's a problem here, but it doesn't sound up our alley. Besides, there's so little to go on that it seems like Brognola wants to use us for bloodhounds instead of pit bulls."

Price raised a questioning eyebrow. "And you gentlemen don't think you can handle sniffing the enemy out before you go for his throat?"

"We didn't say that," Lyons pointed out, "so skip the reverse psychology, all right?"

She offered a strained smile. "You really think I'd resort to that?"

"I think Pol and Lyons have a point," Schwarz said. "I know the chief and Dan Blackpoint go way back together, but why not bring in the Bureau or somebody like that to pinpoint the culprits, *then* bring us in."

"As a matter of fact," the woman conceded, "most of the contractors experiencing sabotage have hired investigators, and there have been internal investigations going on in all branches of the military since the new Administration took office."

"Yeah, Hal's brought in a PI named Randy Walker to check up on Reed-Blackpoint," Grimaldi told the others.

Price nodded. "He's good people."

"Randy's been checking out some irregularities with the Air Force."

"You know him?" Blancanales asked.

"Yes," Barbara replied. "We went to school together. Randy's got top-security clearance."

"Well," Lyons cracked, "if Hal's got Randy, why's he need us?" Everyone knew Ironman didn't like the idea of bringing in outside people, no matter what their security clearance.

"If you want to be accurate, Hal's got nearly twenty-three thousand folks from the Pentagon inspector general's office to turn to," Kurtzman said, patting a four-inch-thick stack of computer readouts resting on an end table beside his wheelchair. "Everybody's churning out their share of data, but there's so much of it that it's hard to get a fix on any kind of solid lead. I'm going to run all this through a few programs and see if I can narrow things down, but in the meantime I think it's good to bring in some outside people. Who knows? Maybe Walker will cut to the heart of things quicker than I can."

"Okay, okay, maybe you're right," Lyons conceded. "Outside of this thing with the truck shipment, though, what other kind of sabotage are we talking about? Is it really life and death or just business?"

"Oh, it's life and death, all right," Barbara said. She turned to Kurtzman. "Could you go over some of the stuff from that subcommittee file?"

Kurtzman picked up a manila file and pulled out several top-security briefs, passing them to Able Team.

"We have test pilots dying when prototype planes suddenly go out of control, research scientists being fried in lab explosions, whistle-blowers meeting untimely ends before they get a chance to make their depositions."

Schwarz skimmed a report on a sabotaged rocket launcher that killed five infantrymen when its warhead exploded inside the firing tube the moment the trigger was pulled. "So these renegades, whoever they are, are playing for keeps," he concluded.

"That's right," Price replied. "So, you see, what happened with Mack last night wasn't just an isolated incident. Not by a long shot."

Lyons read over another one of the security briefs, then passed the file to Blancanales and muttered, "Well, whoever the hell they are, they're gonna find out we play for keeps, too."

CHAPTER SEVEN

"This ties the loose ends into a nice little knot, all right," Mack Bolan said after he finished reading the suicide note on the computer screen in Clark Reed's study. "But it's a little too pat, if you ask me."

Brognola nodded as he glanced over Bolan's shoulder. "My feeling exactly."

"There's no doubt Reed had access to the conversion parts," the warrior said. "I don't have any trouble with that. And the whole revenge rationale makes sense. But it seems to me if he was really trying to make a clean breast of it, he wouldn't have stopped at pointing the finger at himself."

"You think he'd have named his accomplices."

"You bet. The couple in that Trans Am—he doesn't mention them at all. And I know for a fact he couldn't have been one of the men who raided the truck. Those guys had to be my age or younger."

There was a grandfather clock in one corner of the room, and as it began to sound off nine times, Cowboy Kissinger stared at the chimes for a moment, then snapped his fingers. "Hold the fort," he said, crossing the room and picking up a copy of the preliminary notes left by the police forensics team.

"What is it?" Brognola asked.

"Here..." Kissinger skimmed the list for the item he was looking for. "When Reed slumped to the ground, he hit his wrist against the desk and his watch stopped running at 2:02 p.m."

"So?"

"With any luck I'm about to find out," Kissinger told Bolan as he moved over to the computer. The monitor had been cleaned, so they had a clear view as Kissinger ran his fingers along the keyboard, exiting the word-processing program and calling up a menu listing various options. The one he was looking for was halfway down the first column.

"All right!" he exclaimed. "Reed had the computer programmed so that it would automatically save data every ten minutes, provided the keyboard was in use." Cowboy worked the keys to scroll through a directory of all accessible files. "Well, the computer also has a built-in clock, and every time something gets saved, the file registers the time it took in the data."

Now Bolan could see what Kissinger was talking about. "So you should be able to pinpoint when the suicide note was written."

"Right," Kissinger said. A few seconds later he pointed at the screen. "There we are."

"Well, I'll be," Brognola muttered.

The file entry read 2:15.

"So, if my deduction is correct," Bolan said, "the note was written at least three minutes after Reed died."

"Seems a safe bet," Kissinger said, "assuming the computer clock's right, as well as Reed's watch."

"Then it looks like we have another murder on our hands," Brognola said.

Bolan nodded. "And my money says we're looking for the same people I ran into on the truck."

"You're probably right. Look, Cowboy and I'll comb this place one more time. Mack, I think Daniel and Gwen should know about this."

"Will do," Bolan said, heading for the door.

"And you might want to check in with the Farm, too," the big Fed added. "I had Aaron scouting for leads on a few other fronts. Maybe he's come up with something we can use."

Bolan left the study and started down the corridor, passing a collection of framed Natchapo rugs hanging on either wall. Daniel Blackpoint was in the living room, sitting on an overstuffed sofa next to Gwen Reed, the dead man's wife. Bolan joined them and quietly passed along the latest revelation.

"I knew it," Blackpoint said, anger creeping into his voice. "I knew someone was framing him. None of this was like Clark. None of it."

Fresh tears welled in Gwen Reed's eyes. She said nothing, but Bolan sensed that her reaction was different from Blackpoint's. The Executioner wondered if she, like he, suspected that although Reed had been murdered, there was still a lot of truth in the confession that had been attributed to him. Bolan wasn't sure why Reed might have instigated sabotage against his own company, but he had a feeling that evidence would turn up sooner or later linking the old man to foul play. Hopefully that same evidence would point to accessories, as well, especially the party responsible for Reed's death. Bolan wasn't about to get into a discussion of the matter with either Blackpoint or Reed's widow at this point, though, and he excused himself, asking to use the phone. Mrs. Reed told him there was one in the kitchen.

Bolan was on his way out of the room when the front door opened and Homicide Lieutenant Eric Straw entered. "So you boys had your fill yet?"

"Just about," Bolan replied.

The detective had been in a sour mood ever since the Stony Man people had come on the scene. When Bolan told Straw about the time discrepancy, he scowled and shouldered past the big man, who continued on to the kitchen.

Once there, it took Bolan a few minutes to complete the ritualistic series of calls required to ensure that when he finally got through to Stony Man Farm he was talking on a clean line. Barbara Price answered the phone.

"Hi, stranger," Bolan said, smiling at the sound of her voice.

"Mack, I'm so glad—"

"Listen, Barb, we need to talk some business."

"Sounds serious."

"Afraid so."

Bolan's voice took on a more somber tone as he broke the news about Reed's murder and related some of the other findings they'd come up with earlier at the Reed-Blackpoint plant. Then he said, "Hal said Aaron was trying to round up something else for us to go on."

"He's still down in the communications room working on it," she replied. "He did come across an interesting item off the Interpol wire. It might not have any connection, but it might be worth looking into."

"Let's hear it."

"There was this NATO general who died in a fall at a hotel in Monte Carlo," Price reported. "Official word is he was trying to rape some woman in an elevator and there was some kind of scuffle when the doors opened. She shoved him out, and he went over a railing."

"And there are suspicions it didn't go down that way—so to speak."

"Exactly."

"But what's the connection to Arizona?"

"The woman. Her name's Alisha Witt. She's a socialite, runs with the international art crowd and has some kind of chalet in the French Alps. But according to her passport, she's a native of Phoenix. Lived there up until eight years ago."

"Okay," Bolan said. "Still, it seems like a big stretch to plug her into any of this."

"Hear me out, Mack. It seems that before the assault she was at some kind of cocktail party with Herbert Nipree and Khadir Edan. Either name ring a bell?''

''Yeah. Both are in the weapons trade.''

''Exactly. A strange choice of company for an art collector, don't you think?''

''Maybe, but so what? Variety's the spice of life, right?''

''True, but how about this? They've had her under surveillance the past day, and guess who came around to comfort her last night.''

''Beats me.''

''Tomi Leitchen.''

''Leitchen?''

''Makes things interesting, yes?''

''You bet.''

Bolan knew the Puerto Rican by reputation only. He'd started out a few years ago as a two-bit gunrunner working out of a small skiff in the Caribbean and Gulf of Mexico. Along the way he'd knocked off some of the competition, however, and had moved into bigger markets, dealing high-priced weapons to any bidder willing to meet his price, from contras in Central America to terrorists working out of the Middle East. According to most intelligence reports, most of his armament came from stateside sources, both in the form of guns and rifles being phased out by major American manufacturers and surplus inventory wrangled out of military depots through contacts in the armed forces.

"Last report on him that I saw had him working out of the Southwest."

Price chuckled. "Give the man a Kewpie doll. As a matter of fact, my friend Randy Walker has been trying to link Leitchen with missing Air Force inventory for the better part of six weeks."

"Sounds like we're on to something here. How close is Interpol sticking to this Alisha Witt?"

"Round the clock. They're putting a tap on her phones, but my guess is they're probably a little late on that front by now."

"And they figure she offed the general and made it look like rape?"

"Yes, but they aren't letting her know they're suspicious."

The kitchen was dark, and as he listened to Barbara speculate on reasons why the general might have been killed, Bolan gazed out the window over the sink. Suddenly he spotted activity in the backyard. Someone was out there, crouching behind a large cactus.

"Listen, Barb, I have to go," Bolan interrupted. "We've got company."

He quickly hung up and unholstered a Beretta 93-R he'd gotten from Kissinger to replace the one he'd lost to the semi raiders the night before. Kissinger had promised to modify the gun as soon as possible, but for now Bolan would have to make do with its standard features, which varied just enough from his old standby to make the weapon feel unfamiliar in his hand. Not that he doubted his ability to use it.

Crouching behind the kitchen counter, Bolan moved slowly toward a door leading out to the back patio. In doing so he had to give up his view of the outside intruder for several seconds. When he reached the door and peered out through the framed glass, he saw no sign of anyone behind the cactus.

"Damn," he muttered under his breath, slowly turning the doorknob. On a count of three he jerked the door open and somersaulted onto the patio.

A gunshot blasted through the night air, shattering a clay pot to Bolan's right. He rolled to his feet and found cover behind a brick barbecue. Guessing at the trajectory of the shot, he peered through the darkness, trying to spot the gunman elsewhere in the garden. A second shot whistled past his head, driving him back. He circled halfway around the barbecue, then quickly doubled back and lunged from cover, taking a crouched shooting stance and squeezing off a 3-round burst.

Fifty yards away a cactus-limb plopped onto the ground, oozing aloe where it had been severed by 9 mm parabellums. One of the shots had gone through the plant and burrowed into the thigh of the intruder, slowing his flight as he tried to run from the garden.

"Freeze!" Bolan shouted as he took up the chase, picking out cover behind a picnic table next to the garden area. The fugitive fired again, splintering the tabletop, but Bolan wasn't about to hang back and risk losing his prey.

The patio lights flashed and Straw charged out, shouting, "What's going on?"

"Intruder!" Bolan shouted back as he bolted into the open, running a zigzag pattern into the garden. Thorns and pricklers stabbed at him as he plowed through Reed's cacti and succulents, but he tuned out the pain, keeping his eyes on the limping figure ahead of him. Behind him, though, he could hear Straw bringing up the rear, pulling out his service revolver and squeezing off a couple of shots that whipped past Bolan, meant for the intruder.

"Police!" Straw cried out. "Stop!"

The intruder paid no more attention to Straw than he had to Bolan. Scrambling down a weed-choked incline, the man lost his balance and tumbled over a raised sprinkler head that caught his pant leg, ripping the fabric and drawing blood. He landed with a hard thud, losing his gun in the weeds.

Bolan cleared the rise and raced down the incline, hoping to tackle the intruder and wring a few answers out of him. But when the other man came up with the gun and drew on Bolan, the Executioner had no choice but to use his Beretta. At this range and under these circumstances there was no percentage in shooting to wound. Bolan went for the kill shot, drilling the other man in the face.

A return shot flew wide as the intruder crumpled back into the weeds. Bolan hurried to his side, but there was no point in checking for a pulse. The bullet had entered below the man's left eye, killing him instantly.

In the faint moonlight Bolan could make out what was left of the victim's features. He was a Native American without question. A quick search of the man's pockets turned up no trace of identification, but Daniel Blackpoint was able to help out on that end when he came down the hill a few moments later, clutching a flashlight. Straw was with him.

"Either of you know him?" Bolan asked.

Straw took a look and shook his head. "Nope."

But when Blackpoint crouched over the slain man, his features tightened with recognition. He straightened slowly and nodded. "Yes, I know him. His name's Rain Murrer. He's from the reservation."

"Any idea what he was doing here?" Bolan asked, inspecting the intruder's gun.

Blackpoint frowned. "He belongs to NAM, a militant offshoot of the American Indian Movement—the Natchapo Armed Militia."

CHAPTER EIGHT

Cal Ovitz stood smoking a cigarette in the back alley behind the Perimeter Trust building, watching cats roam through a garbage bin stinking of refuse from the Green Orchid Restaurant. When a shift in the summer breeze pushed the fetid smell his way, his stomach churned uneasily. Ovitz had wolfed down a plate of cashew chicken and tangerine beef at the restaurant earlier, and it had been sitting heavily ever since. He took another drag on his cigarette and let the smoke trail out his nose as he waited for the wind to shift again. Down the alley he could see the flashing sign at the front of Rough Trade Hardware—9:34 p.m. and still eighty degrees.

Reaching into his pocket, Ovitz pulled out a fortune cookie and flicked off a scrap of lint clinging to the folds. He cracked the cookie open and ate half of it, tossing the rest out onto the asphalt. One of the cats eyed him suspiciously, then leaped down from its perch and purred its way to the crumbs, taking a precautionary sniff before nipping at the snack with its teeth.

Ovitz straightened out the thin strip of paper that had been wedged inside the cookie. On one side was a scrawl of Chinese characters. He flipped it over for the translation: "You crave the allure of faraway places."

"Ain't that the fucking truth," he growled.

Ovitz held the fortune close to the tip of his cigarette and inhaled deeply, working up the tip's flame until it was strong enough to ignite the paper and light up his lean, tanned face. He watched the fiery glow for a moment, then dropped the burning paper and his cigarette, grinding both under his heel.

At 9:40, dependable as clockwork, the attendant at the parking lot across the alley wandered from his booth and ducked into the back entrance of a doughnut shop. From previous experience monitoring the attendant's rest breaks, Ovitz knew he had no more than ten minutes. He wasn't about to waste any of them.

Striding past the garbage bin, Ovitz nonchalantly vaulted a guardrail separating the alley from the parking lot and strode past a row of idle cars, seeking out a nondescript Honda Civic parked at the end of the row. It was no surprise to find the vehicle locked and wired to a security alarm.

Ovitz was, if anything, primed for the challenge of breaking into the vehicle undetected. He'd come prepared, and as he crouched beside the left rear quarter panel, he reached into his coat pocket and removed a pocket sensor the size of a card deck. One of his most prized inventions put together during his days in Research and Development at the Central Intelligence Agency, the sensor had different reactive modes allowing it to home in on a variety of signals, from simple radio frequencies to radar output and more complex laser and even microwave transmissions.

Once he was able to pinpoint the configuration of the car's security system, Ovitz quickly neutralized the alarm and gained access to the car with the same lock pick he'd used to enter the semi the night before. All in all, the procedure took him less than a minute.

Once inside, Ovitz was forced to lie low across the front seat as another patron appeared in the lot, heading for a Jaguar parked two rows away. From where he was lying, Ovitz was still able to go about his business, using the sensor to detect not only another transmitting device, but also a receiving signal, both inside the glove compartment.

After the driver of the Jaguar drove off, Ovitz sat up. A few seconds more of jimmying with his lock pick and the glove compartment sprang open. Ovitz methodically searched the tight enclosure and located the two items he was looking for. The first, built into the underside of the dashboard, was a compact homing device capable of sending out a constant signal that could be read by an appropriately tuned receiver, allowing for the Civic's location to be traced and pinpointed.

Ovitz quickly disconnected the beeper's wiring, then turned his attention to a thin leather case resting between a service manual and a pair of leather driving gloves. He pried the lid open and stared at the winking lights and whirring of a microcassette. A quick check with the frequency scanner confirmed Ovitz's suspicions—the miniaturized bugging device was tuned in to the state-of-the-art communications system Ovitz had engineered for Tompkins-Ovitz Security Services, which operated out of the top two floors of the Perimeter Trust building a few hundred yards away. Ovitz was familiar with this particular bugging device, made by Inston Corporation, a Mesa-based security firm run by Pat Inston, a former Agency colleague and present-day rival of Tompkins-Ovitz in the private security business.

"Nice try," Ovitz said as he slapped the lid shut and put the case into his coat pocket.

As he was getting out of the car, Ovitz saw a young couple heading toward their Mercedes, parked directly across from the Civic. Putting on an easy smile, he nodded a greeting and strolled across the lot, tapping out a fresh cigarette. He smoked it slowly as he headed past the trash bin, where the cats were munching on a discarded order of chow mein. At the sound of footsteps the animals glanced up at Ovitz, eyes glowing in the overhead floodlights.

"Just me again, you pussies. Here." Ovitz flicked the cigarette, sending the cats scrambling into the shadows, then proceeded into the Perimeter Trust building.

"Evenin', Mr. Ovitz," a balding, middle-aged security guard called out from his post behind a false marble cubicle set next to the elevators.

"Hello, Ken," Ovitz said as he scribbled his name on the ledger logging traffic in the building after normal business hours.

"Hot one, huh?"

"What else is new?" Ovitz leisurely scanned the ledger and placed his finger on the signature of Randy Walker. "Tell me, Ken. Are you familiar with this Walker fella?"

Ken stared at the signature and the time it was entered. "Signed in a couple of hours ago. He's taking that bodyguard seminar of yours, isn't he?"

"That's right," Ovitz said. "Baby-faced guy, probably in his late twenties, early thirties."

"Yeah, yeah...I can place him now."

"Good," Ovitz said. "He ever been by here outside of class? That you know of?"

Ken thought about it, then shook his head. "No, not that I recall. Of course, I just work this late shift, y'know."

"Yeah, I know."

"He might have come another time."

"That's okay. It's not important."

Ovitz moved over to the elevators and pressed the up button. He wasn't about to share confidences with the likes of Ken. Although he had nothing against the old man personally, Ovitz planned to see to it that he was fired at the end of the week.

The way Ovitz had it figured, like the attendant at the parking lot, Ken was a good old boy looking to pad his police pension and stay out of trouble as much as possible, approaching his work with the sort of casual indifference that gave security guards a bad name. Sure, Ken could be counted on to log in legitimate visitors and turn away errant tourists and bladder-pained transients looking for a rest room, but Ovitz knew that if some unauthorized intruder was really determined to get past, it would be relatively easy. Walker was proof of that.

The bell rang and the elevator doors parted.

The elevator was built outside the building, and as Ovitz was hauled up floor by floor, he stared out at the alley and the parking lot as he rode to the seventh floor. The lot attendant was heading out of the doughnut shop with a doughnut clamped between his teeth and a cup of steaming coffee in either hand.

"Stupid shit," Ovitz grumbled.

Rising higher, he could see across the city, past the sprawling campus of the University of Arizona, past Randolph Park to the distant winking of Bergman Air Force Base. Now there was a place with good security... or so they thought.

It had taken Ovitz and Marlowe Tompkins the better part of a year to bypass competition and win a lucrative contract to evaluate existing security systems at the base and propose upgrades on an as-needed basis. But it had been a year well spent, because once they saw how rife with incompetence the base's security was, they were able to initiate a few spin-off enterprises. Between gaining access to high-security material in base computers, siphoning goods from poorly monitored inventories and clandestinely monitoring the Research and Development program for tips to pass along to bidding defense contractors, Tompkins-Ovitz had been able to afford their recent move from a low-rent dive near the freight yards to these new upscale quarters in the heart of the downtown business district.

Ovitz's under-the-counter dealings had not only put him in touch with such upper-crust figures as Alisha Witt and Puerto Rican arms dealer Tomi Leitchen, but also some useful underlings. In particular Ovitz and Tompkins had befriended a couple of low-level Air Force security officials they'd caught in a scheme to smuggle arms from Bergman's overstocked munitions depot. Upon learning that the culprits had family ties to a band of militant Natchapos looking to split off from the American Indian Movement, Ovitz and Tompkins had not only let them off the hook, but they'd also dangled just enough bait to get themselves put in touch with the renegades.

An alliance was struck, with Ovitz and Tompkins doling out far more favors for the Natchapos Armed Militia than they received, writing off the gestures as a retainer of sorts, a way of ensuring that they'd have a reasonably competent goon squad at their disposal in the event they needed some dirty work done at some point down the line. Militants Ellis Hayes and Al Blyford had already been used during last night's raid on the Reed-Blackpoint semi. As Ovitz got off the elevator, he felt in his gut that he and Tompkins might have to call in the rest of their markers with the Natchapos to deal with this new problem of Walker and Inston.

The seventh-floor hallway was quiet, with no sign of activity. The building was new, and most of the offices on this floor were still in the process of being readied for occupancy. Doors were locked, but inside the lights were on and Ovitz could see stacked rolls of carpet, boxes of acoustic tile and thick coils of electrical conduit awaiting tomorrow's work crews. Once finished, the entire floor would serve as offices for Itiz, Seitla and Cruz, one of the hottest law firms in the state, under retainer by not only the Department of Defense and Department of Energy, but also seven of the top ten defense contractors in the Sun Belt . . . and reclusive billionaire T. S. Meyler.

Thanks to a referral by Alisha Witt, Tompkins-Ovitz Security Services had already struck a deal to install a top-of-the-line security system throughout the law firm's suites, but Ovitz figured there was more to be gained from their proximity to Itiz, Seitla and Cruz than a quick onetime job. And so, while installing the alarm and other security systems within the various suites, Ovitz had also set up eavesdropping equipment and seen to the building of an unblueprinted trapdoor and access shaft that would allow entry to the law offices after hours from their own suite a floor above.

But infiltrating law firms was for another time. When he reached the end of the hallway, Ovitz stopped near a door marked Utilities: Authorized Personnel Only. He rapped on the steel-plated door in a coded sequence, then waited several seconds before hearing a dead bolt slide out of place. The door opened, and he stepped into a huge room filled with air-conditioning and heating systems as well as the power boxes for the entire building.

Two men were waiting for him in the room, both of them Natchapos wearing dark clothes. Al Blyford's hair was pulled back as it had been the night before. His brother Zane, two years older, wore his hair short, revealing a deep, jagged scar behind his left ear. Each man held an Ingram MAC-10. A third automatic rested on a condenser unit, along with three ski masks and a black sweater.

"Ready, gents?" Ovitz drawled as he donned the sweater.

"Yeah, we're ready," Al said. There was an edge to his voice.

"Problem?" Ovitz asked.

"Heard on the news that Clark Reed had a little accident," Al said casually.

"Yeah, how about that?"

"They said something about a suicide note."

"Really."

"We were wondering . . ." Zane joined in, glancing at Ovitz as he checked the firing mechanism of his MAC-10. "What if that note named names?"

Ovitz grinned. "I wouldn't worry about it."

"Maybe you wouldn't, but we are," Al Blyford replied. "We weren't there to proofread it."

"Oh, and you think I was?" Ovitz asked.

"You tell us."

"Look, I'm telling you," Ovitz said impatiently, "you have nothing to worry about. Take my word for it."

"We'll feel better if we find out for ourselves," Zane said. "Personally."

"What do you mean?" Ovitz asked.

"We sent one of our guys to have a look around."

"You what?" Ovitz couldn't believe it.

"You heard me," Al said. "But he's not going to find anything that will point a finger at us, right? So, like you said, why worry?"

"Right." Ovitz shook his head and laughed cynically. "Sheesh, these days you can't even trust your friends. What's the world coming to?"

"Not an end, we hope," Zane said cryptically.

Ovitz tried not to show any concern as he finished donning the dark sweater, but he was having trouble getting a fix on the two brothers. Were they just voicing a little healthy paranoia, or were they leading up to something else? Blackmail perhaps?

"These sure are nice weapons," Zane said, stroking his MAC-10. "Be nice if we could get some for all our friends."

Ovitz shrugged. "I'll see what I can do."

"That'd be real nice," Al said. "Real nice..."

Ovitz pulled the ski mask over his head and grabbed the MAC-10. "Okay," he told the others. "Now that we've had our little chat, let's take care of business."

CHAPTER NINE

Marlowe Tompkins had a square jaw, chiseled features and a few raw scars that he always jokingly claimed had been left by the chisel. Built like a runt linebacker about to burst his shirt seams, he paced the conference room at Tompkins-Ovitz Security Services. Before him, three men and two women sat around a polished oak table littered with memos and file papers. Smoke curled from several ashtrays, mingling with steam from plastic cups of coffee. Two other men in loose suits loitered away from the table, one near the doorway, the other next to a large window offering a view of the Auto Club building and night traffic out on Oracle Road and Casa Grande Highway.

"And our third-quarter figures don't look any more promising," Tompkins droned on in a sonorous monotone. A three-foot-long spreadsheet trailed from his meaty hands. He could sense that the others were distracted, barely listening to his presentation. In mid-monologue he suddenly whirled and slammed a big fist against the table, rattling the ashtrays and nearly capsizing one of the coffee cups.

"Look, folks, we got a situation here, okay?" His voice boomed off the paneled walls. "We gotta turn things around and do it quick, or one of these days Joey in Accounting's gonna stroll in here telling us we've gone chapter eleven. That happens and we start cutting deadwood." Grinning at his now-attentive audience, he added, "And the first place we'll be looking for deadwood is right here in this room."

Randy Walker was sitting at the far end of the table. He met Tompkins's grin with one of his own and raised his hand. "Yo, boss," he said, pushing back from the table and reaching for a growth chart propped on a wooden easel behind him. "I got a surefire way to turn things around."

"That so?"

"Yep." Walker grabbed the growth chart with its jagged red line graphing out a steady decline and calmly flipped it upside down, then gestured at it like a magician who'd just pulled a rabbit from a hat. "Voilà!"

There were muffled snickers and snorts throughout the room. Tompkins smiled as well, but it was a menacing smile, void of any trace of good cheer. He waited as Walker took a mock bow and moved back to the table, then resumed. "Now that we've all basked in Walker's so-called wit, how about we do some—"

Tompkins was cut off as the door to the conference room suddenly burst open. Three gunmen charged in, dressed in black and wearing ski masks, waving deadly MAC-10s. One of them, tall and lean, took aim at Tompkins.

"Nobody moves!"

But the two men in loose suits were already in motion. The guy by the door lunged forward, lashing out with a karate chop that sent the gunman closest to him reeling off balance into a filing cabinet. The other man in a suit was already in the process of diving across the oak table, scattering paperwork, coffee and cigarette butts in his wake. Clearing the table, he tackled Tompkins to the floor in such a way that he made himself a human shield, as well as a target for one of the Ingram-toting intruders.

As the other dumbfounded board members froze in their seats, Walker sprang into action, sliding from his chair and yanking out a double-action Colt revolver as he crouched for cover at the table's edge. Behind him the easel toppled backward, landing with a dull thwack on a leather sofa.

Gunfire thundered away in the cramped confines of the office. Two of the intruders were quickly put out of commission, but the tall, lean man was able to use a filing cabinet for cover as he blasted away with his MAC-10 on full-automatic, spitting out its 32-round magazine in a deadly clatter. One of the women at the table slumped forward, knocking over another ashtray and dropping the telephone receiver she had just reached for. Another board member swiveled wildly from the table and crumpled to the carpet.

Walker didn't have a good angle on the last assassin, so he moved to his hands and knees and crept past one of the victims, inching closer to the filing cabinet.

A burst of autofire rattled his way, however, and he collapsed like a broken doll onto the carpet.

Just when it looked as if the last intruder were about to finish off the survivors, the man who had tackled Tompkins rolled out from under the stockier man and came up firing his Browning at the gunman behind the filing cabinet. The lean man dropped his MAC-10 and sagged to the floor, groaning.

For a prolonged moment the room was silent save for the dripping of spilled coffee over the edge of the table. Then, one by one, everyone in the room slowly stirred to life. Those who had taken point-blank hits miraculously showed no trace of blood, and although nearly a hundred rounds of ammunition had been spent, none of the walls or furnishings showed the ravaging effects of 9 mm or .45-caliber slugs.

All told, the most serious damage turned out to be coffee stains caused by the overturned cups. As Walker snatched a paper towel and blotted up a dark puddle on the carpet, Marlowe Tompkins rose to his feet and surveyed the others.

"Not bad on the whole," he said, eyeing the two men in loose suits. "I was probably dead meat along with half the board, but you ended up nailing all the goons."

"Yeah, with my help," Walker boasted as he holstered his Colt. "I plugged the last guy."

"Only because I let you have a shot at me," Ovitz muttered as he yanked off his ski mask. There was a wire dangling from the back of his mask, and at the end of it was a small, two-pronged plug. He carried the mask over to a computer console on the far wall and, after sliding the plug into an adapter, he punched up a program that flashed the image of a ski mask on the screen. A single blinking circle appeared on the forehead area, roughly equidistant between the two eye-holes.

"A good shot, too," Walker said as he eyed the screen.

There was a cord and plug connected to the sweater Ovitz had donned, too, and when he plugged it into the computer and cued the monitor, the others moved in closer to see how many circles appeared on the diagram. Each one represented a gunshot wound Ovitz would have suffered if the Brownings and Walker's Colt had been firing live rounds instead of infrared beams that marked various target sensors woven into the sweater.

Everyone in the room was wearing some form of doctored clothing. The Blyford brothers shed their masks and set their MAC-10s on the conference table. After Ovitz had finished charting his hits, the others took their turns plugging into the computer and determining where they'd been shot during the exercise. As they did so, Ovitz and Tompkins backed away and huddled in one corner of the room, speaking in low whispers. Ovitz did most of the talking, and when they broke from their huddle, Tompkins stole surreptitious glances at both Randy Walker and the Blyford brothers.

Once cumulative scores had been tabulated, Tompkins spelled out the results. "Just like I said. All three intruders ate it, but they took out half of the good guys on the way."

"And if you figure we were Iranians," Al Blyford cracked, "we gladly gave our lives to Allah in the name of the greater good."

"Yeah," his brother sniggered, "Koran kamikazes."

"But you aren't Iranian," Walker observed, taking in the men in black. "I'd guess Natchapo, maybe Apache."

Al laughed. "Shit, we're American. Same as you."

Ovitz didn't want Walker pumping the Blyford brothers for any more information. "Al and Zane are graduates from our last bodyguard school," he interrupted, turning the introduction into a sales pitch. "They both finished with high ratings and top references and they've both been working regularly ever since. The same can happen to any of you if you keep applying yourself for the rest of the classes."

"Sounds good to me," Walker said.

Ovitz led the brothers to the exit. "Thanks for dropping by, guys."

"Hey, always glad to help out," Zane said. Once they were out in the hallway, he eyed Ovitz and winked. "And what goes around comes around, right?"

Ovitz nodded. "I'll be in touch."

"Good," Al Blyford said. "Remember. Automatic subguns. Or rifles."

"Yeah," Zane agreed. "AK-47s would be okay."

"Hey, it's not as if I'm going to the supermarket," Ovitz advised. "I have to see what's available. I've got a feeling we're talking carbines."

"Just give it your best shot," Al told him.

The two brothers turned and headed down the hall. Ovitz watched them, whispering under his breath, "Don't worry, boys. I will. I will."

But dealing with the uppity Natchapos wasn't top priority for Ovitz at the moment. As he returned to the conference room, he casually glanced at Randy Walker, who'd sat back down with the other students around the table. If the young man thought he was under suspicion, he gave no sign of it. Like the others, he had a pen and notepad out, ready for the critique on tonight's training exercise.

"Okay, everybody," Tompkins began, "listen up. And this time I'm not just slinging some corporate mumbo jumbo. From what I saw, there are a few things that could have been done to cut down on casualties. Let me spell them out."

For the better part of twenty minutes Tompkins and Ovitz lectured the recruits on ways to maximize security and protection while serving as bodyguards for corporate bigwigs. They had the spiel down pat, having given variations of the same lecture to more than a dozen similar classes over the past year as part of an intensified ten-step, three-week cram course for which aspiring bodyguards shelled out three thousand dollars apiece in hopes of earning a "diploma" and, more importantly, a job referral that would put them directly to work for an ever-growing list of celebrities and self-envisioned VIPs who desired bodyguards as either a status symbol or genuine shield against threats on their well-being or that of their families.

The Bodyguard Training Seminars were a low priority in the overall scheme of Tompkins-Ovitz Security Services, but it provided a decent front for their illegal sources of income, and also there were those times when Ovitz or Tompkins would come across a student who exhibited the ideal traits that would make him a viable addition to the company's own elite corps of agents who were hired out to firms on a temporary basis.

Properly groomed, the ideal Tompkins-Ovitz security agent was someone who could gain the trust and confidence of an employer and be placed within the inner sanctum of a corporation for the alleged purpose of providing bodily protection for ranking executives and security for high-level company secrets. Once placed, of course, the agent would be in a position to capitalize on his access to sensitive information.

To date, in addition to the Blyford brothers, there were two other such special agents working for Tompkins-Ovitz. Randy Walker had seemed like an ideal candidate when he began his participation in the bodyguard seminar. However, as the class progressed, both Tompkins and Ovitz had begun to suspect that he was no mere aspiring agent.

The quick raid on his Civic had confirmed their worst suspicions—Walker was already an agent working for one of their major competitors, Pat Inston. The question now was who had hired Inston to have Walker infiltrate Tompkins-Ovitz. Had it been Clark Reed, foolishly hoping to blackmail his way out of being associated with the botched sabotage of his company's radar shipment? Or perhaps the law firm downstairs? The Air Force? Or maybe even Alisha Witt? One way or another the partners meant to find out the answer.

Once they'd finished critiquing the night's exercise and had given the students an assignment on tailing procedures to work on during the upcoming week, Tompkins dismissed the class, with one exception.

"Walker," he called.

The young man paused halfway out of the conference room and glanced back at Tompkins. "Yeah?"

"How about sticking around for a second?" Tompkins asked. "We want to go over something with you."

"Sure." Walker lingered behind while the others left. Once he was alone with Ovitz and Tompkins, he cracked his knuckles and nonchalantly began reloading his Colt, this time with live ammunition. "So what's up?" he asked casually.

"We were hoping you could tell us," Ovitz said, tapping out a cigarette and wandering close to Walker.

"Tell you what?" Walker frowned. "I don't get it."

"Well, let's spell it out for you, then."

Ovitz stood directly in front of Walker and pulled out a lighter. When he ran his thumb along the striker wheel, instead of a flame, the lighter sprayed a thin mist directly into Walker's face. He staggered backward, taken by surprise, then tried to raise his Colt to a firing position. But the fast-acting gas overwhelmed him and he toppled forward. Ovitz caught him and eased him into one of the chairs.

The two men exchanged glances. "He's got some bugs planted around here," Ovitz said. "Let's track them down, then we'll take Randy boy for a little drive."

"I...I DON'T KNOW what to say," Alisha Witt whispered, drawing the sheets around her as she sat up and stared at one of the O'Keeffe lithographs featuring barren deserts and shadowed mountains under a soft blue sky. "It's just so... I feel so out of control...."

"Hey, it's all right," Tomi Leitchen assured her, gently stroking her exposed back. They were in bed together, both of them sweating from exertion after their lovemaking. They'd been in bed for nearly ten hours now, drifting off to sleep between frantic gropings. There'd been little conversation, and whenever she did talk, Witt took care to keep up her pretense of the frail victim. She knew she was treading a fine line, indulging in such passion in the wake of what had supposedly happened to her, and as morning light probed through the horizontal blinds, she wanted to make sure Leitchen was still securely in her web.

"I...don't know," she stammered, slumping back in bed and resting her head on his chest. "It's like I needed you . . . needed to do this right away, so I wouldn't keep associating it with what that . . . that animal did to me.''

"Shh." Leitchen fingered her hair, leaned over to kiss the round curve of her ear. "I understand. You don't have to explain."

She turned to him, kissed him lightly on the lips, then looked him in the eye. "Thank you."

"Please . . ."

"No, I mean it. I was feeling so lost, but now . . ." She leaned against him, stroking the muscular lines of his forearm, staring curiously at a small, heart-shaped tattoo on his wrist. "Now I feel safe."

"I'm glad I could help."

The woman managed a smile. "Ali. Call me Ali, okay?"

Leitchen smiled back at her. "Sure, Ali."

She glanced past him, staring at the lithograph again. Although the setting O'Keeffe had painted was of northern New Mexico, it could just as well have been Arizona, where it had all begun for Alisha Witt, years before she'd fled to France and her life as a prostitute in Paris. Raised an orphan, moved from foster home to foster home, she'd learned in Arizona of the need to adapt, the need to rely on one's personal resources to get by in a largely uncaring world. Maybe that was what she needed now—a return to her roots.

"What are you thinking about?" Leitchen asked her.

"Nothing," she murmured, blinking away tears that had come without warning.

"You can talk to me."

"I know." She turned from the lithograph and traced her fingernail along a scar on Leitchen's chest. "I was just trying to figure out what I'm going to do."

The Puerto Rican frowned. "Is there a problem with the police here?"

"No, no."

"Because if there is..."

"No, it's not that. The police were wonderful." She bit her lower lip for a moment, then said, "I'm concerned about the others."

"Others?"

The woman nodded. "Investigators from NATO and Interpol. I think there's someone from British Intelligence, too. I'm afraid they'll try to make it look like this was all my fault somehow."

"Why would they do that?"

"To make themselves look good," Witt snapped bitterly. "They'll protect this general's reputation because it reflects on them. They'll say I was trying to seduce the man for a favor."

"That's ridiculous!"

"No, I don't think so."

"I don't understand. What favor?"

She held her breath tentatively, as if she were wary of taking the Puerto Rican into her confidence. Inwardly, though, she was pleased with the way things were going. She had Leitchen right where she wanted him. Finally she let out a resigned sigh. "I came here to Monte Carlo because I knew the general was meeting with Mr. Nipree and Khadir Edan... about business. Military business.''

Leitchen cocked an eyebrow slightly as he curled a lock of her hair around his finger. "I see," he murmured.

"You do?"

"Well, actually, no." The Puerto Rican chuckled. "To be perfectly honest, Ali, I'm curious why an art dealer would be meeting with these types of men. Besides a friendly game of poker."

"I suppose I owe you an explanation."

"Only if you wish," he said, kissing her hair again. "I'm intrigued by women of mystery."

"Still, I'd feel better if you knew." Witt swallowed hard, then said, "You see, I have some friends...close, dear friends who've invested everything they have into a business that deals with military hardware."

"Oh?" He tried to sound only casually interested, but Witt knew better.

"It's supposed to be very efficient," she explained, leading him along. "A way the armed forces can keep better track of their inventories or something like that. They figure that if there are all these budget cutbacks in the military, there'll be a big demand for better management. You wouldn't believe some of the stories they tell me about the way things are run now. You know, like ordering new replacement parts for jets just because nobody can find the parts that came in two weeks ago. Things get misplaced or mismarked in warehouses. Does any of this make sense?"

Leitchen nodded. "Go on."

"Well, it's taking longer than they, my friends, had hoped to line up the right connections. They have only a few small clients, nothing close enough to what they need to earn a living, much less a profit. In fact they were losing so much money that it looked as if they were going to go bankrupt. So I...I..."

"You put some money into their company."

She nodded. "And when I heard about this meeting down here, I just felt I had to come and see if, if...I don't know, if I could help to land a big contract."

"I see." Leitchen looked past Witt for a moment, idly running a finger back and forth across his mustache. Finally he said, "Perhaps I can help you."

"You?" She did her best to look confused. "But how? Last night at the poker game you said you were involved in shipping."

Leitchen grinned. "That's true. And a lot of my shipments are for the military. Weapons, jeeps...many things. The general was a client of mine."

"Oh, no."

"That's all right," Leitchen said. "He was a pig. I shed no tears for him. And I have many other clients. Some of them might have an interest in the services of this company run by your friends."

Witt's eyes brightened. "Do you mean that?"

"Absolutely," the man assured her. He reached out and dragged his fingertip lightly under her chin. "So let's not be sad anymore, okay? Things will work out."

She let him pull her face to his. They kissed again, then eased back between the sheets. As Leitchen slowly began trailing his lips down her neck and shoulders, he whispered to her between kisses, "Who are these friends of yours?"

"Oh, some people from America," she told him, closing her eyes, deciding to celebrate her victory by enjoying the favors of her suitor one more time. He was, after all, a rarity among the men she'd bedded in that he took care to make sure he pleased her as well as himself.

"I do business with some people in the States, too," Leitchen said. His tongue crept out as he leaned over, teasing the soft flesh of her nipples until they hardened. "In fact, even now I have dealings with some men in Arizona."

Witt's eyes widened. She'd been fondling his back, but she suddenly pulled her hand away. "Arizona?"

"Yes." Leitchen laughed. "It's near California."

"I know that," she snapped, feeling herself tightening with involuntary rage.

Leitchen glanced up at her. "Is anything wrong?"

"These people in Arizona," she asked, "what are their names?"

"Ali, I don't ask the names of your people," he said with a smile. "There has to be a certain discretion, you know?"

"Ovitz and Tompkins," she guessed. "Is that who you're dealing with?"

Leitchen looked puzzled. "But...how did you know that?"

For the first time since the Puerto Rican had entered her suite, Alisha Witt dropped her charade, along with the fragile lilt of her French accent. In a voice that was all rage and all American, she snarled, "Those goddamned sons of bitches!"

CHAPTER TEN

An eighty-seven-car train lumbered down the tracks through the Tucson night. Lights blinked to life and the crossing gate began to lower across Kruk Street. Twenty yards away Al Blyford floored his Mustang and cried out to his brother, "Hang on to your seat belt!"

"What seat belt?" Zane howled as they hurtled forward, speeding under the gate and across the railroad tracks, well ahead of the approaching train.

The engine blasted its horn, and Al stuck his left arm out the window, raising his middle finger at the unseen engineer. "Same to you, fucker!"

As the train thundered behind them, Al proceeded down the street, which ran parallel to the downtown freight yards. There was a string of tenements within spitting distance of the tracks, and Blyford pulled up to the second of the six-story brick buildings and parked under the throbbing yellow glow of a halogen lamp, one of several dozen that lit up the entire area like a videogame arcade.

The men had come to rendezvous with Rain Murrer, their colleague who'd volunteered to raid Clark Reed's house and see if the old man's suicide note had implicated Al, Ellis Hayes or any other members of the

Natchapo Armed Militia in the attempted sabotage against Reed-Blackpoint Enterprises.

"Don't see his car," Al said, scanning the parking lot.

"He'll be here," Zane replied as they got out of the Mustang. "Let's go wait."

Litter was strewed across the asphalt except in one area where a handful of teenagers were shooting basketballs at a netless hoop mounted on a telephone pole. Younger kids watched from the sidelines on Stingray bikes. There were other idlers out in front of the apartment buildings, smoking cigarettes, drinking beer and chattering above the bustle of the nearby depot. The crowd was ethnically mixed, though mostly Indian and Hispanic, and uniformly poor.

"I get tired of this goddamn dump," Al said as he and his brother started up an outside staircase.

"Serves the purpose," Zane reminded him.

"Yeah, yeah, but it still sucks, y'know? Shit, look at the digs Ovitz and Tompkins got. Why can't we have offices like that?"

"It'll happen, Zane. We just gotta play our cards right, that's all."

Branded as outlaws by their fellow tribesmen on the reservation and targeted for arrest because of their sporadic outbursts of violence, the Natchapo Armed Militia was dependent upon a certain amount of secrecy, and the Blyfords had rented an apartment here under assumed names to serve as one of two clandestine hangouts. The rent was cheap enough, and the ongoing drone of rail traffic made it easy for them to speak freely without fear of being overheard by the other tenants, not that any of them were apt to care one way or the other.

The apartment was on the fourth floor. Al unlocked the door and they walked in on two other men, both Natchapos, playing chess on a large cable spool that served as a makeshift table. The rest of the room was equally Spartan. There were a couple of cots set against one wall and an overturned wastebasket in the corner.

"Rain been by?" Al asked the other men as he closed the door behind him.

"Nope," said Timothy Gwynn, a forty-year-old rancher who'd lost the tips of four fingers on his left hand to a grenade explosion during his tour of duty in Vietnam. If the injury presented a handicap, he didn't show it. A fitness buff and weight-training enthusiast, Gwynn, at six foot three and 230 pounds, was every bit as imposing as he had been during his days as a Marine. He dwarfed the other player, Carney Jones, a bookish-looking man in his early thirties. Jones was winning the chess game easily.

"Check," he said, whisking a rook across the board and capturing Gwynn's queen.

"Shit."

On the table next to the chessboard were several stacks of flyers, and as Gwynn pondered his next move, Al picked up one of the sheets and skimmed it. "What's this?"

"Pamphlets," Jones told him. "One's to recall the tribal council, the other's for a demonstration at the Air Force base when they put on their air show next—"

"Christ, not again," Al interrupted.

"Yep," Gwynn said as he used his king to take Jones's rook. "Carney's back on his Martin Luther King trip."

"I'll pass them around every day of the year if that's what it takes," Jones vowed. Almost as an afterthought he evaluated Gwynn's move and countered with his knight, announcing, "Checkmate."

"Shit," Gwynn muttered again.

"If you ask me, this is all these are gonna be good for." Al folded one of the pamphlets into a paper airplane and threw it across the room. His brother batted it down with his hand.

"Well, you're wrong," Jones insisted. "We can win this thing if we just have a little perseverance."

"Bullshit," Al retorted. "The only way we'll win is with a lot of guns!"

"Yippee, the great debate!" Gwynn exclaimed, rolling his eyes as he gathered up the chess pieces.

Jones stared hard at Al Blyford. "We're in the right. If we stick to our position and press our case, we'll win. Violence will only backfire."

"Since when?" Al said with a cynical smirk. For emphasis he reached below the cuff of his denim pant leg and slid an eight-inch Bowie knife from a leather sheath, then took aim and threw it end over end at the map of Arizona posted on the far wall. The blade bit through map and drywall before imbedding in a stud.

"Nice shot," Zane called as he walked over for a closer look.

The knife had all but obliterated that part of the map between Phoenix and Tucson showing a thirty-thousand-acre parcel of Suldowyo National Forest, located adjacent to the largest Natchapo reservation in the state. The land was the center of a growing dispute between the Air Force, which was looking to expand its proving grounds and gunnery ranges, and the Natchapo Indians, who claimed the ground was sacred and should be placed under their sole control as settlement of a lawsuit dating back nearly a century to a treaty between their forefathers and the U.S. government.

The men had grown fed up with what they saw as collusion between the present-day Washington bureaucracy and local council members who stood to gain personally by siding with a proposed compromise that would place the most desirable land into military hands and leave the Natchapos with more than half of the disputed acreage but in scattered, barren tracts whose only resources were subterranean mineral lodes. If passed, the new measure would, in essence, allow the Air Force to develop their share of the land unhindered, while the Natchapos would be forced to negotiate with yet another enterprise managed by the white man, namely energy conglomerates searching for coal, uranium, copper and other ores buried in the desert.

Carney Jones, Timothy Gwynn and the Blyford brothers were only four of seventy members of the Natchapo Armed Militia. Not so coincidentally, the majority of the group's membership, including Gwynn and Al Blyford, consisted of Natchapos who had served tours of duty in Vietnam. NAM was dedicated to taking measures to ensure that the Natchapos weren't sold down the river by the tribal council that supposedly represented them. Their effectiveness, particularly in recent weeks, had been hampered by reports linking several members of the group with incidents of armed robbery and assault that had little direct bearing on any perceived political issues.

And now, once again, the group's founders were at odds over battle tactics. Carney Jones, an admirer of Thoreau, Gandhi and Martin Luther King, had denounced the group's criminal leanings and persisted in advocating a high-profile strategy of nonviolent civil disobedience. The Blyford brothers, while denying any complicity in the aforementioned crimes, were nonetheless all for meeting force with force.

"We gotta show these people we mean business," Zane told Jones. "And the only language they understand is firepower."

"I don't believe that," Jones said.

"Wake up, Carn, will ya?" Al pleaded, his voice edged with irritation. "Shit, if we don't kick some ass, it's gonna be the same old story. Uncle Sam gets the mine, the power companies get the ore and we get the fucking shaft."

"And I don't know about you guys," Zane said as he pried his brother's knife from the wall, "but I'm not gonna piss away my time on some goddamn sit-in. It's time to act."

Another train was coming into the yards, passing so close to the building that the windows rattled. Over the rumbling drone the Blyford brothers drew Gwynn into their plans to escalate their protests against the Air Force. Jones sighed and went to the window overlooking the railroad yard. There were several engines rumbling away, filling the air with the rank smell of diesel as laborers jockeyed loads of freight off the cars. To see everyone bustling away down there, concentrating on business as usual as his colleagues rattled on about revolt and insurrection, filled Jones with a sense of futility.

When he helped to form NAM, Jones had proposed that the acronym stand for Natchapos Against Manipulation. It had been his hope to steer the more radical elements of his tribe away from the militaristic stance often espoused by the American Indian Movement. From the beginning, though, he knew his ideas for civil disobedience and other nonviolent confrontations were falling on deaf ears. Within a week the Natchapo Against Manipulation had become the Natchapo Armed Militia, and within days after that had come the first reports linking the group to a wide range of felonies in the Tucson area.

Jones had stayed on, however, hoping that if he had enough time to press his case, he might eventually win the Blyfords and the other NAM members over. Now he saw that little had changed after all these months. They still saw his position as weak and vulnerable. Al, Zane and all the others held firmly to their belief that might made right, and now it looked as if they were about to make the transition from random violence to all-out warfare in the streets. That thought depressed Jones, and it didn't take long for his sadness to give way to anger.

"Okay," he snapped, turning from the window to face the others. "You want to talk tough, huh? Talk practical?"

"No, what we want to do is *stop* talking," Zane corrected, "and start acting."

"Fine," Jones said. "I'm not sure how you figure on getting this big arsenal you keep talking about, but supposing you do, what do you think's gonna happen next, huh? I'll tell you. You'll whoop up some half-ass war party and go do something stupid, and then we're not only gonna get that shaft you keep talking about, we're gonna get buried in it."

Al sneered at Jones. "Look, it ain't like we're just gonna paint our faces and make some reckless charge on horseback."

"Yeah," his brother said. "We're gonna plan it out, same as you plan out your goody-two-shoes little games of chess, and then—"

Zane's words were drowned out by a splintering of wood as the door suddenly burst inward. Lieutenant

Eric Straw charged through the opening, revolver in hand, followed by two gun-toting uniformed officers.

"Nobody moves," Straw said, glancing around the room. He quickly saw that the only person armed was Zane. "You," he told him, "set that knife down on the table."

Zane hesitated. "What gives?"

"Trick or treat," Straw replied. "Now put the fucking knife down, or I'll take it and carve you a new asshole, asshole."

Zane obliged, complaining, "You ever hear of knocking?"

"Funny, that's what we wanted to ask your buddy."

"Buddy?" Gwynn repeated.

"Rain Murrer," the lieutenant told him. "He was looking to do a little breaking and entering at a friend's house. Tried to shoot me when I caught him."

"Murrer?" Jones said. "Where was this?"

"I think you know."

"No, I don't," Jones protested. "And you're out of line here. You had no right breaking in here like this. We're citizens, just like—"

"Save it for the judge," Straw snapped. "Right now I want all three of you to assume the position. We're going to slap on some charm bracelets and take you downtown."

"What's the charge?" Gwynn demanded.

"Mouthing off for starters," Straw said as he slammed the bigger man against the wall. When Gwynn whirled around and waved a fist, Straw pointed his gun at the Natchapo's face. "Go ahead. My baby here's been wanting to burp all night."

"Tim, just do what he says," Jones advised as he spread-eagled against the wall. "They don't have anything on us, and they know it."

"We'll see about that," Straw said, pulling a piece of paper from his pocket and waving it at Jones. "It's called a warrant."

"Fine," Jones said, gesturing around the sparse room. "Look around all you like."

One of the officers started searching the room as the other helped Straw handcuff the Natchapos and recite their rights. Then Straw asked Gwynn, "What was Murrer doing at Clark Reed's?"

"Clark who?" Gwynn asked.

The Blyford brothers were the only ones in the room who knew the answer to Straw's question, but they weren't about to cooperate.

"Whatever he was doing," Al said, "he was acting on his own—especially if he had a gun. We don't advocate violence."

"Yeah, and I don't scratch my ass when it itches," Straw cracked. "Come on, we'll see if we can't loosen your tongues at the station."

"I'm telling you, man," Al said, gesturing with his head at the pamphlets Jones had run off earlier. "There, look for yourself. We're strictly aboveboard."

As Straw paused to glance over the pamphlets, Zane grinned at Jones, then began spouting Jones's line of rhetoric. "We're peaceful, law-abiding citizens just trying to change the system from within. It's not easy, either, mind you, but we try."

"Yeah," Al said, "you think we like working out of a dump like this? I mean, if we were violent, we'd go out and rob a couple of banks or something so we could rent someplace nice, right?"

"Yeah, that's right," Straw agreed. "And you've done the robbing, so why are you living so low on the hog here? Saving your pennies for a penthouse?"

"Fuck you," Gwynn snarled.

"I take it back," Straw said. "Why don't you guys shut up and wait for your lawyers to come do your thinking for you?"

"Good idea," Jones said.

As the men were led from the apartment and down the steps, Gwynn asked, "What happened to Rain?"

Straw grinned. "He fell down and went boom."

Gwynn fell silent, trying to put it all into perspective. He'd long suspected that the Blyford brothers were involved with Rain Murrer and Ellis Hayes in some kind of extracurricular enterprise. If Murrer had been killed at Clark Reed's place, it stood to reason that he had something to do with the raid on the Reed-Blackpoint radar shipment he'd read about in the papers. Hayes hadn't been seen since the previous night, and rumor had it that he was one of the unidentified victims burned beyond recognition in the Trans Am.

The way it all added up for Gwynn was that Zane and Al were staging some kind of secret power play.

Something that would bolster their control over NAM. But now it looked as if their cover had been blown, and Gwynn was determined to find a way to capitalize on that. He figured if he played his cards right, he might just find a way to place himself at the helm of NAM, which had been his dream since the organization had first been formed.

A crowd of curiosity-seekers had gathered around the trio of squad cars parked by the front curb, and two other officers were busy keeping a clear pathway for Straw and his prisoners. As the Natchapos were ushered into the backs of two of the vehicles, a Ford Taurus rolled into the parking lot and sped over to the squad cars. The police raised their guns, but Straw signaled for them to put them away when he recognized the men inside the Ford.

Bolan was the first one out, followed by Brognola and Kissinger. They beelined to the squad cars, where Straw intercepted them.

"Evenin', boys," he said casually. "Appreciate the assistance, but as you can see, we've got everything under control."

"Oh?" Bolan said. "And what have you found out?"

Straw glared at Bolan and Brognola. "Uh-uh. You showed me up once. Not again." Gesturing at the three men he'd placed under arrest, he boasted, "These are my prisoners."

"And you're going to hold them hostage until you've saved face, right?" Bolan guessed.

"I don't owe you anything, G-man," Straw growled contemptuously. "Now get out of my way and let me do my job."

The Executioner was about to take a step forward, but Brognola grabbed him by the arm. "Let him go, big guy."

Bolan watched Straw circle around and get in one of the squad cars. He wasn't all that surprised at what had just happened. Straw, after all, struck him as the type to go to any lengths to salvage what passed for a reputation. Back at Clark Reed's place the lieutenant had claimed little knowledge concerning the whereabouts of the Natchapo Armed Militia, but obviously he was better informed than he'd let on, since he'd managed to beat Bolan and the others here to the group's hideout.

It had been Bolan's hope to set up surveillance at the tenement and tail some of the NAM members before they caught wind of Murrer's death, in hopes of being led to the masterminds behind Reed's death and the Reed-Blackpoint sabotage. But now, thanks to Straw, the militants were on the alert, and unless the lieutenant had had the good fortune to stumble onto some court-admissible evidence while taking his prisoners into custody, they'd be back out on the streets by morning.

"So, looks like it's back to square one, huh?" Kissinger said as he followed Bolan and Brognola back to the Taurus.

Brognola sighed. "Afraid so."

CHAPTER ELEVEN

During those first few disorienting moments when Randy Walker returned to consciousness, he was aware of a tightness around his chest, and his mind flashed on the symptoms of a heart attack. Was that what had happened to him? Where was he? What day was it? It was all a jumble.

As he struggled to piece things together, Walker tried to move and found he couldn't. As he became more aware of his surroundings, he realized the tightness he was feeling was from some sort of binding around his chest, holding him upright. Concentrating further, he felt a ropelike chafing against his wrists, thighs and ankles, none of which he could move.

And then it flashed on him. Ovitz. The conference room. Cigarette lighter. *"Well, let's spell it out for you."*

They knew. That was it. They'd found him out.

Overhead he could hear the drone of a jet, and off to his left the yelp of a coyote. A hot wind rolled past him, and he felt a slight sting of dust. He was outside.

He slowly blinked and found himself staring down at his feet. It was dark out, but the moon shed enough light for him to make out the rope tethered around his legs, binding him to what felt like a section of cyclone fence. Leaning back, he could feel the cross-diagonal bite of metal poking through his shirt. When he tried to move, the fence groaned under his weight. He turned his head back and forth and saw more fencing on either side of him. He was in some sort of cage.

"Have a nice nap, Randy?"

Walker glanced up and could make out a man's vague silhouette. It was Ovitz, standing a few yards away. Behind him the cage opened out to a dirt field, and twenty yards away another man was standing next to a piece of machinery the size of a gas pump.

"I asked you a question, Randy," Ovitz repeated. "How was the nap?"

Walker's throat was dry, cottony. It was hard for him to talk. When he did, it came out in a hoarse whisper. "Why?"

"Why?" Ovitz stuck a cigarette in his mouth and fidgeted with his lighter. Walker instinctively flinched, recalling the misty gas that had knocked him out, but Ovitz merely lit the cigarette, then put the lighter away. "Tell ya what, Randy boy. How about if I ask the questions?"

Walker said nothing. He looked away, trying to focus on the man in the distance. It had to be Tompkins. But what was he standing next to? It was too dark for him to make out details.

Ovitz took a step closer and blew smoke into Walker's face. "Why'd you bug our offices?"

"Bug? Didn't..." Walker wheezed. "I didn't."

"You didn't? Are you sure about that?"

Walker nodded weakly.

"Bullshit. I guess your memory needs a little jogging."

Ovitz sighed and took a step back from Walker, snapping his fingers. Off in the distance Tompkins reached out to the machine and tugged a switch. Walker heard a metallic creaking, then a springlike sound and a faint whistling in the air. The next thing he knew something struck him on the thigh with a loud thwack. He gasped at the fierce pain that ran up his leg, nearly hurtling him back into unconsciousness. Out of the corner of his eye he saw a baseball fall to the dirt and roll away from him.

"Ball one, low and outside," Ovitz said.

Walker clenched his teeth and writhed as the throbbing pain washed over his entire body. When the baseball rolled to a stop near the rubberized pentangle of home plate, he realized to his horror that he was bound to a batting range backstop.

"C'mon now, Randy, let's have it," Ovitz repeated, "Why'd you bug our offices? And don't say you were just trying to earn some extra credit, okay?"

The more Walker's eyes adjusted to the predawn darkness, the more details he could make out. He couldn't find any signs to give him a clear idea of where he was, but along the horizon he recognized the outline of the Tortolita Mountains and they looked as if they were only a few miles away. That would put him north of Tucson, near Cortaro or maybe Oro Valley.

He strained his ears for sounds of traffic but could only make out the waning buzz of the overhead jet.

When Walker didn't respond, the pitching machine groaned again, sending a second ball screaming toward him. This one came in a little higher, smacking him in the chest. Even though the ropes absorbed some of the blow, he still let out a howl, feeling as if a couple of ribs had been broken.

"Knock it off!"

Ovitz chuckled and turned away from Walker, calling out, "He says he's had enough of the slow stuff, Marlowe. Let's have a fastball, right up around the letters."

"You got it," Tompkins said from the mound as he adjusted the controls on the pitching machine. Walker braced himself as a third ball came slinging forward, swerving as it picked up speed. It whistled past his left ear and wedged itself in the wire mesh of the fence behind him, rattling the entire cage.

"Sorry, wild pitch," Tompkins called. "Let me try again."

"Wait!" Walker gasped.

"Time out on the field," Ovitz chuckled.

Tompkins strode in from the pitching machine, stooping to pick up a baseball bat lying in the dirt. Ovitz flicked his cigarette so that it bounced off Walker's chest. A few ashes burned through his shirt and singed his skin. He grimaced silently, determined not to show any further sign of weakness.

"Tell you what," Ovitz said, peering at Walker. "We'll kinda help you out here, then you can just fill us in on the missing pieces. Does that sound fair enough?"

"You didn't have to resort to any of this," Walker protested.

"Let's not get into that, okay? Now, here's what we figured happened. One of our clients for some strange reason lost faith in our ability to provide the best in security for their operations. Who knows, maybe they have a lot of internal theft. Maybe somebody's selling patent secrets to competitors. Whatever. So this client jumps to conclusions and figures we're to blame. How we doing so far?"

When Walker said nothing, Tompkins moved in, assuming a batting stance and taking a few half swings that brought the bat to within inches of striking Walker in the same spot where he'd been hit by a ball earlier.

"Instead of just going to the authorities," Ovitz speculated, "this client decided to have another security agent check on us, and so he called the good folks at Inston Corporation up in Mesa. And Pat Inston, an old buddy of ours, decides the best way to get the dope on us is to infiltrate us. So he sends along one of his top field agents to pose as some greenhorn looking to get into the bodyguard business. Enter Randy Walker."

Tompkins cocked the bat and swung away, slamming the barrel into Walker's ribs. The PI let out an involuntary cry and felt himself slipping back into unconsciousness. Blood bubbled up his throat and spilled out of the corner of his mouth. Ovitz grabbed Walker by the hair and kept his head from sagging.

"Three questions," Ovitz snarled. "One, who hired Inston? Two, what have you found out so far? And three, who else besides you and Inston are in on this?"

Walker's head was fogged with pain, but he was still clearheaded enough to realize that once he answered those three questions he was as good as dead. There was one chance for survival, and he could only hope it would work.

"I...I can help you," he murmured weakly. The words came hard, because with each breath he felt a stabbing pain in his chest and lungs. "We can be...the same side."

"Same side? What do you mean? Be a triple agent?"

Walker nodded feebly. "It can work. Let me down. Please."

Ovitz and Tompkins looked at each other, then Ovitz pulled a switchblade from his pocket and used it to cut Walker's bonds. As the ropes gave way, the man toppled facefirst into the dirt. Unable to break his fall, he struck his head against home plate and once again surrendered to the black void. The other two men stood over him, waiting for him to come to. Ovitz nudged him with the toe of his cowboy boot. "Guy has a problem staying on his feet."

"I don't trust him," Tompkins said.

"Me neither. But let's see if we can find out what he and Inston know before we get rid of him."

"If they're on us, killing him's only gonna put more heat on us."

"Not if we do it right," Ovitz said. "I figure if we play this smart we can kill two birds with one stone. Put him out of the way and make sure somebody else takes the fall for all this crap with Reed-Blackpoint."

"Sounds good, but who do you figure for a fall guy?"

Ovitz stared out into the Arizona dawn, where a coyote once more howled at the still-present moon. "I wonder," he said, the corner of his lips turning up into a malicious smile. "Is that really a coyote?"

Tompkins turned in the direction of the howl. "What do you mean?"

"I mean, maybe it's a coyote. Or maybe it's Injuns on the warpath."

"Ah," Tompkins said, picking up one of the baseballs and rolling it around in his hand. "Y'know, you might be right. Hell, I hear one of them got shot prowlin' around the suburbs just a couple of hours ago."

"Yeah, it's got all the markings of a full-scale uprising." Ovitz crouched over Walker, who was breathing shallowly but otherwise not moving. "Damn savages. Look at the way they tortured this poor guy. Hell, he's lucky he's still got his scalp."

"Ain't that the truth," Tompkins said. He wound up and threw the baseball at Walker, hitting him in the shoulder. "Seems to me we should do our part as good citizens and show those redskins a little justice."

BOLAN WAS FATIGUED, but his mind was restless and the bruise left by the bullet he'd taken in the semi had been aggravated by the chase through Clark Reed's cactus garden, making its presence known every time he moved. He lay still for a few minutes more, then threw off the covers and got out of bed. He was staying at the Roadrunner, a low-rent motel west of the Tucson city limits. Brognola and Kissinger had rooms down the hall, but it was past one in the morning and Bolan didn't feel like waking them just so he'd have someone to share his insomnia.

There was some milk in the minifridge and he drank it straight from the carton as he fussed with the television, switching channels in search of something that might distract him enough from his thoughts to let sleep creep up on him. The motel wasn't hooked up to cable, though, and all that was on was a talk show with some guy passing off smug put-downs of minorities as humor and a call-in shopping network offering genuine zircon simulated diamond necklaces for fifty-eight dollars and change. Bolan opted for a station that was off the air, letting the test pattern flicker on the screen, giving off a garbled hiss.

He went to the window and drew back the shades. He was on the second floor and had a scenic view of the parking lot and, beyond that, the perimeter of Tucson Mountain Park, seventeen thousand acres of essentially untamed desert, studded with mesas and towering saguaro cacti.

Bolan thought about his current mission. Over the past twenty-four hours it seemed as if he'd been stumbling through an ever-growing cluster of seemingly random names and events, and yet he knew that somehow they all fitted together, and the challenge was for him to find the right way of looking at all of them and making them fall into some kind of order.

Daniel Blackpoint. Clark Reed. Rain Murrer and the Natchapo Armed Militia. Randy Walker and sabotage in the Air Force. Lieutenant Straw. Tomi Leitchen and Alisha Witt. Somehow they were all connected, and it was up to Bolan to find out how. As a man of action, he desired a straightforward approach, but he knew that wasn't going to happen until he'd brought the picture more into focus, until he'd figured out which of the many targets held the key to the mystery.

The likeliest course was to probe the Natchapo question. He could always stake out the jail where Straw had taken the NAM militants netted in the roundup of the tenement. Once the men were released, as he was sure they would be, he could tail them in the hope that at least one of them would be foolish enough to lead him to some intermediary, some other part of the puzzle.

While he was thinking about all of this, a Chevy van exited Pass Road and pulled into the parking lot, sliding to a stop next to Bolan's Taurus. Out stepped Lyons, Blancanales, Grimaldi, Schwarz...and Barbara Price. She happened to glance up at his window and winked when she saw him.

"I'll be damned," he murmured.

By the time Bolan had thrown on a pair of jeans and a shirt, there was a faint knock on his door. He opened it and Price strode in, carrying a small overnight bag.

"You weren't supposed to be flying in until tomorrow," Bolan said.

She gave him an icy stare and glanced past him at the rumpled bed. "What's the matter? You have some love slave hiding in the closet or something?"

"No, that's not what I meant and you know it."

"Oh," she said, turning to leave, "you just want some privacy. I'll just take a room down the—"

"Don't you dare," Bolan said, reaching for her arm. He shook the tote bag from her grasp, then pulled her close. Their lips met hungrily, and when Price bent her legs at the knees, Bolan held her up, swinging her around until their momentum plopped them onto the bed.

When they finally broke the kiss, she stared at Bolan with a look of concern. "When you called back after chasing down that intruder, I told Jack to get the jet started pronto. I wanted to make sure I had another chance to hold you while you were still in one piece."

"Well, congratulations," he told her. "I still am."

"Good. It was a long flight. Let's go to bed."

CHAPTER TWELVE

Tomi Leitchen emerged from Alisha Witt's suite and padded down the hall in his bare feet, lugging an insulated bucket to the ice machine near the elevators. He was wearing one of the hotel's terry-cloth bathrobes, which was thick enough to conceal the bulge of a vintage World War II Luger tucked into the waistband of his pants. Humming nonchalantly, he set the bucket under the machine's spout, then pushed a button that brought a stream of clear cubes tumbling out of an inner reservoir. As he waited for the bucket to fill, Leitchen stole a glance down the hallway. There was a man huddled in one of the phone booths opposite the elevators. He was half-turned so that Leitchen could only see him in profile. From the styling of the man's clothes, the Puerto Rican guessed he was a Londoner, possibly a NATO agent but more likely from British Intelligence. It was equally likely he was the only man handling surveillance on the floor.

On the way back to the room Leitchen encountered a maid who had just emerged from a suite, pushing a large hamper mounted on a wheeled dolly. They exchanged words briefly, then Leitchen returned to Alisha's room and let himself in with the passkey.

"One man by the elevators," he told Witt, who was sitting at the vanity smoking a cigarillo, dressed in a tight-fitting silk teddy.

"And he saw you come out?"

Leitchen nodded. "So he'll have to move farther from the elevators so he won't draw suspicion."

"Or he'll switch off with someone else," the woman speculated.

"Maybe."

"What about the maid?"

"I told her to come by in ten minutes," Leitchen said. He set aside the ice and came up behind Alisha, gathering her hair in his hands. "Her hair's almost the same color, but it's pulled back, like this, and wrapped in a net."

"And her build?"

Leitchen smiled, letting go of Alisha's hair and reaching down the front of her teddy. "Nothing to compare with yours, my love . . . but close enough."

"Good." She held his hand against the swell of her breast for a moment, then drew it away.

"There's one problem, though," Leitchen said, bending over to kiss her pale shoulder. "She's Third World. Guatemala, I think. You could lie on the beach for a week and not be dark enough to pass for her."

"That won't be a problem." Witt put out her cigarillo and opened her makeup kit. "I never have the patience to lie on the beach for an hour when I'm here, much less a week. So I get my tan by the tube."

Opening the kit, she removed what looked to be a half-used roll of toothpaste. When she removed the cap and squeezed some out onto her forearm, however, the substance was the color of mahogany. As she rubbed it in, her skin took on a similar hue.

Leitchen chuckled. "Just like Al Jolson, yes?"

"Somewhat. But this is a little too expensive to use as shoe polish."

"Here," Leitchen said seductively as he reached for the tube, "let me help you rub it on."

Witt swatted his hand. "There's no time for that. I'm just going to do my face and arms. You need to get dressed."

As the Puerto Rican shed his bathrobe and crossed the room to put on his shirt, Witt turned back to the mirror and carefully dabbed the coloring cream on her face.

She'd decided during the night that it was imperative she slip out of the hotel undetected and flee the country. She'd been fortunate to forestall the interrogators for a day, but if she stayed around, she'd eventually have to answer their questions. And even if she was able to convince them for now of her innocence in the matter of General Puckzer's death, she had doubts that her cover could hold under the combined scrutiny of several sophisticated intelligence agencies. Although fleeing Monte Carlo would be tantamount to an admission of guilt, the woman felt certain she could elude capture. If need be, she would merely cast off her identity and take on a new one, just as she was now turning herself from a ritzy fashion plate into a demure member of the working class.

She'd been reluctant to draw Leitchen into her confidence to help with the escape, but as a man with undoubtedly vast experience in such matters, she knew he was a valuable ally, if only for the time being. Once they were free, she'd decide whether to continue their association. In the meantime, however, Witt was already looking ahead to other dilemmas that would be facing her once she reached the States. Maintaining control over T. S. Meyler's financial domain was certainly foremost on her mind, and given the information she'd just coaxed from Leitchen, she felt certain that her fate in that enterprise was now, more than ever before, linked to the way she resolved the matter of Cal Ovitz and Marlowe Tompkins.

The way Leitchen had spelled it out, Ovitz and Tompkins had contacted him through a mutual friend three months ago, saying they were looking to move a surplus of various weapons, mostly older guns and rifles. Although they might have been too obsolete for the U.S. military, the weapons were fully functional, and Leitchen knew of countless clients who'd be more than happy to add such firearms to their arsenals. A deal had been struck, and so far Leitchen had arranged for eight different buys involving two different buyers.

The Puerto Rican hadn't mentioned any names, but from information she'd gathered before even coming to Monte Carlo last weekend, Witt knew Leitchen had been hobnobbing recently with middlemen from Libya and the Colombian drug cartels, both likely candidates for a gunrunning operation.

The fact that Leitchen consorted with global undesirables didn't bother her. After all, she'd had occasion to run in the same circles when it suited her purposes, and back at her mountain chalet she had a trophy diamond the size of a golf ball, testifying to the gratitude of one of Libya's ranking generals after a weekend tryst at one of Khaddafi's Tripoli safehouses.

No, what roused Alisha's ire was the fact that Cal Ovitz was involved in a smuggling scheme he'd never bothered to inform her about, especially when it involved Air Force munitions, as she was sure it did. After all, it had been Alisha who'd used her influence with key Air Force personnel to help Tompkins-Ovitz Security land their lucrative contract at Bergman Air Force Base. Of course, she had benefited from the arrangement, too, using confidential information secured by Ovitz to wage a successful campaign to ensure that a T. S. Meyler subsidiary kept its valuable contract to continue supplying the Air Force with its controversial Nightflasher pilot goggles.

But that was beside the point. If Ovitz and Tompkins were gunrunning behind her back, they might be involved in other clandestine activities, too. Witt figured these sideline activities were probably responsible, one way or another, for whatever mental lapses had led to the failed attempt to discredit Reed-

Blackpoint for falsifying the contents of its equipment shipments to Saudi Arabia.

And that, for Witt, was intolerable.

She had no use for people she didn't feel she could trust. She'd give Ovitz and Tompkins every chance to come clean with her and show that they'd remedied the problems that had been reported to her. But regardless of the outcome, there was no way Cal Ovitz was going to receive the promotion she'd been dangling before him these past months. He'd failed his loyalty test, and if any of her suspicions were borne out, she'd see to it that both Ovitz and Tompkins were disposed of.

Witt was finished with the cream and piling her hair on top of her head when there was a knock on the door. Leitchen checked the peephole and saw the maid eyeing him tentatively.

"If you're not quite ready yet, sir, I can come back in a few—"

"No, no," Leitchen assured her. "We're just on our way out."

He gestured the woman in, and she wheeled the tall hamper past him into the room. When Witt turned around, the maid stared at her, confused.

"Miss?" she said. "You look—"

Before she could finish her sentence, the maid was silenced as Leitchen brought the butt of his Luger crashing against the base of her skull. He caught her as she fell and dragged her to the bed. Together he and Witt quickly undressed her. Then, as Witt changed into the maid's outfit, her accomplice hurriedly emptied the hamper of dirty sheets and towels, piling them on the floor.

The uniform was tight, but once Witt had draped the other woman's hair net over her head, she bore a close enough resemblance to pass casual inspection.

"Okay, let's do it," she said as she gathered a few essentials into a small bag and handed them to Leitchen, who had already climbed into the hamper. He crouched low, placing the bag under him and drawing his Luger, which was equipped with a three-inch-long silencer.

"Can you hear?" Witt asked as she lowered the lid on the hamper.

"Yes," Leitchen replied. "Let's go."

Although the Puerto Rican weighed considerably more than a full load of laundry, the cart was designed well enough to support the extra load, and Witt had little trouble wheeling it out into the hallway.

As Leitchen had predicted, whoever had been working surveillance from the phone booths had left, and she saw no sign of anyone else in the hallway. Once she reached the elevators, she took out the maid's keys, sorting through them for the one that worked the service elevator. The first one she tried fitted the lock, but wouldn't turn it.

"Shit," she muttered. It took her five tries before she got the elevator doors to open and, as she had begun to fear, the fumbling had blown her cover. Across the hall a door opened and a man in a gray suit emerged, heading toward her.

"Excuse me," he called out in a British accent.

Alisha pretended she didn't hear the man and rolled the hamper into the elevator. The doors were beginning to close when the man caught up with her, withdrawing a card from his coat and waving it as he blocked the doorway.

"Interpol," he said, identifying himself.

"No hablo inglés," Witt told the man, but he wasn't buying it.

"I'm sorry, Miss Witt, but I'm going to have to ask you to step out and answer a few questions."

The man was gesturing for her to leave the elevator when the hamper lid swung open. Leitchen popped up like a lethal jack-in-the-box, firing one shot directly into the agent's heart. The man lurched forward, dropping his card. Leitchen climbed out of the hamper and helped drag the agent into the elevator.

"Damn!" he cursed.

"Hopefully he didn't have time to alert anyone else," Witt said as the doors closed. "We might still be okay."

There were two parking levels below the ground floor. Leitchen pushed the button for the first level, and as the elevator began its descent, he pocketed the man's ID and quickly frisked him, coming up with a service revolver. He handed it to Witt, asking her, "Do you know how to use it?"

She nodded, then put the gun into the pocket of her uniform so that she could help Leitchen stuff the dead man into the hamper. They were just closing the lid on him when the elevator stopped and the doors opened on to the parking garage. Leitchen started out, calling over his shoulder, "I'll meet you in the basement. I want to see if anyone's on to us."

Witt felt a twinge of wariness as the doors closed on her. If Leitchen was to walk away, she'd be left with the dead man and a lot of explaining to do should there be more agents in the basement. She took the gun out and concealed it with a loose towel as she grabbed hold of the hamper. The elevator eased down one last floor, then stopped again. When the doors opened, she pushed the cart out, senses on the alert.

There was a bank of washers and dryers built into the wall just off the elevators, and the heat they generated washed over her like a summer breeze. Another maid was feeding sheets and towels into one of the machines and paid little attention to Witt as she kept the towel draped over her gun and abandoned the hamper, heading through the archway to the basement parking lot.

Both she and Leitchen had agreed that it was too risky to use their cars, so she sought out a likely prospect and smiled when she saw a middle-aged woman getting out of a Volvo station wagon twenty feet away. Witt headed for the woman while keeping her eyes open for anyone who might be watching. It seemed, though, that the rest of the lot was vacant. She was wrong, however.

"Wait!" a man called, stepping out from behind a pylon, gun in hand.

Witt was swinging her own weapon into play when a shot echoed through the concrete structure. The man dropped his weapon and spun halfway around before crumpling to the ground. Blood spurted from a gaping wound in his neck. Thirty feet away Leitchen emerged from the stairwell, lowering his Luger.

When the owner of the Volvo opened her mouth to scream, Witt raised her automatic and pumped two shots into her face. As the woman pitched to the ground, Witt quickly crouched over her, grabbing at the keys. Meanwhile, Leitchen turned and took aim at the other maid who had rushed out from the laundry area. One tug on the trigger and the maid was down, too, bleeding from the chest.

"Let's get out of here!" Witt roared, rushing to the Volvo.

As she started the engine, Leitchen slipped in beside her, keeping his Luger out. "We're okay," he told her. "We're okay."

They drove away from the carnage. Witt took care not to speed or otherwise draw attention to herself. She noted with relief that there was a long-term parking pass on the dashboard. When they rolled past the parking attendant, he eyed the pass and lazily waved them through.

As they headed through the streets of Monte Carlo, Leitchen kept an eye open for anyone trailing them. "So far so good," he said after they'd put a few miles between them and the hotel.

"We're still going to have to switch cars at some point."

"Of course," Leitchen agreed. "Then we'll drive to Marseilles and my people will take care of the rest. By the end of the day we'll be on a private jet, heading for America."

CHAPTER THIRTEEN

"Hi. This is Randy. I can't come to the phone right now, but if you'll leave a message at the beep, I'll get back to you as soon as possible."

Barbara Price checked the wall clock as she waited for the tone, then sighed into the receiver. "Beep yourself. Listen, Randy, it's Barb. It's after ten now. Once you're rid of whatever bimbo you spent the night with, give me a call, okay? Like I said before, it's urgent. I'm at the Roadrunner, room 248. If I'm not in, try the Wild Coyote near the airport around noontime. I'm having lunch there with Daniel. Bye."

Hanging up the phone, Barbara leaned back in bed. She was dressed already, but Bolan was shaving in the adjacent bathroom, wearing only his slacks and shoes. She smiled at the sight of his muscular torso, then frowned when her eyes fell on the black-and-blue mark on his left side. "That bullet left a nasty bruise, Mack."

"Would have left worse than that if I hadn't had the vest on," Bolan told her as he guided a disposable razor along his jawline. "Your friend's still not back?"

"Apparently not. It's not like him not to check for messages."

"Maybe you should try his office," Bolan suggested.

"I guess it couldn't hurt to check."

"I'm going to huddle with the team," Bolan told her, throwing on a shirt on his way out the door.

The sun was up and glaring in the morning sky, which was splotched with a few scattered clouds. Bolan headed down the outside deck and rapped his knuckles on the door of the adjoining room. Blancanales answered and motioned him in.

Lyons and Schwarz were seated at a small table, cleaning their Colt Government Model .45s. Brognola growled into the receiver. "Those goddamn idiots!"

"Who's he talking to?" Bolan asked Blancanales as he helped himself to one of the breakfast rolls resting on a room-service tray next to the television.

"Grimaldi or Kissinger. They went down early to run a tail on those NAM guys Lieutenant Straw brought in last night."

"Let me guess. They'd already been released."

"Sounds that way," Lyons said as he rammed an ammo clip into his automatic, then slipped the gun into his shoulder holster.

Brognola confirmed the bad news after he hung up the phone. "Our good friend Straw apparently grilled them for a few hours, then let them go with a tail to see where they'd head."

"And the Natchapos shook the tail," Gadgets guessed.

Brognola nodded. "Two went back to the apartment, but the others got away." He went to pour himself some more coffee, then realized the carafe was empty. He set it down angrily. "I ought to go down there and throttle that lieutenant personally."

"I wonder," Bolan said. "Is there any chance this Straw guy's not just incompetent?"

"What do you mean?" Brognola asked. "That he's in cahoots with NAM?"

"It's possible, don't you think?"

"Hell," Lyons interjected, "the way this mess is shaping up, anything's possible."

Brognola mulled it over for a moment, then glanced at Schwarz and Blancanales. "I think I'll call up Aaron and have him run a check on Straw. In the meantime maybe you two could shadow him for a while."

"Fine by me," Blancanales replied. "But why not Grimaldi and Kissinger?"

"They're on their way to the Air Force base," Brognola said. "Randy Walker was supposed to meet them to go over all the leads they've come up with there."

"Of course! Excuse me for a minute, guys." Bolan backtracked to his room and found Barbara still sitting on the bed.

"Randy's over at Bergman. He's meeting with—"

"No, he isn't," Barbara interrupted.

"No?"

"I just got off the phone with Pat Inston, Randy's boss," she explained. "Randy was supposed to phone in from the base at nine-thirty for a conference call. But he never did. Pat called the base, and the guys at AFI said he hasn't been in all morning. Mack, this isn't like Randy at all. I'm worried.''

She didn't have to tell Bolan; he could see it in her eyes. He went to the bed and sat beside her, offering a brief hug that was more comforting than reassuring. He didn't like the way things were adding up, either.

''Barb, how much do you know about this other assignment he was working on?''

''Not much more than you, I'm afraid,'' the woman confessed. ''It had something to do with checking into all the outside clients who did business with the Air Force, especially in terms of security work and procurement.''

''Do you have any names?''

''No, but Inston should be able to tell us. He's driving down to meet with Daniel and me for lunch. I'm going to see if some of the Air Force people can drop by, too.''

''Good. You know, Randy might be on a stakeout that's paying off and he just can't get clear to make a call.''

''I thought of that,'' Price said, ''but when I mentioned it to Inston, he said Randy's car is fitted with a homing device for just such situations. It's supposed to give off a steady signal so they'll know his position whenever he's doing surveillance.''

''But they aren't getting any readings?''

She shook her head. ''None.''

"Well, I've been in that situation before," Bolan told her, "and that could mean a number of things. He's probably able to override it or disconnect it if he thinks somebody besides Inston might be homing in on him. Considering he's checking out these high-tech outfits, that might be what happened."

Price looked hard at Bolan. "You don't really believe that, do you?"

He met her gaze. There was nothing else he could say.

"He's always been so reckless," she whispered, her voice choked. "Taking unnecessary chances, pushing his luck—he's as bad as you."

"You're pretty good friends, eh?" Bolan said.

Price nodded, trying to smile. "For a long time."

Ten minutes passed. Bolan heard a door open nearby, then close. Three sets of footsteps headed down the walk and came to a halt outside Bolan's room. There was a knock on the door, followed by Lyons's voice. "Mack?"

"Just a second." Bolan went to the door and opened it. Lyons, Schwarz and Blancanales stood on the landing, dressed light but with sports coats concealing their shoulder holsters. They looked ready for business.

"Change of plans," Lyons informed him. "Bear struck pay dirt running computer checks on the Natchapo Armed Militia. He dug deep on as many members as he could, and one address kept popping up on employment records."

"That apartment by the depot?"

Blancanales shook his head. "No. Some body shop out near the desert."

"We're on our way to check it out," Lyons said. "You interested?"

"Start the car up. I'll be right with you."

Able Team started down the steps to the parking lot as Bolan moved back inside the room, slipping his Beretta into its rigging and putting it on before donning a jacket. "I'll still try to make it for lunch, but—"

"I know." Price moved forward and kissed him lightly. "Be careful, Mack. Please."

By way of answer he kissed her back, then turned and headed out the door. Price sat back down on the edge of the bed, biting her lower lip as she stared at the phone, trying to will it to ring. When it didn't, she picked up the receiver and dialed her friend's number. As soon as the recorded message came on, she hung up.

"Randy, where are you?" she whispered.

WHEN RANDY WALKER failed to show up for the scheduled briefing at Bergman Air Force Base, John Kissinger and Jack Grimaldi split off with different Air Force Intelligence officers for updates. While Kissinger conferred with AFI officers looking into procurement and inventory irregularities, Grimaldi chose to mix pleasure with his business and took a much-anticipated tour of the restoration and renovation facility, a fifty-acre sprawl that contained a diverse collection of both present-day and vintage military aircraft.

With its arid climate, the Arizona base was a natural choice for long-term storage of such venerable mainstays of bygone wars as the Spitfire and Boeing B-29 Superfortress, but the site served as more than a mere outdoor museum. Newer craft that might otherwise be consigned to obsolescence were often given a new lease on life after undergoing painstaking repairs and high-tech upgrades.

"And that's gonna be important with all these defense cutbacks," AFI Agent George Sax told Grimaldi as they wandered along a row of Vietnam-era Huey helicopters. "You're not gonna be able to get Congress to cough up the big bucks for a whole new batch of newfangled jets and bombers like they used to."

Grimaldi nodded. "Yeah. Cutbacks are gonna put the screws to a lot of contractors, too, I'll bet."

"That's a fact," Sax said, wiping his greasy hands with his already soiled rag. "Especially the ones that were always on the cutting edge, like Guille/Lance and the Johnny-Ray Works. Hell, if you can't build new stuff, you got no need for a lot of research and development. Know what I mean?"

"True," Grimaldi said. In fact his tour of the restoration facility had a second purpose besides satisfying a flyboy's natural fascination with the planes of yesteryear. At the same time Grimaldi was admiring the aircraft around him, he was keeping an eye and an ear open for any possible connection between the Air Force's elusive culprits and the Natchapo Armed Militia, Alisha Witt, Tomi Leitchen and the parties responsible for the attempted sabotage of Reed-Blackpoint Enterprises and the murder of Clark Reed.

As Grimaldi and Sax looked over the Hueys, some of them still boasting decals and scars from their use in the Vietnam War, the Stony Man pilot felt a rush of nostalgia that took him away from the present and back to his own tour of duty in Indochina. A flurry of images flashed through his mind—the endless chain of aerial missions, undertaken at all hours of day and night; flying through smoke, rain and the retaliatory gunfire of the Vietcong; enduring the screams and howls of the wounded as they thrashed about in the back of the Huey after being hauled off the battle-field. He remembered a worn and battered pocket calendar he'd kept in his flight pack, marking off each day after collapsing in an exhausted heap on his bunk, calculating how much longer he'd have to serve before he could leave the death and carnage behind him. Little had he realized that now, years and years later, he'd still be in the war game, still shuttling men to the field of battle, still living each day as if it might be his last.

Sax had a sense of what was going through Grimaldi's mind, and as they climbed down from one of the Hueys, he asked, "You want to find out if you flew any of these babies?"

"Well, I—"

"We've got most of the flight logs on file," Sax said. "I can check for you."

"Not right now," Grimaldi said. He could indulge his sentimentality later, once they'd wrapped up this mission. Putting himself back on track, he asked Sax, "Are there a lot of Vietnam vets here?"

"Hell, yes," Sax said.

"Any Natchapos?"

"That are vets, too?"

Grimaldi nodded. According to Daniel Blackpoint, a high percentage of the Natchapo Armed Militia had seen duty in Nam, so it seemed worth looking into anyone fitting that category.

"I can't recall any offhand," Sax confessed, "but I'd suspect there's a couple. Of course, we have a lot of Native Americans in the program."

"I've seen a few of them," Grimaldi said. "But I think we might want to check into the vets in particular."

"No problem. We'll head over to Personnel after we finish up here."

As they began to circle back to where they'd started the tour, Grimaldi and Sax were interrupted by the laboring groan of a monstrous diesel tow truck coming up behind them. Stepping back, the men watched the truck roll past, carrying the mangled remains of an Apache combat chopper strapped to a flatbed truck with steel cables. Sunlight glared off the cables and strips of exposed metal where the sides of the aircraft had been ripped apart and twisted from an obvious crash landing.

"Looks like a bad one," Grimaldi said.

Sax nodded. "Yeah. Lost three men on that one."

"Where did it happen?"

"Yuma," Sax said. "Night-training exercise."

"Shit," Grimaldi muttered. "I should've known. Pilot was using Nightflashers, right?"

Sax nodded. "Yep."

Nightflashers were special infrared goggles that amplified moon and starlight to increase pilot visibility during nocturnal missions. They were a strategic boon in that they allowed choppers to fly lower than usual at late hours, increasing the element of surprise in battlefield situations. On the downside, however, the design of the goggles was such that they obstructed peripheral vision, giving pilots only one-quarter of the viewing range they'd have without them. Furthermore, while the Nightflashers illuminated objects in the immediate foreground of their wearer's field of vision, any obstacles farther in the distance actually became darker. These factors, combined with the fact that the goggles decreased visual acuity to twenty-fifty rather than the twenty-twenty vision traditionally demanded of anyone aspiring to join the Air Force pilot program, were pointed out by numerous critics as primary reasons for the startling number of chopper casualties during night-training exercises at bases throughout the country.

Grimaldi knew of several fellow pilots who'd died during such accidents and another two who had refused to reenlist after serving their tours of duty specifically because they'd felt that being forced to wear Nightflashers during night flights was like being forced to play Russian roulette.

"I can't believe they don't just get rid of those damn goggles," he said, "or at least try something else."

"Office politics most likely," Sax told him. "It's like we were just talking about. They've dropped so much money into developing these Nightflashers and buying them for every air base between here and the Atlantic, they don't want to admit they maybe made a mistake. If they did that, some heads would have to roll and—" Sax looked around to make sure no one else was eavesdropping, then said, "And just between you and me, I'll bet some of the big brass are probably getting kickbacks from whoever's making 'em."

"The old boy network," Grimaldi said with disgust.

"Makes sense, don't you think?"

Grimaldi nodded and watched as the tow truck idled at the end of the row. A huge crane kicked into gear, preparing to hoist the demolished Apache from the flatbed. From this angle he could see the spider-webbed windshield, stained with the blood of the pilot who'd gone down with the chopper.

"Well, look on the bright side," Sax said with a cynical smile. "There might be a few parts we can salvage from that Apache and slap onto another one. Save Uncle Sam a few dollars in repair bills.''

''Yeah, right. Listen, George, you stock those Nightflashers here, don't you?''

''Yeah.''

''Any idea who makes them?''

''Jones & Long, outfit out of Phoenix. I think they're owned by that big shot Meyler guy. You know, the nutcase.''

''T. S. Meyler?''

''Yeah.'' Sax glanced at Grimaldi skeptically. ''Hey, you don't think *he's* behind this, do you?''

''Probably not, but we might as well touch all the bases.''

''I guess so.''

''And even if he isn't behind the sabotage,'' Grimaldi said, once more glancing at the ruined helicopter, ''I'd like to figure out how he's managed to keep the Air Force buying up those goddamn goggles of his.''

''You think you can do something about it?''

''Seems worth a try,'' Grimaldi said. ''Don't you think?''

''Hell, yes.''

They headed back to the main office. Halfway there a mechanic in a beat-up golf cart drove out to meet them. Kissinger was riding beside him.

''Find something?'' Grimaldi asked.

''Maybe so,'' Kissinger replied, getting out of the cart and taking the other two men aside. ''We were checking inventory and, among other things, they're missing not only some plastic explosives but also remote detonators."

"Like the one Striker found on that semi?" Grimaldi asked.

"Hard to say for sure, but from the way the big guy described it, I'd say yes. But that's not all. We just got a call from the chief. There's some good news and some bad news."

"All right." Grimaldi sighed. "I'll play. Let's get the bad news out of the way first."

"Alisha Witt and Tomi Leitchen," Cowboy reported. "They gunned their way out of the hotel they were staying at in Monte Carlo."

"They what?"

"You heard me." Kissinger briefly related the details of the escape as he'd gotten them from Brognola, who in turn had gotten the information thanks to Aaron Kurtzman's interception of an Interpol communiqué back at Stony Man Farm.

"Any trace of them after they made their getaway?"

"Zip," Kissinger said, "but Interpol's speculating that they hightailed to Marseilles, where Leitchen has a lot of connections. They'll probably hide out for a while, unless Tomi can score a plane, in which case the thinking is they'll skip the country."

"And go where? Puerto Rico?"

"Maybe. But let's not forget that Leitchen figures into some of the stuff going down here. If we're lucky,

Tomi'll come flying right into our laps, along with Ms. Witt.''

"And that's the good news?" Grimaldi asked. "It seems a little tentative."

"No, the good news is even better. Kurtzman did some cross-referencing through the computers, and it looks like we've pinpointed another base of operations for the Natchapo Armed Militia. We're going to pay a little visit and see if they're sitting on the rest of those explosives.''

CHAPTER FOURTEEN

After Randy Walker's interrogation at the batting range, Marlowe Tompkins set out to lay a trap for the Natchapo Armed Militia. Cal Ovitz, meanwhile, drove north to Mesa where, wearing a hard hat and the uniform of a telephone repairman, he climbed the telephone pole feeding wires to the headquarters of the Inston Corporation and put a tap on all of Inston's phone lines. It wasn't an easy procedure, since Inston had taken numerous precautions against such an intrusion, but the extra effort was worth it. Retreating to eavesdrop over the transceiver in his Camaro, Ovitz's patient wait was rewarded less than two hours later when he overheard the conversation between Inston and Barbara Price, confirming his suspicions that Randy Walker had been spying on Tompkins-Ovitz Security Services on behalf of the Air Force.

Now all that remained was to find a way to determine how much, if anything, Inston had learned from Walker about clandestine activities going on behind the Tompkins-Ovitz business front. Having heard that Inston intended to drive down to Tucson later that morning, Ovitz's course of action was clear, and he focused his sights on the parking garage adjacent to Inston's building.

Like countless thousands of parking facilities throughout the Southwest, the two-story structure featured an auto-detailing service. As head of his own business, Inston felt compelled to have his car reflect his position and paid a monthly fee to have attendants keep his Mercedes 280 in pristine condition. He'd barely driven the day before, so this morning the coupe needed only the slightest once-over. One worker went about plucking dead bugs from the hood and grill-work, using rubbing compound to neutralize any other minute traces of residue from the desert, while the other leaned inside the vehicle, vacuuming the ash-trays and floor mats.

"Vanity, vanity," Ovitz whispered as he got out of his Camaro and quietly closed the door. "It's gonna be your undoing, Pat, buddy."

Carrying a small black satchel, Ovitz crossed the street and casually circled halfway around the parking lot, then slipped into a side door and stole up a flight of steps to the second floor. There were more than thirty cars parked in rows on either side of the driving lanes. Ovitz waited in the stairwell doorway for a man in a yellow Toyota to drive past, then slipped out and quickly made his way to a Chevy pickup with its front window rolled down. Ovitz flipped the lock and opened the door on the driver's side. Cautiously he released the parking brake, then jockeyed with the steering wheel, turning the front wheels as much as possible before the steering column locked in place.

After slipping the truck into neutral, he eased it slowly out of the parking space. As it rolled across a slight incline, the truck gradually picked up momentum, rolling directly for a parked Rolls-Royce. Just as he slipped into the stairwell and started back down the steps, Ovitz heard the jarring crunch of metal against metal as the pickup slammed into the luxury car.

"Holy shit!" the attendant polishing Inston's Mercedes wailed. He threw down his chamois and rushed up the incline leading to the second floor.

"Wait for me," the other worker cried, squirming out of the 280. As Ovitz had counted on, the second attendant haphazardly closed the Mercedes's door, leaving it unlocked.

Once both attendants were out of view, Ovitz beelined to the 280 and yanked the door open. Unzipping his black satchel, he withdrew a transistorized plate no larger than a soda cracker. With expert swiftness and precision he was able to insert it into a cellular-phone system cradled between the two front seats.

Once wired to the phone's circuitry, the plate served two functions. First, it would direct all outgoing calls through another cellular unit in Ovitz's Camaro. While monitoring Inston's calls, Ovitz would have the ability to drown out the other party with a wash of static, and cut in on the call if necessary. Consumers were used to glitches in reception in the Arizona desert, especially outside the major cities, and Ovitz doubted that any interference would draw undue notice from Inston. The plate's second function would cause its circuits to overload when triggered by a remote signal, giving off a wisp of the same gas Ovitz had used to deck Walker the night before.

Mission accomplished, Ovitz quickly checked under the dashboard. As he had hoped and suspected, Inston had installed a combination receiver-radar unit, which included detailed map cards that could be laid over a miniature radar screen to pinpoint homing signals. The system was one of the few joint projects Inston and Ovitz had worked on during their affiliation with the CIA, and the undertaking hadn't been a pleasant one for Ovitz, since Inston had made most of the major breakthroughs and received primary credit for the invention.

"Yeah, but he who laughs last laughs best," Ovitz told himself. He retreated from the Mercedes seconds before one of the attendants scrambled back down to the ground floor. Once across the street, Ovitz slipped back behind the wheel of his Camaro and tapped out a cigarette. Now he only had to wait.

Less than a half hour later Inston and Donna Long, a trim redhead, entered the parking structure and got into the Mercedes, paying little attention to the heated argument taking place between the parking attendants and the apparent owner of the crumpled Rolls-Royce.

Once the Mercedes rolled out of the lot and into traffic, Ovitz began tailing in his Camaro. On the seat beside him a receiver picked up the conversation between Inston and his secretary. By the time they reached the county line, Ovitz had overheard enough to realize that although there were suspicions, Inston had no concrete proof linking Tompkins-Ovitz Security Services to any criminal wrongdoing. In fact, at the same time Randy Walker had been enrolled in the bodyguard school, he was also investigating three other Tuscon-based outfits with Air Force contracts.

"That's all we need to know," Ovitz muttered once Inston and Long had ceased talking and turned up the Mercedes's car radio. Picking up his cellular phone, Ovitz punched a number and waited for Tompkins to come on the line.

"Yeah?"

"All systems go. Inston's on his way with his secretary. They don't know squat."

"Good."

"Where are you?"

"About five minutes from the reservation."

"Perfect," Ovitz said, keeping an eye on Inston's Mercedes. "Go ahead and snap on Walker's homing signal and Inston will be on his way to the ambush."

"Okay, it's on," Tompkins reported. "Now I gotta go drum up some Injun trouble."

"I'm sorry, but I don't see the point of staying around here all day," Carney Jones said, cleaning his glasses with his shirttail, then slipping them back on and going to the window overlooking the freight yard. There was a shabbily dressed man down in the weeds near the fence, rummaging for bottles and cans. Even from this distance Jones could tell the man was an undercover cop working surveillance. "So what if we keep a few cops out of commission for a few hours?"

"Hey, it was orders from Big Al," Timothy Gwynn replied, making no attempt to hide the sarcasm in his voice. "When the Big Chief speaks, we do what he says, right?"

Jones turned from the window and eyed Gwynn curiously. "You know, Tim, all these years I've known you and still I can't get a bead on you."

"Oh?" The man glanced up from the block of wood he was whittling with a jackknife.

"One minute you're preaching violence along with Al and Zane, the next you're siding with me against them. Where do you really stand?"

Gwynn smiled sardonically and pointed the knife's blade at his chest. "I look out for number one. That's where I stand."

"Maybe that's part of our problem," Jones said. "Everybody's got their own agenda, so we never rally behind one plan of action."

"I feel a lecture coming on." Gwynn yawned and shaved a strip of wood off the block, which was slowly taking the shape of an eagle's head.

Jones grabbed one of the stacks of pamphlets from the makeshift table. Gesturing at the other pile, he said, "Why don't you grab those and we'll go pass them out near the base? The cops'll probably follow us, but at least we'll be doing something constructive."

"Hey, speak for yourself." Gwynn nodded at his handiwork. "I'm making a belt buckle."

"Fine, suit yourself." Jones headed for the door. "I'll be back later."

Gwynn held up the stubs of two fingers, making a *V*. "Peace, man," he called out with the stoned drawl of a sixties pothead. "Power to the people."

"Too bad you think it's a joke. Any sort of real effort and we could make it happen."

Gwynn didn't bother responding. He focused on his whittling until Jones was out the door and heading down to the parking lot, then calmly folded the knife and slipped it into his pocket. Rising from the table, he moved from window to window, watching Jones leave and monitoring the response of the man in the weeds. The undercover cop stooped, half burrowing his head into the trash bag he'd been filling with cans and bottles. Gwynn suspected he was using a walkie-talkie or remote mike to announce Jones's departure and make sure the Natchapo followed.

Gwynn wasn't planning to stay in the apartment all day, either. He went to a third window facing the inner courtyard and eased it open. Climbing out, he could see a couple of children playing stickball below, and he waited until he was sure they were distracted, then stood on the windowsill and reached for a lightning rod anchored to the edge of the roof.

Even without the tips of four fingers he was still able to secure a firm enough grip on the rod to pull himself up. The roof was flat, so it was easy for him to make his way to the other side of the building, where he pried open a trapdoor and climbed down a steel ladder to an inner stairwell.

Once down the steps, he glanced out the small window on the exit door, which opened out to a thin strip of parched lawn dotted with dog excrement. Beyond the lawn was the street and a bench where five people were waiting for a bus. Gwynn stayed put for another ten minutes, then a bus rumbled up to the stop and idled as it took on the new passengers. The Natchapo jogged out of the building, nearly bowling over a withered old man who was out walking his leashed Chihuahua.

"Hey, watch where you're going!" the old man wheezed.

Gwynn ignored him and slipped aboard the bus just before the driver was about to close the front doors. He paid the fare and headed to the back, plopping down next to a matronly woman with a lapful of yarn. As the bus pulled away, he crouched over slightly so that he couldn't be seen by anyone outside. Once he was sure he'd gotten away, Gwynn moved to another seat and relaxed, letting the scenery roll by as he planned his next move.

Last night at the police station he'd pretended to fall asleep during a lull between questioning. As he'd hoped, he'd overheard the Blyford brothers huddling together and trading whispers. He'd only picked up snatches of conversation, but it had been enough for Gwynn to realize Zane and Al's secret undertaking had something to do with weapons. Later, when the brothers had split off from Gwynn and Jones after their release, Gwynn felt certain they were getting ready to make a move, and now that he'd gotten Jones and the cops out of his way, Gwynn was determined to find out what was going down.

For weeks now Gwynn had been intrigued by the brothers' outside activities, and not only out of mere curiosity. To Gwynn's way of thinking, the Blyfords commanded control over the Natchapo Armed Militia primarily because of their contacts. If he were to gain access to those same people, Gwynn figured, there was no reason why he couldn't bolster his own standing in the group. Hell, if he played his cards right, he could even wind up taking charge. Of NAM's seventy-odd members, he figured he could count a dozen as firmly in his camp, which was more than Carney Jones could say but still considerably shy of the number of Blyford loyalists. However, if he could get the lowdown on what Al and Zane were up to and find a way to turn the information against them...

The bus took Gwynn downtown, past Tucson Museum, then up Campbell Avenue and across the Rillito River. The route extended all the way to the edge of the reservation, but Gwynn got off a few blocks earlier and headed down a long cul-de-sac to Ideal Auto Body and Salvage. Inside a row of adobe-style service bays facing the street, men could be seen spraying paint, replacing fenders and otherwise tending to disabled vehicles. Those cars that were beyond repair were stacked in crumpled heaps in the sprawling lot behind the body shop. For a small fee customers could scavenge amid the wrecks for cut-rate parts.

Gwynn sauntered up to one of the bays, where a fat-bellied man was pulling masking tape off the windshield of a freshly painted Nissan.

"Hey, Mike," Gwynn called.

"Mornin', Timmo," the fat man said, talking around a thick wad of bubble gum. "Hear you got hauled in for the third degree last night."

"Yeah, but they didn't find out shit." Gwynn glanced around. "I take it Zane and Al came by. They still here?"

Mike shook his head and blew a huge bubble as he wadded the tape into a ball and heaved it at a waste bin against the wall. It missed but stuck to the side of the basket. "Left about half an hour ago."

"Any idea where they went?" Gwynn asked.

"No, but they got a call from somebody."

"Who?"

"Dunno," Mike said. "You might want to check with Diton. He took the call."

Gwynn smiled. Diton was one of his closest friends. "He out back?"

Mike nodded and started in on one of the side windows. Gwynn left him and circled around the service bay to the back lot. There were a couple of customers huddled over the remains of an old Dodge station wagon, trying to pry a water pump and alternator out of the wreck. Elsewhere, some fellow NAM members were salvaging parts from a couple of cars that had been towed in earlier that morning. Gwynn exchanged greetings as he walked past, talking above the yelping of a yellow-toothed rottweiler that strained at its leash inside a large wire cage.

Back at the far end of the lot, barely visible behind a towering heap of used tires, was a small cinder-block structure that had served as a filling station back when the main road had run through the yard and linked up with the nearby highway. Now it was fenced off from the rest of the compound and overrun with weeds. Three pumps rose from a slab of cracked concrete, posting prices that dated back to some bygone era when a gallon of premium went for less than forty cents. Propped against the building's east wall were several old billboards layered with peeling cigarette ads. To the casual eye, it appeared the old station had been long abandoned, but a closer look revealed a current telephone line running to the roof and a fresh gleam to the brass dead bolt on the front door.

The gate wasn't locked, so Gwynn let himself in and walked through the weeds to the door. It opened before he could get to it. A tall, solidly built man in grease-stained coveralls waved Gwynn inside.

"Hey, man, what's up?"

"Hey, Diton. I was looking for Zane and Al," Gwynn said. "Mike says I just missed 'em."

"Righto."

The windows in the main working area were boarded up save for peepholes allowing a view of the salvage yard. An overhead light shone on a long table mounted against the far wall. There were two other men standing at the table, using an assortment of galvanized pipes, wiring, timers and explosives to make homemade time bombs. They'd pieced together nine of them already, along with more than two dozen Molotov cocktails that had been carefully placed in a liquor case with cardboard dividers.

"Looks like we're stepping up production," Gwynn observed. "We getting ready to make a move?"

"Seems that way, don't it?" Diton said.

"Al and Zane . . . they wouldn't happen to be out on a weapons run, would they?"

Diton shrugged. "Hell, they don't tell me anything. You know that."

"Yeah, but you got two ears," Gwynn said, gesturing at an old rotary phone mounted to the nearby wall. "You must have heard something when they got that call."

"Not much. All I caught was something about the old Baines mine."

"That's good enough. Thanks, man."

"Hey, stick around, why don't you?" Diton said. "Al wants fifty bombs by tomorrow. We could use some help."

"I saw Dave and Galzie ducking around in the yard. I'll send 'em back," Gwynn told him as he grabbed a set of car keys from a nail jutting out from the doorjamb. "I got an errand to run."

THE BLYFORD BROTHERS RODE across the desert hard-pan in Al's old Mustang, windows open to let in the scant late-morning breeze. The sun beat down on the barren land, and up ahead waves of heat rippled above the horizon, giving the illusion of water. They were on the reservation, but miles from the nearest living quarters, and the road they were on was seldom used and half-covered by drifting sand.

"Why the hell did he drag us way out here?" Zane complained.

"He wants to make sure we're alone," Al guessed, squinting as he drove through a whirlwind of dust and sand. "He was probably worried we'd bring along the whole gang and try to wrangle the guns for free."

"Not a bad idea." Zane opened the glove compart-ment and pulled out a .38-caliber revolver. As they passed a weathered sign reading Baines Mining & Drilling Co., he took aim out the window and squeezed off a shot that punched a hole through the *O*.

"Quit wasting ammo," Al chided.

"Shit, bro, we'll have plenty more soon enough."

"Let's get it in our hands first, okay?"

"Yeah, yeah." Zane pulled the gun back into the car and set it on his lap. Turning his attention to the radio, he twirled the tuning knob to pull in an oldies station and started to hum along to a Jan and Dean surfing anthem.

It had been three hours since the brothers had been released from custody along with Timothy Gwynn and Carney Jones. Aware that they were under police surveillance from the moment they'd left the station, the group had quickly split up, with the understanding that Jones and Gwynn would take a circuitous route back to the apartment near the freight yards and stay there the rest of the day. Zane and Al, meanwhile, had played cat and mouse with their tails, leading them downtown and then losing them in traffic before doubling back outside the city limits to the salvage yard.

There was a message for them, and when they'd returned Marlowe Tompkins's call, he'd told them he'd lined up a cache of M-1 rifles. Zane and Al had been hoping for something more potent, but the carbines were still an improvement over the motley assortment of handguns and hunting rifles that made up the present arsenal of the Natchapo Armed Militia. With the increased firepower it would be far easier to escalate their violent campaign against the white man.

After driving another eight miles, the Blyford brothers came upon the scattered ruins of the old Baines mining project, a venture initiated by Natchapo tribesmen in the late sixties, only to be abandoned a few years later when the ground failed to yield enough wealth to turn a profit. Over the past two decades the elements had taken a toll on five wood-framed dormitories and a brick ore house, giving the site the dreary look of a ghost town.

Al pulled to a stop alongside a small hut that had originally served as a machine shop. It was in a poor state of repair, pocked with holes where rust had eaten through the metal walls.

"This is the place," Al said, killing the engine.

"Nice and cheerful, huh? Shit. It looks worse than our place at the salvage yard."

"Low overhead keeps the prices down," Al joked as he got out of the car. Like his brother, he was armed with a .38 revolver. He looked around for a trace of another vehicle but didn't see any. Starting for the hut, he said, "Let's check it out."

Passing through the doorway, they found the interior of the hut filled with cobwebbed workbenches and old lathes. Dust motes danced in various beams of light pouring in through the rotting walls. The air was hot and reeked with the smell of decay.

"Over there," Al said, gesturing at one corner of the enclosure, where a large, hulking form lay buried under a layer of thick, weathered canvas. They approached it warily, guns at the ready as they peered into the wavering shadows along the hut walls. As they got closer, they could see footprints in the dust.

"Looks like they brought it in from the back," Zane said, tracing some of the prints to a rear loading area.

"Yeah." Al set down his gun and leaned over, grabbing a corner of the canvas. "Let's see what we got."

Together they yanked the tarp away, stirring up clouds of dust.

"Jackpot," Zane said, mouth widening into a grin.

Resting in neat stacks on the wooden floor were several large crates stamped with Air Force markings. Al pulled out his Bowie knife and used the thick blade to pry the lid off one of the crates. Inside, as promised, was a neat row of Air Force-issue carbines nestled in packing material. Al whistled with admiration as he picked up one of the rifles and tested the firing mechanism.

"Nice. Real nice."

"Amen," Zane agreed as he ran his finger along the rifle's barrel. "With these mothers we're gonna raise some definite hell."

"I wouldn't count on it."

The Natchapos glanced back at the entrance to the hut. Marlowe Tompkins stood silhouetted in the doorway with an M-16 cradled in his gloved hands.

"Tompkins . . ."

The M-16 barked to life, pumping 5.56 mm ammo into Zane's chest. He reeled off balance and crumpled to the floor, leaving Tompkins with a clear aim at his brother. Al grabbed for his Bowie knife, but as he turned to throw it, Tompkins raked him with a burst of semiautomatic fire. Al staggered backward onto the weapon crates, and the knife fell harmlessly to the floor.

The echo of gunfire lingered for a few moments and was followed by the clatter of rats fleeing through the shadows. Then the hut was silent. Tompkins breathed the cordite stench as he kept the M-16 trained on the two Natchapos. Blood seeped from the mangled corpses, and from the contorted way they were lying, it was clear that neither had survived the ambush.

Leaving the hut, Tompkins sprinted across the hardpan until he reached a small, lone butte, behind which was parked Randy Walker's Honda Civic. The windows were down and Walker was sprawled across the back seat, gagged with duct tape and bound tightly at the wrists and ankles. He'd tried to wriggle free but had only managed to wedge himself at an angle that had shifted his weight onto his broken ribs, immobilizing him with pain. From the slightly panicked look in his eyes, Tompkins could tell Walker had heard the gunfire.

"Don't worry. You'll get your turn," Tompkins promised, starting the engine. As he shifted the Civic into gear and drove back to the hut, Tompkins grinned at Walker in the rearview mirror. "See, here's what I figure happened. You found out me and Ovitz were clear, so you shifted your focus to these war-crazy Injuns. Came out here snooping on them, only they caught you in the act and worked you over trying to find out what you knew."

Circling behind the hut, Tompkins parked and opened the back door. As he leaned in, Walker suddenly kicked outward, expending what little strength he'd managed to store up while waiting in the car. Tompkins teetered backward slightly, but the blow wasn't forceful enough to knock him off his feet. He grabbed Walker by the ankles and jerked as hard as he could, yanking the investigator from the car. The man's head struck the door frame, opening a wide gash and spilling blood into the dirt.

"Yeah, yeah, you put up a valiant effort," Tompkins said, shifting his grip to take hold of Walker by the armpits. "But it just wasn't in the cards for you to get away."

Tompkins dragged Walker into the hut and shoved him down into a heap next to the weapon crates. Blood trailed from his head wound, stinging his eyes, but he could still see Zane Blyford lying next to him, mouth agape, dark eyes staring vacantly.

Tompkins leaned over and tore at the duct tape covering Walker's mouth. Involuntary tears welled in Walker's eyes as the tape pulled against his lips. He gulped in the dusty air and tried to swallow, but his throat was so parched that he wound up choking, and with each cough his broken ribs jabbed against his lungs. Yet again Walker found himself hovering close to the verge of unconsciousness.

As he calmly loaded one of the carbines, Tompkins told Walker, "You were a real trouper. Took your lumps and kept your mouth shut. You were in bad shape, but at least you were still alive. Then one of the NAM lookouts came rushing in, saying that someone was coming." Tompkins idly aimed the carbine at Walker. "Somebody panicked. Bad news for Randy Walker."

Tompkins pulled the trigger. Walker's head snapped back as the bullet slammed into his face, obliterating flesh, cartilage and bone before lodging in his brain. He fell back and lay still, his blood beginning to mingle with that of the Natchapos.

The killer carried the carbine back to the window and calmly glanced out, waiting for a telltale cloud of dust to announce the arrival of the Mercedes carrying Pat Inston and his secretary.

''Next,'' he whispered with anticipation.

CHAPTER FIFTEEN

The dust-covered Chevy van carrying Mack Bolan and Able Team pulled off the main road and rolled to a stop before the locked gates leading to the Rillito Drive-in. Lyons was behind the wheel. He rolled down his window and glanced up at a man perched on the scaffolding that ran along the base of the complex's huge marquee.

"Hey!" he shouted.

The man on the scaffold was wearing headphones and bobbing his head to himself as he went about putting up new film titles on the sign. He had his back turned to the van and obviously hadn't heard Lyons.

"Stupid jerk," Lyons muttered.

"Let me take care of it." Bolan slid out of the van. His face smeared for camouflage and wearing fatigues over Kevlar body armor, the Executioner looked braced for combat. He had the silencer fitted on his Beretta, and one well-placed shot took care of the padlock on the gate. As Bolan waved the Chevy through, the man on the scaffold turned and gaped at the intruders.

"Hey," he called, yanking off his headphones, "we're not open till dusk!"

"Federal agents," Bolan replied. "We aren't here for the movies."

"Well, they haven't made the popcorn yet, either." The worker stepped over a box of two-foot-high letters and moved toward a ladder leading to the ground. "I'm gonna call security."

"Why don't you let us worry about that?" Bolan shouted, making sure the worker got a good look at his Beretta.

"Okay, man, no hassle," the man said, holding his hands out. "Don't shoot me. I got kids."

"Look, if you're smart, you'll get down from there and go across the street. It's not likely to be safe around here for a while."

"I'm gone, man. I'm gone."

As the man scrambled down from the scaffolding, Bolan climbed back into the van. Lyons drove past the vacant ticket booths and around a curved wall leading to the outdoor facility. All five screens rose from the outer perimeter of the lot, which was empty save for the countless rows of speaker posts and a two-story projection booth-concession area situated in the middle of the complex. There were a few cars parked next to the building, and as the van approached, an overweight security guard ambled out, munching on a wispy cone of cotton candy. When he spotted the van, he dropped the cone and went for his gun, bellowing, "Hold it right there!"

The van pulled to a stop next to the other vehicles.

"Federal agents!" Bolan repeated, climbing out and flashing his cover ID.

"What?" The guard eyed his credentials suspiciously, licking cotton candy off his fingers. Glancing up at Bolan, he asked, "Why the getup? And how'd you get in here?"

"I picked the lock."

"Huh?"

"We don't have a lot of time to chat, okay?"

The other doors of the van swung open and Able Team piled out. Like Bolan, they were dressed for battle. Schwarz and Blancanales clutched modified M-16s and had their Government Model .45s tucked away in shoulder harnesses while Lyons lugged a high-powered Ruger rifle. All three men had lightweight binoculars dangling from their necks and walkie-talkies clipped to their waists, along with foot-long bolt cutters.

"Holy shit," the guard muttered. "What the hell's going on?"

"Never mind," Bolan replied. "Round up anyone inside and get them out of here. Now!"

The security guard warily retreated to the concession area and headed back in through the swinging doors. Bolan suspected the man would be making some desperate phone calls, but Brognola had already alerted the local authorities and warned them of what was about to go down, so he was pretty sure they'd be able to proceed without interference.

Bolan led Able Team to the picnic area adjacent to the concession stand and pointed in the direction of one of the screens as he spelled out a quick battle plan. Lyons normally commanded all Able Team field operations, but he readily deferred to his peer in this situation, offering only a limited input before the group split up.

The Executioner and Lyons moved out together, heading directly for the nearest screen while Schwarz and Blancanales fanned out in separate directions, dodging speaker posts as they made their way to the cyclone fence enclosing the drive-in. Behind the guardrail that ran parallel to the fence was a three-foot-wide strip of land filled with thick hedges and bits of trash. Schwarz hurdled the rail, then squeezed between the bushes as he took out his bolt cutters and began snipping at the fence, making a hole just large enough to squeeze through. He couldn't see Pol, but he knew Blancanales was doing the same thing a couple of hundred yards away.

When Bolan and Lyons reached the base of the huge screen, they circled behind it and climbed up an iron ladder to a catwalk that afforded a view over the back fence, nearly ten feet away. Beyond the fence was a fifty-yard-wide stretch of uneven terrain heaped with mounds of fill dirt and littered with illegally dumped furniture and old appliances. Beyond that was another fence surrounding the back acreage of the Ideal Auto Body salvage yard. Bolan and Lyons could make out the mountain of old tires and the roof of the old filling station.

Lyons took hold of his binoculars and slowly panned the salvage yard for signs of a lookout. "Seems all clear," he said, lowering the glasses.

"Good. Why don't you stay posted here just in case, though?"

Lyons nodded. He unslung his Ruger, then handed his bolt cutters to Bolan. "If the shit hits the fan, I'll be down in no time flat."

Bolan grinned. "I bet you will."

As the Executioner started back down the ladder, Lyons pulled out his walkie-talkie to tell the rest of the team it was all right for them to proceed.

It took Bolan less than a minute to cut his way through the fence and enter the no-man's-land between the drive-in and the salvage yard. In the hot glare of the sun he got down on his belly and began the long crawl. The roll of the terrain was such that he couldn't see either Schwarz or Blancanales on either side of him, but he was sure they were out there, inching along toward their mutual target.

Halfway across, the warrior moved into a half crouch, using an undulating row of dirt mounds for cover as he made his way forward. Up ahead he scanned the length of fencing around the salvage yard, trying to calculate the best point of entry. Glancing to his right, he finally caught a glimpse of Schwarz, who was huddled behind an overturned refrigerator, his face pressed to his walkie-talkie. When the two men made eye contact, Schwarz signaled another all-clear.

As he ventured from the dirt mound and once more crawled his way along the littered ground, Bolan spotted Blancanales off to his left. Pol had already reached a section of the fence roughly fifty feet away from the old service station and was going to work with his bolt cutters.

Bolan continued on a straight course, and as he drew closer, he saw that there was a gate directly behind the old service station. It looked newer than the rest of the fence, and he guessed that it had been installed by the Natchapos as an alternative escape route in the event they were raided from the direction of the body shop.

There was an old freezer half-buried in the dirt less than ten feet away, its lid rusted open. Bolan moved behind it and found he had a clear view of the gate. He decided to stay put. With any luck Blancanales and Schwarz might flush out some of the Indians and send them fleeing through the gate into his clutches.

All in all, it looked as if things were going well on this front. As he lay in wait, Bolan wondered how Kissinger and Grimaldi were doing on their end.

JACK GRIMALDI TURNED OFF Campbell Avenue and started down the dead-end street to Ideal Auto Body and Salvage. He was behind the wheel of a dinged and battered Ford pickup that Air Force agent George Sax had appropriated from one of the base maintenance men. Besides bodywork, the vehicle was also in need of a tune-up, and the engine bucked and jolted as Grimaldi shifted gears. He grinned at Sax, who was riding beside him. "Nothing like traveling first class, huh?"

"Long as it does the trick," Sax replied, giving the Ford an affectionate pat on the dashboard.

The windows were down, but both men were sweating in their T-shirts. There was no way they could have worn coats or bulletproof vests without tipping their cover, and the only guns they could carry were small .22s tucked into ankle holsters under their baggy jeans. As they pulled into the driveway, Grimaldi was already casing the service bays, looking for cover if the lead started flying.

Most of the workers at the shop were Native American. Grimaldi guided the pickup toward the service bay where two men were working on a late-model Nissan. A stocky man was blowing bubbles as he buffed the chrome grillwork, and a second guy in a gauze mask sprayed primer on a back quarter panel.

Grimaldi stopped the pickup and got out, reaching into the truck bed for a large toolbox. He made a point of not looking at the piled heap of canvas just behind the driver's seat. Kissinger was huddled out of view beneath the covering, drenched in perspiration, both hands on an AK-47 assault rifle, ready to spring into action at the first sign of trouble.

The fat man strolled away from the Nissan, wiping his hands on the buffing towel. "Howdy," he called out casually to Grimaldi.

"Hi. Hot one today, huh?"

"Yep." The other man nodded and glanced past Grimaldi at the pickup. "Quite a wreck you got there."

"Ain't that the truth," Grimaldi replied. Hefting the toolbox, he added, "Want to replace a few things under the hood, and my buddy needs some parts for an '82 Accord."

The Natchapo shifted his gaze to George Sax, who was still inside the pickup. He popped another bubble, then looked back at Grimaldi. "We got a couple of old Fords and three, maybe four Accords that haven't been picked over too bad."

"Great, Mike," Grimaldi said, noting the other man's name stenciled above his shirt pocket. "Close by or should we drive there?"

Mike gestured behind the body shop. "They're just a few rows back in the yard. You gotta check in at the cashier's station, though. Have your boxes checked and all that shit."

"Boxes checked?" Grimaldi asked, trying to keep a straight face. He had his .45 automatic and five ammo cartridges concealed in the box and wasn't crazy about a search.

"Yep, standard procedure," Mike explained. "Got too many people trying to smuggle out carburetors with their lug wrenches. Know what I mean?"

"Yeah, seems fair enough," Grimaldi said, thinking fast. "Let me just drive around and park first so we aren't blocking the way."

"Good idea." The fat man pointed behind the building. "There's a couple of parking spaces next to the hubcap racks."

"Thanks."

As he lugged his toolbox back to the pickup, Grimaldi signaled to Sax, who slid behind the wheel and started the engine. It turned over noisily, spewing a blue-black cloud of smoke out the tailpipe. Putting the toolbox back near the canvas, Grimaldi whispered to Kissinger, "We'll try to park in the shade."

"Thanks, pal," Kissinger hissed back from beneath the tarp. Of course, more ideally they'd find a place to park where Cowboy could slip out undetected and help them search the grounds for the Natchapo Armed Militia's hideout.

At least that was the plan.

LIEUTENANT STRAW PULLED away from the doughnut drive-through window, ripping the lid off his vanilla milk shake. He goosed the accelerator and lurched into traffic, passing the Perimeter Trust building and the Green Orchid Restaurant. At the corner he stopped for a traffic light and popped a couple of antacid tablets into his mouth. He chewed them angrily, washing them down with the milk shake.

His ulcer was acting up, and he had any number of people to blame for his discomfort. Those damn interlopers from Washington, his ex-wife, the frigging Natchapo Armed Militia, Police Chief McPall, the inept bunglers from his department who'd let Timothy

Gwynn sneak away from Parquason Apartments...
Hell, some days the list just seemed to go on forever.

The light changed, and he started up Oracle Road in
his unmarked sedan. He figured he'd drop by to see his
attorney about mounting some kind of defense against
his ex-wife's call for an increase in her alimony pay-
ments. Yeah, sure, he'd just gotten a raise to go with
his recent promotion, but there was a lot more stress to
contend with, and Straw wasn't about to endure it so
that his ex-wife could upgrade her wardrobe and afford a couple of extra trips to the beauty parlor each
month.

Straw took out some of his aggression on the steering wheel, jerking it so that he could swerve around the
slow-moving car ahead of him. When the other driver
honked his horn and waved a fist at him, Straw flashed
the finger and sped forward, then cut sharply in front
of the other car, forcing the driver to slam on his brakes
to avoid a collision. Then Straw gunned his engine and
pulled away.

As Straw rolled past West Miracle Mile, his dashboard transceiver bleeped to life with a call from the
undercover agent who'd been working surveillance on
Parquason Apartments when Timothy Gwynn had
given him the slip.

"Got something, Lieutenant," the officer reported.
"Some old fart says Gwynn nearly flattened him while
he was out walking his dog about an hour ago."

"And?"

"And he says Gwynn got on the bus."

"Which bus?" Straw said, finishing his shake and wadding the paper cup.

"Line 502," the officer reported. "Runs north-south on Campbell Avenue. And the end of the line is the reservation."

"Aha!" Straw said with a grin. Oracle Road ran parallel to Campbell Avenue, and he was already heading north, just passing over the Rilitto River. "Nice job, Merez. You'll get off my shit list yet."

Straw signed off, not bothering to tell the other officer that he knew of a likelier destination Gwynn was headed for than the reservation. He flashed his turn signal and hung a right at the next light. He was only a couple of miles from Ideal Auto Body and Salvage, and although he'd yet to come up with solid proof the yard was a front for the Natchapo Armed Militia, his gut instincts told him his luck was about to change.

Much as Straw wanted to track down Gwynn on his own so that he could claim sole credit, he was also wary of getting bogged down with some kind of runaround while the militant slipped away. Reluctantly he patched through a call to the station, requesting backup. To his amazement the dispatcher informed him that a square-mile area including the auto yard and the Rilitto Drive-in had been declared off-limits by Chief McPall.

"What?" Straw raged as he turned onto Campbell Avenue. "You're joking, right?"

"Nope. Apparently there's some activity involving federal agents and—"

"No way!" Straw interrupted, shutting down his transceiver. As he approached Darrow Avenue, he unbuttoned his coat and pulled out his gun. He wasn't going to let those goddamn G-men show him up again. No way.

Barreling down the one-way street, Straw pulled out his portable flasher, rolled down his window and set it on his roof. Up ahead he saw an old Ford pickup parked out in front of one of the service bays, and he recognized the man about to climb into the front seat as one of the federal agents.

"Oh, no, you don't."

Straw slammed on his brakes, skidding to a halt in the driveway. Leaping out of the car, he flashed his badge and aimed his gun at the fat Natchapo standing a few feet away from Grimaldi.

"Freeze!" he shouted. "Get your hands up!"

"Make up your mind," Mike retorted. "You want me to freeze or put my hands up? I can't do both."

"Hands up and shut up!" Straw railed, moving closer.

"I don't believe this," Grimaldi muttered under his breath.

"I can handle this, G-man. Take a hike."

"I don't think so," Grimaldi replied.

But Straw was already closing in on the fat painter. "I'm looking for Timothy Gwynn," the lieutenant said. "And don't tell me he hasn't been here!"

"Gwynn?" Mike said with a frown. "He plays for the Padres, right?"

"I'm warning you, lardass!" Straw snarled. "I'll turn this two-bit dump upside down if I have to."

"Yeah? You got a warrant?"

"Yeah, right here!" Straw thrust the gun into Mike's face. "You wanna read the small print, just shoot your mouth off again!"

As Mike calmly regarded the officer's weapon, Straw detected activity in one of the other service bays out of the corner of his eye. He whirled and drew a bead on the Natchapo near the Nissan, who'd set aside his painting gun in favor of a double-barreled shotgun. Before Straw could pull his trigger the gun bellowed, smacking him in the chest with so much force that his feet shot out from under him.

Falling to the pavement, the lieutenant's last sight was that of his own blood and guts spilling out of his suit. He felt a vague sensation of pain, followed by a wave of chilling cold that left him numb. Within seconds his life was over.

But the war had just begun.

THERE WAS LITTLE TIME to curse Straw for blundering onto the scene. The trigger-happy gunman in the service bay still had another round in his shotgun, and Grimaldi had to make sure he wasn't going to be the next recipient. He lunged away from the pickup, snatching Straw's fallen gun and rolling across the pavement to the cover of a mailbox. Mike retreated to the bay as the other Indian's shotgun erupted a second time. Buckshot clanged off the mailbox, leaving dents and a few small holes. Unscathed, Grimaldi poked his head over the top of the box and shouted, "Drop it!"

The Natchapo had no intention of surrendering, however. Hunched behind the Nissan, he cracked open the shotgun and fed two fresh shells into the breech. Nearby Mike rummaged through a workbench for a snub-nosed .38, and a third Natchapo materialized in the office doorway, driving Grimaldi back to cover with blasts from a Colt .45.

Inside the pickup George Sax leaned low across the front seat, snapping open a second toolbox. Like Grimaldi, he'd stashed away a side arm, in his case a military-issue Beretta. Once he had it in his hand, he rolled down the passenger window, then rose into view, drilling the gunman in the office.

The shotgun bellowed again, and the Ford's windshield shattered, pelting Sax with a combination of glass shards and deflected buckshot. His scalp and the side of his face ran red with blood, but none of the hits had been direct enough to prove fatal. He blinked blood from his eyes and lay low for a moment, switching his Beretta to its 3-shot mode.

Meanwhile, Kissinger threw off the tarpaulin in the back of the truck and rose into view, letting loose with the AK-47. Bullets riddled the Nissan's paint job and drew a howl from the man with the shotgun. Pitching forward, his weapon fired wild, pummeling a wall calendar with a picture of a half-clad woman holding a crescent wrench.

Mike only bothered with one lame shot at Kissinger, scarring the hood of the pickup, then turned and fled through a back door. Grimaldi moved out from behind the mailbox and sidestepped Straw's body. Sax sat up inside the pickup, a horrific vision with his blood-soaked scalp and smeared face.

"George?"

"I'm okay," Sax muttered. "Let's get those bastards!"

"Amen," Kissinger called out from the back of the truck. "With any luck we can nip this in the bud."

CHAPTER SIXTEEN

The moment he heard shots in the distance, Bolan knew something had gone wrong. Although he and the others had arrived on the scene heavily armed, they were wary of the possible presence of explosives and didn't want to resort to gunplay except as a last resort. They feared that a shoot-out in such volatile surroundings would present a threat, not only to the combatants but also to innocent civilians in surrounding neighborhoods. Bolan had been counting on stealthy penetration of the NAM stronghold and a chance to pinpoint the location of the explosives before taking action. Now, obviously, that was out of the question.

The Executioner normally took the offensive when faced with a battle situation, and it was with great reluctance that he stayed put behind the wasted freezer, keeping a vigil on the back gate. As the gunfire resumed, his war-trained ears sorted through the sounds. The shotgun blasts were unmistakable and told him that the enemy was involved in the shooting, since none of his crew was armed with such a weapon. The other shots were less distinguishable, although the last burst of rhythmic fire sounded as if it might be coming from Kissinger's AK-47. Nothing that Bolan heard, however, clarified the circumstances behind the shooting, much less the outcome.

As the shots subsided and were replaced by sounds of shouting within the compound, Bolan glanced along the back fence, catching a glimpse of Blancanales wriggling through the gap he'd created with his bolt cutters. Seconds later a shot rang out from in front of the old pump station. Bolan couldn't see who had fired it but guessed that a Natchapo had come out of the building and spotted Blancanales.

His suspicions were confirmed by the return fire of Pol's M-16, which tore through Fred Diton, Timothy Gwynn's close friend. The tall Indian staggered around the side of the filling station and into Bolan's view, looking to take cover behind the old billboards. Bolan raised his Beretta and lined up the man in his sights, but held his fire when Diton suddenly teetered to one side and slumped to the ground, leaving a trail of blood on the billboard.

Moments later the back door of the pump station swung open and a shorter man in dark coveralls slipped outside, cautiously holding a shoe box as if it contained something he was afraid to drop. Bolan guessed the man was probably trying to make a run for it with the explosives, and he smiled to himself as he saw the man free one hand to feed keys into the back gate.

"That's it," Bolan whispered as he crouched low behind the freezer, holstering his Beretta. "Come to papa."

The gate creaked on its hinges as it swung open, and although more shots were sounding throughout the salvage yard, Bolan was able to concentrate on the footsteps heading his way. He held his breath, and when the other man ventured past, he sprang upward and outward. Capitalizing on the element of surprise, Bolan was able to snatch the shoe box with both hands without upsetting its contents. In nearly the same motion he pivoted to one side, using a modified karate kick to upend his adversary, sending him sprawling backward into the dirt.

Quickly recovering, the man went for a gun tucked inside the front pocket of his coveralls. Bolan shifted his grip on the shoe box, holding it close to his body with his left hand so that he could use his right to go for his Beretta. He won the draw and pumped a single shot through the militant's heart, killing him instantly.

Bolan lowered his gun and inspected the shoe box. He was right. Inside were the explosives and remote detonators Kissinger had reported missing from Bergman Air Force Base. Furthermore, Bolan recognized them as similar in design to the bomb device that had nearly blown him sky-high the other night.

There was little time for reveling in this bit of good fortune as a shadow suddenly swept across the ground into Bolan's field of vision. He ducked as a gunshot gouged at the lid of the nearby freezer, missing him by mere inches. Someone was firing at him from the roof of the old filling station. The sun was directly behind the building, half blinding Bolan when he peered up.

"Damn!" Bolan cursed as he put down the shoe box in the soft dirt at the base of the freezer. His vision was blurred with the sun's fiery afterimage, and there was little he could do but crouch low and hope he wouldn't be picked off. A second shot pinged off the freezer, and he felt a metal shard sting his cheek.

Bolan could hear a steady outpouring of renewed gunfire inside the salvage yard, and yet it was another shot coming from behind that drew his attention most, since it resulted in a groan from the station rooftop and the loud thump of a Natchapo gunman falling to the ground.

The warrior kept blinking until the spots faded before his eyes, then he risked a glance over the freezer. The fallen gunner had landed headfirst near the gate, but his pant cuff had caught on a section of the fence, holding one leg up in the air.

Leaving the explosives shielded by the freezer, Bolan moved out and glanced back at the drive-in. He could just make out Carl Lyons on the catwalk behind the nearest screen, lowering his Ruger rifle. Bolan signaled a thumbs-up.

"Nice shot, Ironman," he called out softly. Then, Beretta in hand, he moved forward toward the gate, ready to join the fray.

GADGETS'S SHOULDER was bleeding where he'd scraped it against a section of fresh-cut fence while crawling into the salvage yard. He could feel the whole back of his shirt clinging wetly to his skin, but he couldn't be bothered with stopping to inspect the wound. It wasn't going to be fatal—he knew that much—and with all the gunplay going on around him it was more worth his while to focus on dodging bullets.

After coming through the fence, he'd found himself at the base of the huge mountain of old tires, which gave off a rank odor under the oppressive rays of the sun. Gadgets gave them a wide berth as he headed in the direction of the nearest gunfire. He was halfway around the pile when he spotted Kissinger and Grimaldi, who were pinned by cross fire in the Ford pickup, which Grimaldi had apparently crashed into the hubcap rack.

The passenger door suddenly swung open, and George Sax rolled out and hit the ground running, headed for a stack of used engine blocks. Kissinger and Grimaldi tried to cover him, but Sax took a slug and fell into a wounded heap amid scattered chrome wheel covers that glinted in the sun like oversize jewels. He tried to crawl to cover, but a cross fire of shots rattled across the hubcaps and burrowed into him. He slumped facedown into the dirt, dropping his gun.

"George!" Grimaldi shouted. The man didn't move, however.

Schwarz was less than thirty yards from Sax's assailants—two Natchapos crouched behind the gnarled remains of a Porsche. One had a single-action rifle, the other a cheap .28-caliber revolver. Schwarz braced his M-16, and once they turned at the sound of the rifle's safety being released, he fired away, spending half his ammo clip to make sure that when the men went down they stayed down.

Having evened up the odds, Schwarz signaled to Kissinger and Grimaldi, then veered to his right, stalking cautiously between stacked rows of flattened sports cars. There was motion at the base of the stack to his right, and he was about to fire when he saw that it was a pair of terrified teenagers cowering on either side of the toolbox they'd brought into the lot.

"Stay put," Schwarz advised them as he moved past. From the looks on the youths' faces it was clear they weren't planning to go anywhere.

AFTER DOWNING Fred Diton, Blancanales had moved away from the filling station, anxious to lend Grimaldi and Kissinger a hand. Rather than taking the most direct route and risk exposing himself to fire, he veered by the colossal compactor unit and zigzagged through a maze of older model cars that had been compressed into tight cubes of metal.

The frenzied yelps of a dog brought him up short before he cleared the salvage heaps. He held his M-16 ready for firing and slowly inched his way to the corner, relaxing slightly when he saw that the dog was still tethered inside its cage. However, being confined didn't prevent the rottweiler from charging and leaping against the fence, nearly toppling it under its weight. Blancanales reflexively moved back, and the motion saved his life as a bullet rammed into the dirt where he'd been standing.

Diving sideways, Pol scrambled to cover behind one of the compacted cubes. More shots showered down around him. He was able to place the source of the shots and glanced up, spotting a sniper posted atop the crane used to feed cars into the compactor. The gunman drove Pol back with another volley, then crawled down into the crane's cab. Seconds later the crane's engine spit out a cloud of smoke and groaned to life.

Blancanales rose to a crouch and sputtered a series of shots at the crane, pocking the metal frame and shattering the windshield. The man inside the cab was lying low, however, and if he was wounded, it wasn't mortally, because he was still able to work the controls. The huge girdered arm of the crane began to swing upward, dangling a wrecked Lincoln Continental at the end of a huge electromagnetic slab.

As the car hovered toward him, Pol broke from cover, sprinting in the opposite direction, only to be brought up short by yet another spray of gunfire from an unseen assassin. Short of retreating the way he'd just come, Blancanales's only other opening was to his immediate left. He veered sharply, twisting his ankle in the process. Falling off balance, he landed hard against an old truck chassis, dropping his M-16 as the wind was knocked from his lungs.

He struggled to catch his breath and fight off a black wave of dizziness. He could hear more gunfire close by and was vaguely aware of the shadow of the Lincoln as the crane swung over him. He knew he had to move out of the car's path before the crane operator cut the power to the electromagnet, but his body refused to respond to his commands.

As two tons of instant death dangled directly above him, Pol sensed someone come up from behind and grab him under the arms.

"Hang on, hombre," Schwarz said as he dragged Pol away. Overhead, the Continental swayed for a moment longer, then suddenly plummeted. Metal screamed against metal as the car slammed into the truck chassis and raised a cloud of dust near where Pol would have been dismembered—if not killed outright—by the falling vehicle.

"You all right, Pol?" Schwarz asked.

Blancanales regained his breath and glanced back at the Lincoln, then shook his head and grinned at Schwarz. "Probably be a while before I eat pancakes again, but, yeah, I'm okay."

Schwarz helped him to his feet. "Afraid your rifle got buried on you."

"Better that than me," he observed, drawing his Government Model .45 from his shoulder holster. "Besides, I still have this. And there's a couple of slugs in it with somebody's name on them."

Limping slightly to favor his twisted ankle, Pol led Schwarz back toward the compactor. The Natchapo who'd nearly succeeded in crushing Blancanales was climbing down from the crane. Pol dropped into a firing stance, using a two-handed grip on the .45 to steady his aim. The second the man touched the ground, Pol pulled the trigger. Screaming, the Indian grabbed at his side as he fell backward. Behind him was another row of scrap metal, and he managed to squirm behind cover as Schwarz followed up Pol's shot with the chattering of his M-16.

"No way am I letting that guy get away," Pol said, starting to take up the chase with a stagger-step, grimacing each time his injured foot hit the ground. He didn't get far before Schwarz reached out and grabbed him by the shoulder.

"Let me get him for you," Schwarz suggested. "You need to give that foot a rest."

Pol knew Gadgets was right and reluctantly hung back as his partner sprinted around the steel maws of the compactor. There was a trail of blood left by the wounded Natchapo, and Schwarz followed it back toward the rear of the lot. The gunfire was diminishing around him, and at one point he caught a glimpse across the lot at where Kissinger and Grimaldi were rounding up a few militants who'd decided to surrender rather than fight to the death.

The man Schwarz was trailing wasn't about to give up, however. When Gadgets spotted him passing through the front gate to the old filling station, the wounded Natchapo turned and drove him back with blasts from his handgun. When the weapon fired on an empty cylinder, he discarded it and rushed into the brick building.

Schwarz broke into a run, slowing only when he was through the gate and coming up on the doorway of the old station.

"Stay back!" the man inside screamed. "Stay back or I'll blow everything up!"

From where he was standing, Schwarz could see through the doorway, and when the Natchapo flicked a lighter, he saw that the man was holding a home-made Molotov cocktail. Behind him on the bench were countless other bottles with cloth wicks poking out of their necks.

"I'm warning you! One wrong move and I light this!" The man's voice was high-pitched, and Schwarz doubted there was any point in trying to reason with him. By the same token he wasn't about to try gunning him down, either, because in the time it would take him to raise his M-16 and fire it, the Indian could easily ignite the bomb, no doubt setting off the other explosive cocktails. In that case both of them would die instantly, and the resulting fireball would easily spread to the nearby mountain of tires. He didn't even want to imagine the destruction that would result from a blaze of that magnitude.

"Back away!" the Natchapo demanded. "Drop your gun and back away!"

Schwarz decided to play along, at least for the moment. Any chance of averting an explosion seemed worth it. As he moved back, Gadgets was able to see the roof of the filling station, and to his amazement he saw Bolan, gun in hand, squatting near the trapdoor that had been used by the sniper Carl Lyons had shot during the early stages of the battle.

"Okay, this is what I want!" the Natchapo cried out inside the building. "I want a car...and a first-aid kit. Get it and—"

The man suddenly heard something and glanced upward. Three high-powered bursts from Bolan's Beretta slammed through the trapdoor opening. Two ravaged the Indian's face and another ripped through his throat at a downward angle and lodged deep in his chest. Death came quickly and the man fell forward. The unlit Molotov cocktail shattered on the floor, spreading a pool of gas. The lighter dropped from the man's hand but didn't go out. Flames licked across the concrete floor, igniting the puddle and engulfing the Indian.

Schwarz dropped his rifle and charged for the building, passing through the doorway just as Bolan dropped down through the trapdoor. As Gadgets grabbed a towel and began swatting at the flames, Bolan quickly moved to the rear bench, placing himself between the spreading fire and the other bottles of gas. There were too many of them to gather up and remove from the building, so Bolan concentrated on trying to keep the flames from reaching them.

At one end of the bench were two faded twenty-five pound bags of grass seed, apparently left over from some neglected plan to seed the land behind the station. Desperately Bolan dragged one bag forward and propped it up as a buffer in front of the firebombs.

Then he hurriedly tore open the other bag as he hauled it toward the blaze, which was growing despite Schwarz's flailings with the towel. Bolan upended the bag and directed the outpour so that the seeds fell directly on the fire, smothering most of the flames. Meanwhile, Schwarz closed in and was able to put out the rest.

Coughing through the stench of smoke and gas fumes, Bolan and Schwarz lingered in the structure for a few moments longer, making sure the fire didn't come back to life. Once they were satisfied it wouldn't, they strode outside and drew in welcome breaths of fresh air.

There was no gunfire in the yard now. As the two men slowly headed toward the body shop, they saw corpses littered about, every bit as lifeless as the ruined cars around them. It was a dismal sight, and having survived the bloodbath was small consolation.

"Never seems to get easier, does it?" Schwarz observed.

"No," Bolan agreed, "it sure as hell doesn't."

CHAPTER SEVENTEEN

Pat Inston was coming up on the junction between interstates 8 and 10 when the radar-receiver in his Mercedes flashed on, indicating that the homing signal in Randy Walker's Honda Civic was once again operative. Donna, his secretary, was familiar with the radar unit and checked the digital readout measuring the strength of the signal, then placed an appropriate overlay on the radar screen, pinpointing the location of the Honda.

Inston got off the highway, taking side roads toward the far perimeter of the Natchapo reservation as he put a call out to the Highway Patrol, requesting routine backup. Thanks to the device he'd rigged to Inston's phone, Cal Ovitz had intercepted the call, disguising his voice and using a steady stream of background static to further shield his identity as he assured Inston that a plainclothes officer in an unmarked vehicle would be dispatched.

"Why do you think we need backup?" Donna asked as Inston hung up the phone. A pretty, vivacious woman, she preferred the safety and security of her desk job to this unexpected field assignment. There was concern in her voice.

"Just a standard precaution," Inston told her. "Nothing to be concerned about."

But it was clear that his words were falling on deaf ears. As Donna looked back at the radar screen, her fingers nervously drummed the armrest beside her. They drove past the bullet-riddled Baines Mining sign. Inston tried to change the subject. Gesturing at the buildup of desert sand on the front hood of the Mercedes, he complained good-naturedly, "Gonna need another car wash after this, eh?"

"Looks that way," Donna replied, putting on a lame smile.

They traded more small talk over the next few miles, then fell silent as they approached the mining site. Once he spotted the Blyford brothers' Mustang parked in front of the hut, Inston eased the Mercedes off the road and headed for the cover of the nearby butte.

"Well, Randy must be tracking whoever owns that Mustang," Inston said, scanning the grounds. "I don't see his car anywhere, though."

"Signal's getting stronger," Donna told him, keeping her eyes on the radar screen. "Maybe he's parked behind the hut."

"Could be." Inston noticed a set of car tracks in the sand. "Looks like that's where those are headed, at any rate."

Donna took her eyes off the radar screen and looked around for signs of activity on the wide-open plain. Finally, off in the distance behind them, she spotted a dust cloud on the access road. "That must be the Highway Patrol guy."

"Yeah." Inston turned off the ignition and unbuttoned his coat to reveal the butt of his Colt automatic. Donna gasped at the sight of the gun.

"Mr. Inston, I thought you just told me—"

"I know, Donna, I know. This is just in case."

The car phone rang, startling both of them. Inston picked up the receiver.

"Inston here."

"Broderick Crawford here," Ovitz barked gruffly over the line.

"What? Is this some kind of joke?"

"Yeah." Ovitz chuckled. "I guess you could say that."

"Well, I'm not laughing, Officer."

"No? Well, maybe some laughing gas will help."

Inston glowered, his face reddening with anger. He was in the process of slamming down the receiver when the knockout gas was released from the phone unit. Donna let out another involuntary gasp, then slumped to her right.

"S-s-setup," Inston muttered, reaching for his Colt. The gas overcame him and he sagged forward, landing hard against the steering wheel. Outside the car, a startled jackrabbit took flight as the Mercedes's horn blared shrilly through the morning air.

Marlowe Tompkins charged out of the hut and jogged to the car. As soon as he dragged Inston clear of the wheel, the horn went silent. Moments later Ovitz's Camaro pulled up alongside the Mercedes.

"How'd it go?" Ovitz asked as he got out of the car.

"Like clockwork. We better get moving quick with these two, though, or the coroners are gonna trip us up."

"Right."

Ovitz opened the Mercedes and pulled Donna out, slinging her over his shoulder. Tompkins did the same with Inston. As they headed back to the hut, Ovitz briefed Tompkins on the conversation he'd overheard between Inston and Donna on their way to the reservation. "So it wasn't just us," he concluded. "They were checking all the security outfits under contract with the Air Force."

"That's a relief," Tompkins said.

"No shit. That means if we can just throw everyone off the scent here, we might be able to come out of this smelling like a rose."

"I sure as hell hope so." Tompkins shifted his grip on Inston before entering the hut. "'Cause we've gone past the point of no return."

Ovitz followed Tompkins into the hut, eyeing the twisted corpses sprawled across the floor. "Christ, what a mess!"

"Just wait till we're finished."

Tompkins eased Inston down to the floor just inside the doorway. The M-16 was propped against the nearby wall, and Tompkins carefully placed it in Inston's hands, then shifted the investigator's body to make it look as if he were taking cover behind an old work-bench. The assault rifle slipped from Inston's fingers to the floor and Tompkins had to prop it back in place.

"Okay," he said, stepping back to admire his handiwork. "So Inston barged in here trying to play hero and gunned down our two little Indians here, right?"

"Yeah, that's how I figure it." Ovitz laid Donna on top of the rifle crates, then crouched beside the un-moving figures of the Blyford brothers and Randy Walker. "But unfortunately Inston's not going to be around to collect any medals."

"Yeah, tough break." Tompkins grabbed the car-bine he'd used to murder Walker and crouched beside the body of Zane Blyford. He took aim at Inston, who was still out cold. Gunshots echoed once again off the walls of the hut. Inston jerked in place, then sprawled forward, half his face obliterated by the impact of two direct hits.

Tompkins placed the carbine in Zane's hands to make it look as if he'd killed Inston just before dying. Ovitz glanced at Donna. "What about her? Should we give her Inston's Colt and make it look like she was in on the raid?"

Tompkins shook his head. "I don't think they'd buy it. Odds are Inston would have had her stay out in the car."

"Well, if she stayed out in the car and Inston killed everybody when he burst in here, how do we account for her?"

Tompkins thought it over and smiled. "Somebody got away," he decided. "Yeah, somebody lived to fight again, and he ran into Donna as he was making his getaway and decided to get rid of her."

"Sounds good." Ovitz ran a finger along a stretch of the woman's exposed right thigh. "Of course, we're dealing with savages here, right? So he wouldn't just get rid of her. He'd probably drag her out of the car and get his rocks off, then kill her."

"Or maybe he'd kill her first, then play with her a little," Tompkins speculated. "That sounds a little sicker, don't you think?"

Ovitz nodded, picking the woman up once again. She was still out cold and dangled limply in his arms. "Sorry, love," he told her, "but this just hasn't been your day."

"Okay," Tompkins said. "Let's take care of her, then grab the van and haul these rifles back to the shelter."

As Ovitz started to carry Donna out of the hut, something caught his eye. Gesturing at it with a nod of his head, he told Tompkins, "Hey, why don't you grab that Bowie knife?"

"What for?"

"I think the woman needs a haircut," Ovitz said with a smile.

THE WILD COYOTE WAS an outdoor café on Palo Verde Road, roughly between Tucson International and Bergman Air Force Base. The desert motif extended to the decor, which featured everything from sand-print tablecloths to cactus-shaped salt and pepper shakers and menus in the shape of prospecting pans. The twenty-foot-high plaster coyote perched above the kitchen roof drew in a steady tourist trade, but locals frequented the café, too, most of them drawn by the near-legendary house special—Howl-at-the-Moon-Five-Alarm Chili.

With the constant drone of air traffic overhead, the Wild Coyote was also an ideal place to exchange confidential conversation without fear of eavesdropping. That, along with the close proximity to both Reed-Blackpoint Enterprises and the air force base, made it a natural rendezvous spot for Barbara Price to meet with Daniel Blackpoint, Pat Inston and members of Air Force Intelligence. Price also hoped Bolan and Randy Walker would be dropping by, too.

"I keep going over everything in my mind," Blackpoint told her, "and I just can't make any sense of it. Clark was like a father to me. And the company—it meant everything to him. To have tried to sabotage things... It's too unreal."

"I guess sometimes we just don't know people as much as we think we do." Price took another sip from her margarita and glanced at the hostess station, where a woman dressed like a rodeo sweetheart was taking reservations over the phone. She was hoping she'd see that at least some of the other men had shown up and were waiting to be led to their table, but there was only a middle-aged couple, taking each other's photos with the giant coyote in the background.

"Worried about Walker, aren't you?" Blackpoint asked.

Price turned back to face the man. "A little."

"I'm sure he's okay."

She changed the subject. "Daniel, do you have any idea who might have killed Clark Reed? Any idea at all?"

"I've been asking myself that ever since I found out it wasn't suicide. I have to think it was whoever talked him into the whole sabotage thing. It's the only answer that makes sense."

"And whoever that is must have something to do with the Natchapo Armed Militia, right?"

"I guess so," Blackpoint said, his jaw tightening in a sudden pique of anger. "Damn them, anyway! My people struggle all these years to make some decent strides, but these rabble-rousers get carried away and undo everything we've tried to accomplish."

"But they're just a small minority of the tribe," Price said. "They don't represent the Natchapos any more than AIM or—"

"Oh, I know that and you know that," Blackpoint snapped with frustration, "but your average person on the street doesn't. He's going to see headlines about subversive Indians and lump us all together as savages out on the warpath. It's not fair!"

She hadn't told Blackpoint about the raid that Bolan and Able Team were making on the NAM stronghold across town, and given the man's dark mood, she couldn't see any good reason to bring it up now. She tried to change the subject again. "Do you think maybe somebody's been using both Reed and NAM as part of a plan to take over your company?"

Blackpoint thought it over as a waitress came by to refill their water glasses and ask if they wanted to order yet.

"A couple of more minutes," Price told her.

Once the waitress left, Blackpoint said, "I suppose it's possible, but more likely somebody's out to destroy us, not just take us over."

"Why?"

"Because we have a head start on most other companies in terms of dealing with all these defense industry cutbacks and layoffs. We saw it coming a few years ago, so we've already focused our efforts on ways to adapt. It's going to give us an advantage in landing contracts, both in the private sector and with the military."

"But you'd have lost military contracts if the sabotage had succeeded."

"Most definitely," Blackpoint admitted. He fell silent for a moment as an F-16 fighter flew by, coming in low for a landing at the nearby air base. Watching the jet touch down and begin to taxi toward one of the hangars, he suddenly frowned. "Unless..."

"Unless what?"

"Well, I'd have to check with my attorneys and some people with the Pentagon to be sure about this, but I think if the company was sold, or subject to a take-over, the new management might be able to evade any of the penalties we'd have faced for security breaches or trade violations."

"I think you might be right," Price replied, seeing what Blackpoint was leading to. "If you are, the sabotage might have been a way someone was looking to lower your company's value and make it ripe for a takeover."

Blackpoint nodded, offering a rueful smile. "I think we're on to something here."

"Well, we'll discuss it with the others," Price said, glancing back at the hostess station, "if they ever show up."

"They will." Blackpoint pushed himself away from the table. "In the meantime I think I'll make a few quick calls and see if I'm right about this penalty thing. Why don't you go ahead and order some appetizers?"

"Good idea."

As Blackpoint got up and headed for the pay phone, she scanned the menu, then flagged down their waitress and requested some tortilla chips and guacamole. Sitting back, she watched a couple of fighter jets take off from the air base, sunlight gleaming off their triangular wings.

Her reverie was soon interrupted by the low drone of rotor blades, and as she turned and looked behind her, Price was surprised to see a helicopter setting down on a strip of undeveloped hardpan less than fifty yards from the Wild Coyote.

A door swung open as the chopper idled on the ground, and Mack Bolan leaped out, ducking low until he cleared the rotors. As he approached the outdoor café, she slowly rose from her table and moved past bewildered customers to meet him. One part of her felt relief at the sight of Bolan, but the circumstances of his arrival and the solemn look on his face sent a cold chill through her.

"What is it?" she whispered hoarsely.

"It's Randy," Bolan told her. There was no need to go into details, not just yet. He took another step forward and put his arms around her. "I'm sorry, Barb."

CHAPTER EIGHTEEN

The walls of the panel truck wending along the back-roads of Pima County were stenciled Tucson Geological Survey Team, but Cal Ovitz wasn't a geologist and neither he nor Tompkins was headed for a survey.

Snapping his cigarette out the open window, Ovitz swerved around a tumbleweed lying in the middle of the cracked asphalt road, which was overrun with weeds and drifting sand. It had been nearly fifteen minutes since he'd spotted any sign of civilization other than power lines stretching across the desert, but finally he came upon a turnoff leading to a barbed-wire-topped fence surrounding a vast tract of land reaching miles back to the foothills of Holwell Mountain. A sign said the land was available for lease, but judging from the rust on the fence and the sun-faded lettering on the sign, there hadn't been any takers for some time.

Ovitz left the truck running as Tompkins got out to unlock the gate and swing it open. After Ovitz pulled in past a boarded-up guard station peppered with buckshot, Tompkins closed the gate again, then got back into the truck. Neither had spoken much for the past hour, and they proceeded silently down a barely visible dirt road leading to Holwell Caverns, a one-time film lot that had flourished in the fifties and early sixties when westerns were still popular. Long since abandoned, the site, like the Baines mining project forty miles away, was half-buried by sand and succumbing to the elements, but the facades of a few Old West storefronts still rose tall along what had once passed for the main street of Dodge City. The old buildings didn't seem nearly as out of place as the rambling wooden roller coaster and rusting hulks of several ancient rides that had been used in the schlock B-horror classic *Amusement Park from Hell*.

Tompkins-Ovitz Security Services was in charge of keeping an eye on the property, a job that amounted to little more than twice-a-week checks to make sure squatters or vandals hadn't strayed this far from the real world in search of cheap thrills or a place to lay their heads. Ovitz had sought out the assignment and settled for less than a standard fee because the isolated area was well suited for some of the sideline enterprises he and Tompkins had become involved with.

Driving through the open mouth of a huge clown face that served as the entrance to the amusement park, Ovitz circled around the roller coaster and parked next to a dilapidated funhouse built into the base of Holwell Mountain.

The two men went behind the truck and opened the rear doors. Stacked in back were the crates of Air Force carbines he and Tompkins had removed from the NAM hut in the desert, along with a weathered leather valise. Tompkins hauled out a handcart, then they put their collective strength into hauling out the first of the crates. After they secured it to the cart, Ovitz guided the load around the side of the funhouse while Tompkins went ahead and unlocked the entrance to the service area.

It was dark inside. Tompkins left the door open while he fired up a butane lamp, which cast an eerie glow on the backside of the funhouse ride. The cobwebs were real, but the mummy and werewolf, both covered with dust on their spring-loaded mounts, were obviously fake and far less frightening from this perspective than they were years ago to children who saw them jump out of nowhere while being whisked by on a fast-moving rail car.

Pushing the handcart, Ovitz followed Tompkins past other props, long-dormant machinery and half-gnawed electrical cords that lay like dead snakes amid rat pellets dotting the concrete floor. Halfway around, the two men stopped before a workbench and shelving unit, both of which were piled high with old motors, cables and spare parts for the funhouse ride. Tompkins leaned over the workbench, fingering a toggle switch hidden behind one of the support struts. There was a dull snapping sound behind the shelves, and when Tompkins tugged at the unit, it swung open.

"After you," he told his companion.

Ovitz wheeled the crate through the secret opening. Tompkins followed, and the light of his butane lantern bounded off jagged walls of limestone, revealing a huge natural cavity. The air was stale, cool and dry, a perfect environment for storage.

The current owners knew of other caves honeycombed throughout Holwell Mountain, but when they hired Tompkins and Ovitz they'd had no idea there was this other chamber, which had been transformed into a makeshift bomb shelter during the film lot's heyday. Ovitz had researched old blueprints to pinpoint the cave, not that he and Tompkins were interested in being protected from atomic bombs. On the contrary, these days one was at greater risk of being blown to bits here in the shelter than anywhere else within nearly a fifty-mile radius.

The Air Force carbines were only the tip of the armament iceberg. Through their various connections, in recent months the two men had skimmed inventories at various Arizona weapons depots, selling off some items and stockpiling the rest. Stacked elsewhere in the dark enclosure were crates of fragmentation grenades, rocket mortars, assault rifles, claymore mines, plastic explosives, detonator caps and even some missile components.

"Getting pretty filled up in here," Tompkins remarked as he helped his partner transfer the crate to a corner of the cave already crowded with similar cargo.

"Yeah, but I'm lining up a couple of deals, so we'll be fine." Wheeling the cart back out of the cave, Ovitz added, "Mortilson's got a lead on some people who're drooling for claymores and frag grenades, and I'm sure Tomi Leitchen'll buy as many of these carbines as we can get our hands on."

"Yeah, you're probably right. Maybe we should lie low for a while."

Ovitz grinned. "Getting cold feet?"

"Not really. I just don't think we should push our luck. With all this shit that's been going on, we ought to wait and see if we've got ourselves in the clear, that's all."

"We still have some loose ends with Alisha Witt," Ovitz reminded his partner.

"That's different. That doesn't involve—"

"Wait a second!" Ovitz put a finger to his lips and set the handcart aside. Pulling out his Browning automatic, he eased toward the doorway. Tompkins cut off the fuel flow to the lamp and the flame died out, turning the chamber dark save for the light filtering in from outside. Both men could hear a sound coming from the vicinity of the panel truck. Then a man's voice shouted, "Sweet Holy Jesus!"

Ovitz darted outside. Standing behind the panel truck was a bewhiskered, ruddy-faced prospector who looked to be in his late thirties. The old leather valise was lying half-opened in the dirt at his feet, and his eyes were wide open in a look of bewilderment even before he turned and saw Ovitz emerging from the funhouse, gun in hand.

The prospector wore a small backpack, and whatever was stored in it kept Ovitz's first shot from shearing his spinal cord as he ducked around the side of the truck.

"Goddamn it!" Ovitz roared as he gave chase.

Running like a man possessed, the prospector scrambled over a railing and leaped onto the old roller coaster. A gunshot ripped through wood a few inches from his face as he started up a sloping incline, seeking out a precarious footing on the rusted tracks.

While Ovitz hurdled the rail and followed, Tompkins stayed on the ground, pulling out his automatic and drawing a bead on the prospector. He got off one shot that drew blood from the man's hip, slowing him down. The prospector stopped at the crest of the incline, thirty feet above the ground. Gasping for breath, he stared down the tracks. Ovitz was closing the gap between them.

"Don't shoot!" the prospector pleaded, clawing at the straps of his backpack, trying to draw it in front of him for cover.

Tompkins fired again from the ground. A slug pierced the prospector's chest. As if that weren't fatal enough, Ovitz blasted away with a second shot that caught the man squarely. He dangled for a moment, then toppled over the railing, splintering the wooden framework below and bouncing off one of the idle ride cars before splitting his skull open on the counter's concrete foundation.

Ovitz climbed down and joined his friend alongside the body. Tompkins quickly rifled through the man's backpack, finding only prospecting tools and a well-worn bible.

"Just a drifter," he pronounced.

"Well, let's leave him for now and get the rest of the rifles put away."

"Yeah."

The two men headed back to the panel truck. Ovitz crouched over the leather valise, sticking the Bowie knife and Donna Long's bloodstained scalp back inside along with a thin stack of Natchapo Armed Militia literature and stolen Air Force documents. As he tossed the valise back into the truck, Ovitz pointed at one of the rifle crates. "Let's keep that one to go with this satchel."

"You figured out who you're going to plant it on yet?"

"Yeah, I got it all figured out."

Together the men hauled out a second crate and began wheeling it into the funhouse. Assured that their latest crisis was behind them now that the prospector lay dead, neither man bothered scanning the rest of the grounds. If they had, they might have been able to make out the distant outline of a 1985 Nova parked on the horizon. Behind the wheel of the car was Timothy Gwynn, peering at them through binoculars. He'd spotted them as they were leaving the Baines mining site and had followed them, hoping to find where they kept their cache of weapons.

Now he knew.

THE MEDIA HADN'T YET caught scent of the killings at the old Baines mine, but the vultures had. Two of them ert breeze on their wide, dusky wings. Three others had dispensed with reconnaissance and were perched on the scraggly limb of a desert oak next to one of the old barracks, warily eyeing the paramedics who had beat them to the bodies. Two ambulances were backed up near the front entrance to the hut, and another half-dozen vehicles were parked nearby as their occupants roamed the site of the shoot-out, trying to piece together what had happened. In addition to several County Sheriff officers and three men from the Highway Patrol, there were also two men in suits from Air Force Intelligence. They were questioning a trembling eleven-year-old Natchapo boy whose dirt bike was propped against the side of an old, dust-caked jeep. The youth's parents stood nearby.

A helicopter soon appeared on the horizon, and as it drew closer, the drone of its rotor blades chased away the circling vultures, who set down on the spindly oak near their winged counterparts. Jack Grimaldi was at the chopper's controls, having procured the craft from the Air Force in order to cut down the time needed to get to this remote corner of the Natchapo reservation. Riding with him were Bolan and Barbara Price. Able Team was still sorting through the carnage at the Ideal salvage yard, and John Kissinger had gone with Daniel Blackpoint to Bergman Air Force Base to confer with Hal Brognola and other AFI personnel about the latest developments.

After disembarking from the chopper, Grimaldi headed to where the boy was still being questioned.

Bolan stayed close to Price, leading her toward the paramedic vans. "You don't have to put yourself through this," he told her.

"I'll be okay," she whispered hoarsely.

When they reached the paramedics, Bolan explained that the woman was a friend of Randy Walker's. The two attendants exchanged glances. One of them shook his head and gestured at one of the body bags laid out inside the van.

"He took it in the head," the man told Bolan. "She doesn't want to see that, trust me."

Tight-lipped, Price stared into the van. She made a move forward as if to push her way past the attendants, then pulled back. Tears welled in her eyes and her chin began to tremble. "Randy..."

Bolan placed a hand on her shoulder. She turned and leaned into his embrace, burying her face in his shoulder. "I'm sorry," Bolan told her, feeling bitter anger at the emptiness of his words. "Come on."

Gently he led Price away from the ambulances and over to an old water well. There was a wooden bench beside it, and once he'd gotten her to sit down, Bolan crouched before the woman so that they were eye to eye. As he waited for her to bring herself under control, the warrior glanced to his right and saw the County Sheriff's officers carefully searching Pat Inston's abandoned Mercedes.

"I said I wasn't going to do this," Price murmured, reaching for a handkerchief to dry her eyes.

"Don't worry about it."

She squeezed Bolan's hand and smiled tightly. For a moment neither spoke, then she managed to say, "Listen, just give me a few minutes to get a grip on myself, okay? I'll be all right."

"Sure."

He stood and went to catch up with Grimaldi, who'd just ventured into the hut. "What happened?" he asked.

"Hard to say for sure," Grimaldi replied. "The Indian kid said he was just riding his bike out here when he saw the Mercedes and a Buick parked out back. He took a peek in here and got an eyeful. Pedaled to the nearest phone and called his folks, and they called the Highway Patrol. You know the rest."

There were chalk marks amid the blood on the floor, indicating where the bodies had been found. Pointing to the outline closest to Bolan, Grimaldi said, "Inston was there with an M-16. Walker over here, bound at the wrists and ankles. Paramedics said it looked as if he'd been worked over with some kind of club. From the looks of it, Inston must have burst in during some kind of interrogation and nailed the Natchapos, but not before they got their licks in with a carbine."

"Carbine?"

Grimaldi nodded. "M-1. Same make as those missing from Bergman. There's a whole case of them over here."

Bolan walked past the other chalk outlines and crouched beside the wadded length of canvas that had covered the stolen rifles. The opened crate on the floor was clearly missing one rifle.

"So what do you figure?" Bolan asked. "The Natchapos were stealing arms, Walker got caught spying on them and was being interrogated when Inston showed up and started blasting away?"

"That would make sense, except for a couple of things."

"Go on."

"First off," Grimaldi said, pointing at the floor, "see that stain there by your left foot? There's a dry area where something stopped the blood from spreading. Something oblong, probably heavy."

"Another case of M-1s?" Bolan speculated.

"At least one more, I'd guess. However many there were, they were moved after the shooting, which means there had to be survivors, and not just Inston's secretary."

"Secretary?"

"Donna Long. Cops say they found her purse out in the Mercedes."

"But not her?"

"Nope. They're searching the grounds."

Given the circumstances, neither man held out any great hope of finding the woman alive, but both felt she might hold a key to discovering what had really happened.

"We could cover more ground in the bird," Bolan said.

Grimaldi nodded. Leaving the hut, he went to start up the chopper. Bolan met briefly with the authorities, then stopped by to check on Price.

"I'll be okay."

"You're sure?"

She nodded. "Go. It's important that you find the woman."

Bolan jogged back to the chopper and climbed aboard. Grimaldi jockeyed the controls and lifted off while the Executioner glanced down the access road. Both ambulances were making their way away from the scene of the massacre. Grimaldi took the chopper in the other direction, over the old mining camp and surrounding desert.

"Well, if she's alive, we'll probably have a hostage situation on our hands," the pilot remarked.

"Or she might have fled on foot. If she did, she's out of her element. Whoever survived that shoot-out is going to track her down."

"You think it might be Timothy Gwynn?" Grimaldi asked. "Remember, he didn't turn up at the salvage yard."

"Possibly," Bolan said. "We need to access Inston's records and try to find out who he and Randy were closing in on."

"I can fly up there once we get through—"

"Wait," Bolan interrupted, pointing toward the base of the mountain. "I see some tire tracks down there."

"Let's check them out." Grimaldi banked the chopper slightly, changing course. "Looks like they're headed for the mouth of that old mine shaft."

Bolan peered down, spotting a length of long-neglected railroad track stretching out from a tunnel at the base of the mountain. The track ended near the remnants of an old depot, now little more than a crumbled foundation of cinder block choked with weeds and littered with beer cans. It was amid the weeds that both men caught their first glimpse of the woman.

"Let's bring it down," Bolan suggested.

Grimaldi landed in a clearing next to the mine. Inside the shaft Bolan could see a deserted Honda.

"Randy's car," he observed.

"Let's check the woman first," Grimaldi said.

Ducking under the rotor wash, the two men streamed through the rippling weeds until they came to the body of Donna Long. It wasn't a pretty sight.

CHAPTER NINETEEN

It was late afternoon. A white stretch limousine left Tucson International Airport and headed north through rush-hour traffic for the heart of downtown. Tomi Leitchen and Alisha Witt were sipping champagne in the back seat, their privacy ensured by tinted windows. A three-thousand-dollar sound system pumped a Duke Ellington ballad over speakers mounted in the door panels and behind the lushly padded seats. As Leitchen and Witt clinked their glasses together, the Puerto Rican gestured around him and toasted, "To a lady with taste."

"I'll drink to that."

"You know, Ali," Leitchen confessed after he drained his glass and started pouring a refill, "I still don't know what you want me to do about Ovitz and Tompkins."

"In good time, Tomi," she replied. Through the window she spotted the Perimeter Trust building rising above the smaller structures around it. She imagined Marlowe Tompkins and Cal Ovitz up in their luxurious suite, going about their business with no idea she'd come to town to deal with them. The thought made her smile. Ah, but she enjoyed baiting a trap. She enjoyed it almost as much as she enjoyed watching it spring on her prey.

"Now seems as good a time as any," Leitchen pressed.

"What's with all this shoptalk, Tomi?" Witt asked, smiling invitingly at the Puerto Rican. "You know, I have a saying—'pleasure before business.'"

"I thought it was supposed to be the other way around."

"Maybe for some."

She set her champagne glass aside and flicked an intercom switch that put her in touch with the chauffeur. "Jack, do us a favor and keep us in the city a while longer. I want to show Mr. Leitchen the sights."

"Yes, ma'am," came the disembodied voice over a small speaker on the control console.

Leitchen frowned. "See the sights? I thought we were going to your place in the country."

"Eventually." She reached for the console again, flicking another switch. The music stopped, and suddenly the limo was filled with the sounds of the city around them. It was as if they were in a convertible.

"I had microphones mounted on each fender," she told Leitchen. "Clever, yes?"

"I guess so. But why?"

"Well, here we are able to hear and see everyone around us, and yet nobody can see or hear us."

"True," Leitchen said, "but I still don't see—"

"It's exciting, don't you think?"

Witt gently took the glass from Leitchen's hand and held it close to her, tilting it so that champagne spilled down the front of her blouse. "Oh, clumsy me. That's the last of the champagne, and you look like you're still thirsty, Tomi."

The limo was stopped at an intersection, and pedestrians crossing the street were staring at the tinted windows. Leitchen could see their inquisitive faces, and even though he knew they couldn't see him, he felt as if he were on public display. It was a disconcerting sensation at first, but the feeling soon passed, aided by the sight of Alisha lying back in the seat beside him, drawing a finger along her blouse where she'd spilled the champagne. Aware that she had his attention, she smiled seductively, brought her finger to her mouth and licked it gently with the tip of her tongue.

"Mmm," she cooed, slowly closing her lips around her fingertip and drawing it into her mouth.

Leitchen reached out and unbuttoned the woman's blouse, then leaned forward and licked at the champagne on her neck. Its sweetness mingled with the slight tang of perfume. He kissed his way down to the swell of her breasts and worked his tongue behind the sheer material of her lace bra, seeking out her nipples.

"Yes," she said, pulling the man on top of her and jerking at his belt. "That's my Tomi, my lover man..."

The traffic light changed and the limo pulled forward, rocking the twosome slightly in the back seat. Witt tugged down Leitchen's zipper and reached inside his pants.

"Just for you, baby," he told her. "It's just for you."

"Good, because I want it all."

AN HOUR PASSED before Jack was given the okay to leave the Tucson city limits and take the highway to a verdant twenty-six-acre estate overlooking the Santa Cruz River. The limo passed through a security gate and started down a long paved road flanked by citrus groves. Sated from their lovemaking, Witt and Leitchen stared out at the scenery, watching gardeners tend to the trees.

"Quite a spread, Ali."

"Thank you." The woman snickered as she slipped back into her skirt. "I liked yours, too."

The Puerto Rican smiled indulgently. Once past the groves they came to a flat clearing. Leitchen could see a half-dozen horses prancing in a green field near the river. Up ahead was a huge three-story Tudor-style mansion, sheltered partially from the heat by towering sycamores. Far off in the distance, beyond the horse stables and tennis courts, was a fifty-foot-high brick tower, looking like a mislaid turret from a medieval castle.

"Water tower," Witt explained. "It can get dry out here."

"Ah..."

The limo pulled around to the back of the mansion, stopping near a five-car garage. Leitchen could see workers diligently polishing a Jaguar, a Chevy Blazer and a vintage Italian Avanti. The chauffeur got out of the limo and opened the rear door, then stood back as Alisha and Leitchen stepped out. The Puerto Rican eyed the chauffeur warily, but Jack showed no sign of being aware of the lovemaking that had been going on behind his back all the time he'd been driving.

"See that Gregory tends to our luggage, Jack," Witt told the chauffeur. "I want to take Tomi to see the horses."

"Yes, ma'am." Jack bowed slightly and headed up the cacti-lined walk leading to the mansion's back patio.

Witt, meanwhile, slipped an arm through Leitchen's and led him the other way toward the stables. The gunrunner glanced around at the manicured grounds, the heliport next to a sculpture garden, the Olympic-size swimming pool surrounded by landscaped arrangements of boulders and stone tiles. "Very nice."

"I like it."

"This place . . . it belongs to your friends?"

The woman nodded. "A few of us own it jointly. Since we're always on the move, it usually works out that whenever one of us comes by, we can have it to ourselves."

"A nice arrangement."

"Perhaps I can talk to the others about letting you have a key."

Leitchen shrugged. "Perhaps."

Reaching the fence, Witt leaned against the post. She called out to one of the horses, and it began trotting toward them. Leitchen brushed a strand of hair from her face. "This has all been very nice, Ali," he told her, "but I'm beginning to feel like a gigolo."

"Oh, Tomi, stop."

"I mean it," he said. "I'm a man of action. I need to do my work."

"Of course . . ."

The horse came to a stop alongside the fence. Witt gently fingered its mane and stroked the side of its face.

"You were going to tell me how you wanted me to deal with Ovitz and Tompkins," the Puerto Rican prompted.

"Yes, I know. They've offered you some weapons, right?"

"Yes. A small shipment of carbines and also some ammunition. But they hinted there was more."

Witt reached for a salt block lying on the ground. "Well, I think the first thing I'd like you to do is find out how much of an arsenal they have and, if possible, where and how they got it."

"I'll see what I can do. What else?"

She held the salt block through the gap in the fence so that the horse could lick it. Without taking her eyes off the beast she nonchalantly told the Puerto Rican, "I also want you to ask Ovitz and Tompkins to kill me."

DUSK WAS APPROACHING. As the sun dipped low toward the horizon, a thin band of clouds rolling in from California took on the same rusty hue as the reddish mud that served as mortar for the scattered cluster of large log-walled hogans that were home to several Natchapo clans, including the Blyford and Jones families. Shunning the more formal village structure of neighboring Hopi and Pueblo tribes, most Natchapos lived in these smaller groups as shepherds.

A flock of several hundred sheep dotted the grounds around the huts, and any other night the pastoral setting might have passed as a tribute to the Natchapos' sense of harmony with nature. But tonight there was little sense of peace or tranquillity. The air was heavy with sorrow and rage as families struggled to come to terms with the deaths of the Blyford brothers and the other Natchapos who had fallen during the bloody siege at the salvage yard.

Some of the family members were crammed into the largest of the hogans, where a memorial prayer service was being offered for the dead. Those who hadn't embraced Christianity observed this grim day in the privacy of their homes, and the twilight was pierced with occasional cries of sorrow and pleas to the *yei,* the gods of the Natchapos. Still others congregated on a plateau situated off to one side from the hogans, faces lit by a huge fire as they listened to Carney Jones speak of the need to protest this latest tragedy without resorting to violence.

Jones's voice carried in the still night, and although Cal Ovitz couldn't make out the words, he felt confident that the Natchapo had his colleagues' attention and would keep them away from their homes for at least another half hour. Ovitz didn't figure he'd need much more time than that.

He was spying on the Indians from inside his panel truck, concealed behind a wall of sagebrush on a fire-break in the hills three hundred yards away. He'd been there for over an hour, using high-powered binoculars to monitor the movements of the various families. In particular he focused his attention on a hogan located at the edge of a wash that dipped down to the banks of the Santa Cruz River. Ovitz knew from previous clandestine rendezvous with the Blyford brothers that Jones lived there with his parents, grandmother and two cousins, one of whom had been among the fatalities at the salvage yard.

The first stars were coming out when Ovitz saw the hut's front door swing open. Nine people filed out amid much wailing and chanting. An older woman had to be held up by two young men to keep from collapsing in her grief. Making its way by torchlight, the procession headed toward one of the other hogans, where the survivors of the Blyford brothers lived. By Ovitz's count the hogan was now vacant. It was the opportunity he'd been waiting for.

Setting aside his binoculars, the man slipped quietly from the panel truck. He was dressed in camouflage fatigues and had streaked grease under his eyes. The slain prospector's backpack was strapped to his shoulders, and he clutched his Browning automatic as he cautiously dug his heels into the soft sand of an embankment leading down to the river.

A summer-long drought had left countless boulders and rocks protruding above the waterline. Ovitz had no problem finding a dry footing as he made his way across the riverbed. Reaching the other side, he walked along the bank until he came to the wash leading up toward the hogans.

Darkness had set in, and there wasn't adequate moonlight to penetrate the shadowy darkness of the wash. After stumbling twice over unexpected rises in the terrain, Ovitz cursed and unslung the backpack, taking out a pair of Nightflasher goggles he'd brought along for just such a situation. The frames normally had to be affixed to a pilot's helmet, but Ovitz had adapted this pair with a thick elastic band and swivel mounts so that he could slip them on and flip them up out of view when he didn't need them.

Peering through the lenses, he scanned the ground for obstacles a few yards ahead of him, then raised the goggles as he advanced. It was a tedious process, and the constant shifting between the Nightflasher and regular vision began to give him a headache, but the device proved worthwhile, helping him to avoid several pitfalls and a precariously sharp outcrop of rock jutting from the sand.

Once at the top of the rise, Ovitz slipped the goggles back into the backpack and took out the battered leather valise containing part of Donna Long's scalp, the NAM pamphlets and a few items that had been taken from Pat Inston's Mercedes, items meant to point a finger of suspicion at Inston's company rather than Tompkins-Ovitz Security Services.

Holding the valise in one hand and his Colt in the other, Ovitz slipped into the nearest hogan. Because the opening faced away from the other structures and there were no windows, he was able to use a small flashlight to make his job easier. During the summer Carney Jones's family, like most Natchapos, slept outside, and so the hogan was sparsely furnished and roomy despite the low ceiling of strapped logs. Ovitz moved along the walls, carefully inspecting several crudely made shelves stocked with food staples and clothing. Behind one cupboard was a gap wide enough to conceal the leather valise. After he wedged it into place, Ovitz snapped off the flashlight and started toward the opening.

Suddenly he froze.

There were footsteps outside the hogan, heading toward the open doorway. He glanced around quickly. There was only one way out and nowhere to hide. He was trapped.

Ovitz stole forward and crouched beside the doorway, finger on the trigger of his automatic. With any luck he could surprise and overpower whoever came in the door, but if necessary he was prepared to shoot his way out.

When no one appeared in the doorway and the footsteps retreated slightly, Ovitz feared he'd been found out and someone was heading off to warn the others. Not about to let himself be outarmed and outnumbered, Ovitz decided to take his chances. He charged out the doorway, almost colliding with a spindly legged ewe that was about to wander into the hogan. Startled, the ewe bleated and trotted away, spreading panic to some nearby sheep.

Ovitz bolted the other way, leaping over the edge of the wash. He landed feetfirst at an awkward angle, lost his balance, then somersaulted down the incline, losing the goggles from his backpack as he slammed his shin against a boulder.

Cursing under his breath, Ovitz leaned close to the dirt for cover. In the darkness he wasn't able to see the fallen goggles. Up on the rise he could hear shouts above the wailing of the sheep. He debated making a run for it, but feared he'd be seen trying to cross the river. Staying put, he raised his Colt to firing position, ready to blast away at anyone who might wander into view.

Seconds plodded as he tried to sort through the sounds up above. The outcry of the flock slowly faded, and he was able to pick up the exchanges between Natchapos investigating the disturbance. At one point Ovitz could make out the silhouette of a man against the moonlight. He drew a bead on the man's head and waited for him to turn around.

The other man retreated, however, calling out to his comrades, "Probably just another coyote."

Ovitz exhaled slowly, but stayed put another five minutes until quiet had once again settled over the desert. Then, limping slightly to favor his bruised shin, he backtracked to his panel truck.

A couple of tumbleweeds had become wedged between the underside of the vehicle and the desert floor. Pulling them free, Ovitz was about to cast them aside when he changed his mind and carried them to a nearby rock formation. Even in the dim light he could still see where he'd placed a crateful of Air Force M-1 carbines between the two largest boulders. He used the tumbleweeds to provide further cover, then went back to the truck, where he quickly wiped the grease from his face and changed out of his fatigues before getting behind the wheel.

It was a fifteen-minute drive before Ovitz tracked down the nearest pay phone, located in a booth outside a liquor store just beyond the reservation. There were Natchapos sitting in two dust-covered pickup trucks parked out front, drinking beer as they shouted to one another over the blare of country music from a Gallup radio station. Ovitz parked on the other side of the lot and rummaged through a kit bag for a press-on mustache and a pair of nonprescription glasses. In the bright light of day they'd probably be easily detected as fakes, but at this hour Ovitz was confident they'd do the job. He donned a Phoenix Suns ball cap to round out the disguise, then got out and strode to the phone booth.

Slipping coins into the appropriate slots, he called information, then disguised his voice as he asked for the number of the nearest FBI field office. The operator gave it to him and he dialed again. As he waited for an answer, he glanced through the front window of the store and saw the owner, an overweight man in his midsixties, watching him. Ovitz shifted position, turning his back to the owner.

After three rings, a toneless voice told him, "Federal Bureau of Investigation."

"Yeah. It's about them killings."

"What killings?"

"You know what I'm talking about. Out by the old Baines mine."

"Who is this?"

"Don't matter who I am. Just listen up, 'cause I know the one that got away—the one that scalped that broad."

CHAPTER TWENTY

Mack Bolan was two exits away from Randy Walker's temporary apartment in Tucson, and it only took him five minutes to reach the new complex on the outskirts of town. Idle bulldozers and other pieces of heavy equipment lined the unpaved streets, and sawhorses mounted with blinking lights straddled deep gashes in the earth where sewer lines were to be installed. Walker's apartment building was the only completed structure in sight, although the skeletal framework of other complexes rose from nearby concrete foundations, and huge mountains of stacked lumber suggested that work was proceeding at a clip to match the city's rapid growth in recent years.

Bolan pulled into a lot behind the apartments. Half the units were rented, and there were several cars parked out front, but he saw no sign of Able Team's minivan. He got out of the car and headed up the walk. The staircase leading up to Walker's apartment on the third floor was cordoned off with yellow strips of plastic declaring the area off-limits to the public. Bolan had planned to wait out front, but as he looked up at Walker's apartment, he thought he saw a beam of light glance off the curtains. At first he figured it might have just been a reflection from the halogen lamps illuminating the parking lot, but his instincts told him otherwise.

Heading for the stairwell, the warrior unbuttoned his suit coat, and as he started up the steps, he quietly withdrew his Beretta. A party was in progress in the apartment directly below Walker's and Bolan could smell the aroma of pizza on the second-floor landing. A stereo was blaring, and people were talking loudly above the music. He hurried up the next flight of stairs, pausing to gently peel back one of the police strips so that he could reach the third floor.

Another advisory notice was posted on Walker's door, which Bolan assumed would be locked . . . unless an intruder had picked the tumblers and left it unlocked to allow for a quicker getaway. Thankful for the noise downstairs, the Executioner slowly closed his fingers around the doorknob and turned it.

It wasn't locked.

Slowly the warrior leaned against the door, testing the hinges. They didn't creak, so he opened the door wide enough to slip inside, then drew it closed behind him. Crouched in the front entryway, he froze for a moment, waiting for his eyes to accustom themselves to the darkness. He could feel the bass throb of the stereo vibrating the floor under his feet, and it was difficult for him to tune out the music and revelry downstairs and concentrate on sounds within Walker's apartment. Just off to his right the refrigerator hummed in the kitchen, and a hanging clock in the living room ticked off the seconds.

Although both the shades and drapes were drawn, enough light filtered in from the parking lot for Bolan to eventually make out a den full of furniture. An archway at the end of the hall led to the bedroom and bath.

Halfway across the den Bolan froze again, hearing the unmistakable metallic snap of someone releasing a gun's safety. He placed the sound as coming from the bedroom and instinctively dived forward. Almost simultaneously he heard the distinctive *pfft* of a silencer and the shattering of a glass tabletop behind him.

Bolan's suit coat ripped at the seams as he rolled and took cover behind a wet bar. Waiting only long enough to suck in a quick breath, the warrior lunged to his feet, firing three quick blasts through the archway. His Beretta was even quieter than the intruder's weapon and just as destructive, burying 9 mm rounds into the vents of a wall heater and gouging a hole in the bedroom door frame. However, he missed his would-be assailant, who retreated through the bedroom and began fumbling with a window.

The Executioner charged the back hallway, diving once more as he came within range of the bedroom. A line of gunfire stitched the wall beside him, and he felt the sting of plaster against his back as he flattened himself against the carpet.

Hearing the bedroom window slide open, he sprang to his feet. Someone dressed in black and wearing a ski mask was slipping out the window. Bolan raised his Beretta and fired again, shattering the glass. He raced into the bedroom, hurdling an overturned chair as he made his way to the window, and leaned out.

Although the apartment was on the third floor, it was only a two-story drop to the roof of a cabana overlooking the complex's swimming pool and hot tub. The intruder was on the roof, and Bolan leaned back from the bedroom window as a gunshot shattered a flowerpot on the sill. When he glanced back out again, he saw the other man leap off the far side of the cabana roof and drop from sight.

Bolan had made enough jumps in his time to know how to cushion his landing when he leaped onto the roof. Crouching and rolling on impact, he felt only the faintest jab of pain shoot up his legs. It was a much shorter jump to the ground, but he still somersaulted to one side, making himself as difficult a target to hit as possible.

The intruder didn't shoot at him this time, though. The warrior rose to his feet and looked around. The pool area was surrounded by a high security fence. Bolan figured the only way the man could have fled was through a gateway next to the cabana. He took up the chase, shoving the gate open and running along a walk that led back to the parking lot. He was about to check the lot when he detected motion out of the corner of his eye. Fifty yards away, at the end of a cul-de-sac, a figure was darting into a maze of six-foot-high lengths of concrete sewer pipe. Bolan shifted his course and headed away from the parking lot.

He checked the sewer line, but the man was nowhere to be seen. In addition to the pipe the storage lot was stocked with steel rods and girders, more lumber and a few portable rest rooms—all places for a gunman to hide. Bolan was wary of blundering into an ambush. He slowly circled around the conduit, staying close to the stacked lumber.

"Come on, come on," he whispered, peering at shadows cast by the nearest streetlights, looking for signs of movement.

As he inched along, Beretta at the ready, Bolan suddenly heard a sound above him. As he glanced up, a bundled stack of four-by-fours began to tumble, dislodging other lumber until an avalanche of wood was thundering down on him.

Bolan's quick reflexes saved his life as he dived under the curve of the nearest sewer pipe. The pipe took the brunt of the slide, but a few hundred pounds of lumber pinned the warrior to the ground. He'd dropped his gun during the commotion, and as he grimaced under the weight pressed against his legs, he stretched out his hand, reaching for the Beretta. His forearm began to cramp as he got two fingers on the barrel, and he quickly pulled his hand back.

Waiting for the muscles to relax, Bolan heard the nearby sound of a motorcycle being kick-started. As the engine came to life, a single headlight suddenly glared in Bolan's eyes. The intruder let up on the clutch and surged forward, heading directly for him.

The Executioner concentrated on dragging his legs out from under the lumber. He had one foot out and was working on the other as the motorcycle bore down on him. Realizing he couldn't get out of the way, Bolan pressed himself as flat against the ground as possible and braced for the inevitable.

The bike struck his left thigh first, and the front end bounced upward so that the intruder's full weight was on the back tire as it rolled over Bolan. He thought he could feel something break, but he didn't have much time to dwell on it, because as the sound of the bike's engine faded in his ears, Bolan felt a cold chill wrap around his forehead and spread down his back. His vision became blurred with bright flashes of light, then a sudden curtain of black was drawn over everything.

CARL LYONS DIVERTED his gaze to avoid the headlight glare of the oncoming motorcycle. Once the bike passed, he resumed looking for the right turnoff to Randy Walker's apartment complex. Schwarz was riding shotgun. Blancanales and Grimaldi huddled in back with John Kissinger, who was spelling out the one part of the mystery he'd been able to get a handle on.

"Inston and Walker couldn't have been in cahoots with the Natchapo Armed Militia," he insisted, "either with the sabotage at Reed-Blackpoint or this whole inventory scam with the Air Force."

"I'll buy that," Schwarz agreed. "And NAM's not in it alone, either. They're getting outside help, probably from one of the outfits Randy was doing surveillance on."

"Well," Grimaldi said, "I think Bear hit the nail on the head when he turned up that CIA link between Inston and those two guys running the bodyguard school."

"Tompkins and Ovitz?"

"Yeah, them."

"Let's not forget Tomi Leitchen," Lyons reminded the others. "Seems to me he's involved, too."

"Yeah, but not on his own," Schwarz said. "Hell, he was in Monte Carlo when this whole thing— Hey!" he interrupted himself, staring out the windshield. "What's going on up here?"

As they drew nearer to the apartment complex, they saw people milling around outside, some of them staring up at the third floor and pointing, others making their way toward a nearby lot filled with building and sewer supplies.

"There's Mack's rental," Schwarz stated as they pulled up and parked. "Anybody see him?"

"Negative," Blancanales replied, getting out of the minivan and looking around. His gaze drifted quickly to the shattered third-floor window. "But my guess is either he found something or something found him."

Blancanales and Grimaldi headed up the steps to Walker's apartment while Lyons and Kissinger queried a few onlookers. Because everyone had been inside when the gunfight had erupted, there were conflicting stories as to what had happened. Finally a young man with shoulder-length hair appeared at the edge of the supply lot, shouting, "Hey, there's some dead guy back here buried under a ton of wood!"

Lyons and Kissinger sprinted past the sewer pipes and were led to Bolan. Contrary to initial reports, he wasn't buried and he wasn't dead. Lyons had no trouble finding a pulse, and once he and Kissinger put their collective strength into shifting the fallen lumber, they were able to pull Bolan free. He came to a few moments later.

"It's all right, Striker," Lyons told him. "You're all in one piece."

"You sure? My left leg . . ."

"Can you move your toes?" Lyons asked.

Bolan tried, then shook his head. "Nothing."

"What happened?" Kissinger asked.

Before the Executioner could respond, Lyons turned to the crowd of party-goers closing in around them. "One of you call for an ambulance!" he snapped. "The rest of you beat it!"

As the crowd dispersed, Bolan related his run-in with the intruder and the chase that had brought him to the cul-de-sac. When he explained how he'd been run over by the other man's motorcycle, Lyons cursed loudly.

"What's the matter?" Bolan asked.

"We drove right by some biker on the way here! Shit, all I had to do was veer a little to my left and I could have sent that bastard flying."

"There'll be a next time."

Off in the distance an ambulance siren sounded, and by the time it arrived at the apartment complex, there were other wailings in the night, announcing the approach of the local authorities. After a spot check of Bolan's legs, the paramedics offered cautious optimism on his chances for full recovery, then loaded him onto a gurney so they could transfer him to the ambulance. Lyons and Kissinger broke away and headed back to the apartment complex. Schwarz and Blancanales were just coming down the steps.

"Find anything?" Lyons asked.

"Yeah," Gadgets reported. "A big envelope with some Air Force procurement memos and a roster for the Natchapo Armed Militia."

"Where was it?"

"In the bedroom. Taped under the bottom drawer of a filing cabinet."

"Do we know if anyone searched there earlier?"

"It wasn't mentioned in any of the reports I saw," Kissinger said. "So my guess is no. But I'll make a few calls and double-check, okay?"

Kissinger headed off, and Lyons started laying out possibilities. "Okay, if the cops checked under that filing cabinet and didn't find anything, then obviously our mystery guest planted it there. But, of course, there's a chance the envelope was there all along, in which case maybe Randy's not as clean as we hoped."

"I can't believe that," Blancanales said.

"Well, I sure as hell don't *want* to," Lyons replied.

The argument became moot when Kissinger returned from the van a few moments later. "No," he reported, "there wasn't any envelope under the filing cabinet this afternoon."

All four men shared a look of relief, but then Kissinger added, "There's something else. The FBI just raided the Natchapo reservation. They've arrested Carney Jones for the rape and murder of Donna Long."

MARLOWE TOMPKINS pulled up in front of his ranch-style house on Tucson's east side, guiding his motorcycle to a stop next to the panel truck parked in the driveway. Cal Ovitz got out of the truck and finished a cigarette as his partner unlocked the garage door and put the bike inside.

"Shit, and I thought I got myself dirty," Ovitz said, noticing grime and a few tears in Tompkins's clothes. "What did you do, go motocrossing on the way back?"

"I'm not in the mood for wisecracks," Tompkins snapped.

The garage was spacious, with more than enough room for his motorcycle, BMW and a work area. Tompkins went to a huge cast-iron sink near the workbench and lathered his hands with soap.

"You plant the stuff?" Ovitz asked him.

"Yeah. How about you?"

"No problem. I called the Bureau, too. They should be swooping down on those rednecks like the U.S. Cavalry about now."

"Good." Tompkins grabbed a towel off the bench and dried his hands. Ovitz took a closer look at his partner's superficial wounds as well as the troubled expression on his face.

"Hey, what's up, Marlowe?"

The man hesitated for a moment, then said, "I got paid a surprise visit at that kid's apartment."

"Cops?"

Tompkins tossed the towel across the room into a hamper overflowing with unwashed laundry. "I can't be positive, but I think it might have been the same guy we ran into on the semi."

"What? Are you kidding?"

"Like I said, I can't be sure. I didn't get a good enough look at him." He went on to describe the brief exchange of gunfire and the chase across the grounds of Walker's apartment complex to the supply lot.

"Who the hell is that guy?" Ovitz wondered out loud. "Part of security at Reed-Blackpoint?"

"Probably," Tompkins replied, "but I'm not about to try setting up a new contact there just to find out."

"Man, this sucks," Ovitz complained, taking a final drag on his cigarette and flicking it into the sink. "Do you think he got a look at you?"

"What was there to see? I was wearing the ski mask, same as in the semi."

"Which means he probably made a connection," Ovitz speculated. He suddenly lashed out, slamming his fist on the rear trunk of the BMW.

"Hey, take it easy!"

"Don't you get it?" Ovitz yelled. "If that guy figures you're one of the people who were in on the semi thing, he's gonna find that stuff you planted and figure it's just that—planted."

"Well, there's not a hell of a lot we can do about it. But if you ask me, he's not going to be in any shape to conduct a search. Hell, if I nailed him as bad as I think I did, he might have cashed in his chips and we're getting ourselves all bent out of shape over nothing."

"I hope to hell you're right," Ovitz said. Then he added ominously, "For both our sakes."

"Look, we're both a little on edge, okay?" Tompkins punched out a code on his security system before unlocking the door to the house. "Let's have a drink."

"Good idea."

Inside, Tompkins's place was decorated in a western motif that included several high-priced sculptures of cowboys on horseback and two paintings of cattle runs by a well-known artist. There was an answering machine on the bar, and Tompkins checked for messages as Ovitz poured a couple of bourbons straight up.

"Evening, Mr. T," Tomi Leitchen's voice sounded over the machine's tape. "I'm in town about our little deal. I think we can make it bigger. How about you or Mr. Ovitz give me a call, okay? I'm staying at the Walk Inn."

Tompkins turned off the machine and glanced at his partner. "What do you think?"

"I don't know." Ovitz drained his bourbon and poured a refill. "With all this shit going down, I really wanted to lie low for a while."

Tompkins sipped his drink and stared out a picture window at a view of downtown Tucson. A few moments passed, then he said, "Maybe we can have it both ways."

"What do you mean?"

"Why don't we hear Tomi out, see if we can work a deal that gets us out of town for a few weeks? Give the heat a chance to blow over?"

Ovitz shook his head. "No can do."

"Why not?"

"For starters, we've got two more sessions of that damn bodyguard class to get through. And then there's the home stretch on this gig we've got going with Alisha Witt."

"*You've* got going with Alisha Witt," Tompkins corrected. "Remember, I don't want any part of that bitch."

Ovitz's eyes narrowed. "Shut up."

Tompkins shook his head in disgust. "She's got you so pussy-whipped you're blind. I'm telling you, she can't be trusted."

"What makes you so fucking sure?"

"I feel it in my gut, okay? She's bad news."

Ovitz finished his second drink in another long gulp, then he picked up the phone and dialed Tomi Leitchen's number. "Let's just drop it, okay?"

"Fine by me. Not like I'm the one who brought it up."

Leitchen answered his phone on the third ring. "Hello?"

"Hey, Leitchen, how's it hanging?"

"Ah, Mr. Ovitz."

"You bet. I'm over at Tompkins's place. We got your message."

"Obviously, or you wouldn't know I was here."

Ovitz laughed into the receiver. "Oh, Tomi, always with the jokes. What's this about sweetening the deal?"

"Let's meet and we'll talk."

"I've been running around all night, Tomi. Don't play games. Just spell it out for me."

"You know me, Mr. Ovitz," Leitchen drawled. "I don't like telephones. I like to do business face-to-face."

Ovitz sighed. "Okay, okay. When?"

"I'm not busy now."

"Just a sec." He cupped his hand over the receiver. "He wants to meet tonight."

Tompkins shrugged. "What the hell? Why not?"

Ovitz uncovered the mouthpiece. "We're on our way."

As Ovitz hung up, Tompkins finished his drink and started unbuttoning his shirt. "Give me five minutes to take a quick shower and change."

As Tompkins headed off down the hallway, his partner poured himself a third bourbon, trying to blunt the rage welling up inside him. It wasn't the first time they'd clashed over Ovitz's involvement with Alisha Witt. Not by a long shot. In fact their differences went back to the first time they'd met with the woman several months ago. They'd talked business over dinner, and from the outset it had been clear to Ovitz that they both found Alisha desirable as more than a business partner. But by the time they'd finished dessert, it was equally clear that Alisha favored him over Tompkins, and Ovitz was sure that a lot of Tompkins's bad-mouthing was nothing more than jealousy. All the same, he was getting fed up with it.

"But in a while it won't matter," he muttered to himself. No, in a couple of weeks the mess with Inston and the Natchapos would be history for Ovitz, and so would Tompkins. Once Ovitz helped Alisha seize control of Reed-Blackpoint, she'd take him on as her partner and he'd leave this Tucson hellhole behind once and for all. He'd go to Europe and live the good life.

"Yes, sir," he said, reciting his favorite mantra. "The good life."

"What's that?" Tompkins called out from the hallway.

"Nothing," Ovitz told him, knocking down his third drink. "Nothing at all."

CHAPTER TWENTY-ONE

Most of the sensation had returned to Mack Bolan's leg by the time he was brought to the hospital. X rays turned up no broken bones, but the attending doctors insisted that "Mike Belasko" spend a few days going through a battery of tests to ensure there was no permanent nerve or tissue damage. The Executioner refused to go along with the recommendation, just as he refused to take any sedatives or painkillers that would immobilize him for the night. There was no way he was going to sit on the sidelines while his enemies were out there in the night somewhere, having twice succeeded in fleeing after their attempts to kill him.

Upon his arrival at the hospital, Brognola initially sided with the medics, but when Bolan made it clear he had no intention of staying bedridden, the big Fed again ran the necessary interference to secure the Executioner's release.

"You're sure it was one of the same guys from the semi?" Brognola asked as they drove away from the hospital.

"I'd bet my life on it."

"Well, aside from the evidence they planted, they didn't leave any other clues at the apartment," Brognola said. "But we might be close to a breakthrough on another front."

"Yeah? What's that?"

The big Fed got onto the highway and started north for the Natchapo reservation. "Well, as near as we can figure, at the same time you were at Walker's apartment, your friend's partner was out at the reservation trying to set up one of the Natchapos for raping and scalping Pat Inston's secretary."

"You caught him?"

Brognola shook his head. "No. As a matter of fact, the Bureau fell for the setup and arrested Carney Jones after they got an anonymous phone tip. They found part of the woman's scalp in his hogan, along with some Air Force papers and a NAM roster."

"Carney Jones," Bolan said, recalling the name. "He's one of the guys Straw brought in last night, right?"

"That's right. The black sheep of the group. He's the one who's been pushing for civil disobedience instead of open warfare."

"But you just said the Feds found that woman's scalp in his—"

"Yes, they did. But you see, the thing is, at the time of those killings out at the old mine, Jones was clear across town, passing out protest flyers just down the street from the Air Force base. AFI tailed him there from the apartment and followed him right up to the point where he returned to the reservation after hearing about the shoot-out at the salvage yard. He's clean.''

"So where does that leave us?'' Bolan wondered out loud.

Brognola gestured at a road sign announcing the upcoming exit to the reservation. "Able Team's searching the grounds around Jones's hogan. We're hoping to find something that'll put us on the scent of whoever's behind the frame-up.''

"Able?'' Bolan said. "Isn't that a little risky? If it comes out that we were the ones behind that raid on the salvage yard, we're apt to have a riot on our hands.''

"That's not likely to happen,'' the big Fed told him, flashing his blinker and changing lines. "Any witnesses from that shoot-out are either dead or behind bars, and as far as the public's concerned, it was a SWAT team that made the raid. Able Team's just another batch of faceless Feds as far as the Natchapos are concerned. Some of them are even helping with the search.''

They got off at the next exit. And as they reached a checkpoint at the edge of the reservation, Bolan saw that while some of the Natchapos might have agreed to aid Able Team, another group had gathered inside the checkpoint, waving quickly made placards and shouting antigovernment slogans at the National Guard troops that had been brought in to man the entrance. A few media vans had shown up, and cameras were rolling, taking in the demonstration for the eleven-o'clock news.

Brognola flashed credentials at the sentries manning the gates, and the rental car was waved through. Some of the protestors drifted over, venting their rage on Brognola and Bolan. Even with the windows rolled up they could hear the chants denouncing their arrival, and twice the car was struck with clods of dirt that exploded on impact, leaving dents on the hood and front fender.

"Nice to feel wanted, isn't it?" Brognola said, as he pressed his foot on the accelerator to put more distance between them and the protestors.

"Can't really blame them, can you?"

"No," Brognola confessed with a sigh. "No, I really can't. And the thing is, before all this the NAM group was really looked down on by the people here because they were so prone to violence."

"And now they're being looked on as martyrs, right?"

"By some, yes, I think so."

"One way or another I'll be glad when this whole mess is finally over," Bolan said.

Rounding a bend, the men saw a helicopter hovering in tight circles above the wash that ran alongside Carney Jones's hogan. A spotlight beamed down from the aircraft, aiding the search crew on the ground.

"Grimaldi?" Bolan asked.

Brognola nodded, guiding the car over a series of ruts to a clearing where Able's van was already parked. As he got out of the car, Bolan grimaced with the pain of his first step. Passing the embers of an abandoned campfire, he followed Brognola to the edge of the wash. Lyons had just climbed up from the river and he was holding something.

"Some kind of night goggles," Ironman told them, inspecting the modified Nightflashers. "Whoever planted the scalp probably used them to sneak up on the hogans."

"Air Force issue?" Bolan asked.

"Probably." Lyons handed over the goggles.

As Bolan looked at the goggles in the light cast down from Grimaldi's chopper, Lyons grabbed his walkie-talkie and keyed the microphone. "Hey, Jack, take a peek at these goggles, will you?"

"Hold them up."

Bolan held the goggles in the air as Grimaldi brought the chopper down lower, stealing a glance from behind the controls.

"Yeah," the Stony pilot confirmed, "they're Nightflashers. Made by some subsidiary of T. S. Meyler."

"Okay, thanks," Lyons said. "Why don't you swing across the river and see how Gadgets and Pol are coming along?"

"Roger."

Lyons was about to clip the walkie-talkie back onto his waist when it crackled to life again.

"We're on to something over here," Pol reported. "Found ourselves a crateful of M-1 carbines."

Lyons and Bolan glanced across the river, following the beam of Grimaldi's chopper until it illuminated the cluster of rocks where Schwarz and Blancanales had unearthed the weapons cache.

"There's some tire tracks, too," Pol said. "They look pretty recent."

Lyons keyed his walkie-talkie. "Good work. Call Grimaldi down, then ride with him and see where the tracks lead to. With any luck you'll wind up at a pay phone where they put through that call to the Bureau."

"Will do."

Lyons clipped the walkie-talkie onto his belt. The chopper swooped down across the river, landing close to the rock pile where Blancanales and Schwarz were waiting.

"I think we're finally getting somewhere," Lyons commented.

"I hope so," Brognola said. "I certainly hope so."

Bolan continued to stare at the Nightflasher goggles, trying to make some kind of connection. "Meyler... He's that offbeat billionaire, right?"

"Yeah," Brognola replied, "that's the guy."

"Does he make a lot of his money on defense contracts by any chance?"

"I'm not sure. I can look into it, though."

"Yeah, do that," Bolan said. "If he's got a lot riding on Pentagon dollars, he'd be in competition with Reed-Blackpoint for a lot of business, right?"

"Depends on what products he's involved with."

"I think Mack's got a point," Lyons said. "Hell, Barbara was telling us back at the Farm what a cut-throat business that's becoming these days. It wouldn't be unheard-of for a guy like that to pull some heavy punches trying to muscle away a share of the market from Blackpoint."

"We'll get right on it," Brognola promised.

"Meanwhile," Lyons told them, snapping on his flashlight, "I'm going to check the wash and the river again to see if I can find anything else."

As Ironman started down the slope, Brognola and Bolan headed the other way. Kissinger had just come into view, walking alongside one of the tribal elders. Both men looked concerned.

"What's up?" Brognola asked.

"I'm worried," the older man said. "About thirty members of the Militia haven't been accounted for. We've checked their homes, and I've made some calls off the reservation. Nobody's seen them since late this afternoon."

"You think they're going to retaliate for what happened today?" Bolan asked.

The Natchapo nodded grimly. "If I know them at all, yes."

"And you have no idea where they might be?"

The elder shook his head. "Most of their weapons were probably at the salvage yard, but that won't stop them. They'll get their hands on something, then they're going to lash out."

Bolan stared past the group, watching the storm clouds rolling in across the desert. It was an ominous sight, and combined with the old man's dire prediction, the Executioner feared the worst. If the NAM renegades were to resort to terrorism, there'd be more than rain drenching the Arizona soil. There'd be blood, much of it shed by the innocent.

THERE WAS A PREEXISTING contingency plan in the event of a raid like the one that had taken place at the salvage yard, and during the hours following that shoot-out, the surviving members of the Natchapo Armed Militia, alone and in small groups, had fled to the desert, taking various alternative routes to a single destination—Mission San Jacques. The gleaming whitewashed church and its adjacent grounds served not only as a place of Christian worship for more than seven different Indian tribes, but also as an educational facility...and, as far as the Militia was concerned, a place of sanctuary, where they figured they could avoid arrest in a worst-case scenario.

Of course, the men knew better than to flaunt weapons and spout political rhetoric around the mission. As a front, members of NAM had long been part of an intertribal baseball league that played regularly at the several diamonds laid out on the hardpan behind the church. Accordingly, when they had begun to congregate throughout the afternoon, little suspicion had been cast their way. They had played ball throughout the afternoon and into the evening, pretending surprise when other tribesmen passed along word of the double tragedy that had befallen the Natchapos earlier in the day.

Timothy Gwynn had been among the first to arrive at the mission, which was less than twenty miles from the old Holwell Cavern film lot. As he heard the details of the shoot-out at the salvage yard and the killings at the Baines mine, he'd registered the appropriate shock and sense of outrage. But inwardly, he felt a growing excitement and anticipation, because for him these were fortuitous circumstances, a conspiring by the fates to usher him into a position of power within the Militia. After all, he'd avoided the separate bloodbaths that had claimed Zane and Al Blyford as well as half the group's membership. If that wasn't enough of an omen, as he'd logged the arrival of the survivors, it became clear to him that, with the exception of his good friend Diton, most of his closest allies were still alive.

As night fell over the mission and the various tribesmen drifted off into separate groups, the Militia had gathered, far from earshot of the others. As Gwynn had hoped, his friends stood behind him when he laid claim to the leadership of NAM, and he was able to win over the few dissenters once he divulged that he'd discovered the means by which the Militia could effectively retaliate against the forces that had tried to bring them down.

Now, several hours later, the renegades, piled into five dust-caked pickup trucks, were converging on the dilapidated ruins of the Holwell Caverns Amusement Park. A sixth truck remained back near the entrance to the lot on the chance that Cal Ovitz or Marlowe

Tompkins might return. Gwynn rode with the lead vehicle, and after they parked, he guided the others to the run-down funhouse.

"I saw them haul the rifles in there," he told them.

One of the militants struggled briefly with the lock, trying to spring it with a crude pick, but when he failed, another Natchapo drew a .44 Magnum pistol and motioned for everyone to stand back. He fired a round at the lock, battering it enough so that the bolt could be easily jimmied free.

Using flashlights, the men poured into the service area and began searching for the crates. They spread out and scoured the ride itself as well as the backstage area without finding anything. It didn't take long before seeds of doubt began to form in the minds of Gwynn's newfound disciples.

"Are you sure about this?" groused Don Kellan, a Blyford loyalist who'd been one of the least inclined to back Gwynn as the outfit's new leader.

"Positive," Gwynn shouted back. He was beginning to lose patience himself. He wondered if perhaps Ovitz or Tompkins had doubled back after leaving the site. There were other grumblings, and Gwynn worried further that he was in danger of losing control of the men as quickly as he'd gained it. Finally, however, his friend Jerry Salpen, a tall, jug-eared man wearing an ever-present Atlanta Braves cap, stumbled upon the hidden switch by the workbench and triggered the openings of the concealed door.

"Yes!" Gwynn cried out as he helped Salpen and another Natchapo pull the door open.

"Holy shit!" Kellan exclaimed when he flashed his light into the cavern and laid eyes on the wealth of munitions secreted inside. The other members of the Militia voiced similar sentiments as they entered. The dead prospector lay rotting in one corner, and a handful of rats fled from his corpse when beams of light flashed their way.

"I can't believe all this!" Salpen dragged his hand over a box filled with fragmentation grenades. "We're gonna be able to kick some real ass now! We'll make those bastards pay."

"Yes, we will," Gwynn promised, smiling triumphantly. "First let's see what we have here, then we'll figure out where to strike, and when."

CHAPTER TWENTY-TWO

Tomi Leitchen was paying a bellhop for two-fifths of room-service Kentucky bourbon when Tompkins and Ovitz arrived at his room at the Walk Inn.

"C'mon in," he told the men as he stuffed two twenty-dollar bills into the bellhop's hand. "Here, keep the change."

"Thank you, sir." The bellhop waited for Ovitz and Tompkins to enter, then strode out of the room. Leitchen put out a Do Not Disturb sign, then closed the door and threw the dead bolt.

"So good to see you," he beamed, extending a hand to Ovitz.

"Likewise. You remember Marlowe."

"Of course." Leitchen shook hands with Tompkins, then gestured at the bourbon. "I even remembered what you like to drink. Help yourselves."

"What a guy," Ovitz said, cracking the seal on one of the bottles.

The room was far more modest than the suite Leitchen had stayed at in Monte Carlo, but it still had its share of comforts, including a spacious living room with overstuffed leather furniture. As Ovitz poured drinks for everyone, Tompkins settled into an armchair next to the coffee table.

"You're in town early," he told the Puerto Rican. "The deal was set for next week."

Leitchen nodded. "Very true, but in my business sometimes things change. In this case for the better."

"So you told us." Ovitz stayed on his feet, nursing his drink as he paced before a stone fireplace. "How about if we get a little more specific?"

"Yes, of course." Leitchen sat down across from Tompkins and propped his feet on the coffee table. "I've met some new people. Very well connected. They represent a lot of buyers—Third World mostly. There's much demand for product, and it seems they have a lot to spend."

"My kind of people," Ovitz commented.

"Exactly, and of course I thought of you two right away." Leitchen sampled his drink, then said, "Tell me, besides the carbines we discussed earlier, what else do you have to offer?"

Tompkins and Ovitz exchanged glances, then Ovitz told the Puerto Rican, "It's not like we put out a summer catalog, ya know? Some stuff we have on hand, other stuff we can get hold of—if the price is right."

"Like a wholesaler," Leitchen ventured.

"I guess you might say that."

"But can't you be any more precise about this 'stuff'?" Leitchen asked. "I mean, if I knew exactly what you had access to, I could steer you to the right people."

"That so?" Ovitz said.

"Let me give you an example. Since the Iraqis were caught up in that sting a while back trying to buy nuclear triggers, they've been desperate to link up with a new supplier. Why, I even read in the papers today that it looks like they were trying to do some business under the counter with a firm right here in Tucson. Reed-Blackpoint. Have you heard of them?"

"Quit beating around the bush, Tomi," Ovitz answered evasively.

"Very well," Leitchen said. "I think perhaps these new friends of mine might be able to broker for the Iraqis and get you top dollar for, say, old fuel rods."

Ovitz shook his head. "Haven't got 'em."

"And you can't get your hands on any?"

"Not likely."

"I see. And would that be because they aren't part of standard Air Force inventory?"

Ovitz stopped pacing and stared hard at the Puerto Rican. "Why do you say that?"

Leitchen shrugged. "Just guessing. Arizona is, after all, mostly an Air Force state. It only makes sense that you'd be getting your goods from them."

"Time out." Ovitz set down his drink and wandered over to the television set. He turned it on, cranking up the volume until the room was loud with the play-by-play of a Rangers-Angels ball game. Then he pulled out his pocket sensor and began waving it around the room, eyes on the dial.

"What's this all about?" Leitchen demanded.

"Just a precaution. You're beginning to sound like some kind of undercover G-man."

Leitchen laughed. "I am?"

"Matter of fact, yeah." Tompkins pulled out his automatic and let it rest in his lap. He eyed Leitchen skeptically. "Be a real shame if we found out you were trying to set us up."

"Well, you can look all you like." Leitchen stood up, unbuttoning his shirt and pulling it open so that the men could see his bare chest. "See? I'm not wired. I have nothing to hide. I should take this as an insult."

"Take it any way you like," Ovitz called out from the bedroom. He returned moments later and waved his sensor around the kitchen, then finally flicked it off and turned down the volume on the television. "Okay, where were we?"

Leitchen finished his drink and buttoned his shirt, grumbling sullenly. "I was just about to ask you to leave."

"Come on, Tomi," Tompkins said. "Don't get sore. Sit down. Let's talk."

Ovitz ventured over with the bourbon and refilled Leitchen's glass. The Puerto Rican eyed him angrily, but took the drink and sat back down.

"Okay," he said. "You want to know the truth? I asked you about your Air Force connections because I think I can bring you a wider base of suppliers to tap from. Okay? I want to make us all a little richer."

Ovitz quit pacing and sat down on the edge of the coffee table. "We're listening."

"One of these new people I've met is a woman. She knows a lot of money people, and not just in the military. She's someone who can generate business even when the arms market is flat. Artworks, computers, hotel chains—she has her fingers in many pies, so to speak."

Ovitz felt the back of his neck reddening. He couldn't believe what he was hearing.

"This woman," he said hoarsely, "what's her name?"

"Witt," Leitchen replied casually. "Alisha Witt."

"Son of a bitch," Tompkins muttered.

The Puerto Rican feigned surprise. "Oh, you know her?"

"Yeah, we know her," Tompkins said.

"Then you know how well connected she is."

"You could say that," Tompkins replied.

Ovitz's whole face was flushed now. He stood again and turned away from Leitchen as he tried to get a grip on himself. This couldn't be happening, he told himself. Alisha and Tomi Leitchen? It wasn't possible.

"She says she wants to be partners with me," Leitchen said, "but I'm thinking I'll play along with her, meet her people, then get rid of her and join forces with you."

Tompkins grinned, enjoying Ovitz's obvious discomfort. He told Leitchen, "This is awfully big of you, Tomi, but why so generous? Why not handle this alone?"

"Because of this," Leitchen said, clutching the skin of his forearm between his thumb and index finger. "I'm a brown man, and this is a white man's world. I have to be realistic."

Ovitz knocked back his drink and poured another one. With as much forced calm as he could muster, he asked, "And what makes you think you can get the information you need from Alisha?"

"Oh, I have her wrapped around my little finger," Leitchen boasted with a light laugh. Clutching his groin, he chuckled and said, "Well, actually I have her wrapped around something bigger than my finger, but...you know what I mean."

"Yeah, we sure do," Tompkins sniggered. "Right, Cal?"

Ovitz said nothing. The bourbon burned its way down his throat and turned to lead in his stomach. He wanted to yank out his Browning and empty it into the Puerto Rican's smirking face. Another, even darker urge focused his rage on the woman he felt had betrayed him.

"Right," he finally muttered.

"Oh, she's a piece of work, I tell you," Leitchen went on. "We met in Monte Carlo at a poker game. She was hustling me and three other men. One was a general from NATO. She had his tongue hanging halfway out of his head all night, and when he tried to follow her to his room, what does she do? She kills him!"

"What!" Tompkins exclaimed.

Leitchen laughed. "You heard me. Knocked him off a fifth-story railing and then went crying to the authorities that he tried to rape her."

"Maybe that's what happened," Ovitz said coldly.

Leitchen shook his head. "No, I don't think so. This woman, she's a...what do you call it? A nymphomaniac. Yes, a nymphomaniac. She just can't get enough!"

"Gee, where have I heard that before," Tompkins wondered aloud with mock innocence, eyes on his partner.

Ovitz busied himself with a cigarette. He filled his lungs with smoke, then vented it in an angry cloud. "Hey, look, Tomi," he snapped, "we aren't in a fucking high-school locker room, all right? You want to crow about your sex life, save it for somebody else."

"Hmm, seems I struck a nerve. You and her, you have something going on?"

"Let's talk business, all right?" Ovitz retorted.

"But I am," Leitchen insisted. "I'm just trying to figure something out, that's all."

"Figure out what?" Tompkins asked.

"Well, if you must know," the Puerto Rican said, breaking into a laugh, "she wanted me to hire you two to kill her."

"What?" Tompkins was shocked.

"That's what she said," Leitchen insisted. "What I can't figure out is why."

Ovitz was dumbstruck. None of this made any sense. Alisha was his lover, his ally. They were going to carve out an empire together. And now she was trying to get Tompkins and him to kill her? Why? What the hell could be going on in that woman's mind?

Suddenly Ovitz began to smile. In a flash it all came to him. This was a test. Alisha was testing his loyalty. She hadn't slept with Leitchen at all; it was just part of a story she'd had the Puerto Rican concoct to see how he, Ovitz, would react. Of course! That had to be it! And so far he'd proved himself, letting his anger show. Leitchen would report that he'd defended Alisha from the get-go. But that wasn't enough, he reasoned. There was need for a grander gesture, a true indication that Ovitz was a worthy ally for her.

"You're smiling, Mr. Ovitz," Leitchen observed. "Do you know why she'd make this bizarre request?"

Ovitz pulled out his gun and aimed it at Leitchen's face. "One more bad word about Alisha Witt and you're dead."

"Mr. Ovitz..."

"Understand?" He flicked off the gun's safety. "Do you understand?"

Leitchen's gaze locked onto the gun's lethal barrel. "Y-y-yes," he stammered.

"Louder!" Ovitz demanded.

"Yes, I understand!"

Ovitz lowered the gun slowly but kept his eyes trained on the Puerto Rican. "You know what I think this is all about, Tomi? I don't think Alisha mentioned anything about Marlowe and me killing her. No, I think that's your idea."

"No, I swear—"

"I think you came here hoping you could bait one of us into killing her so you could move in on her turf," Ovitz said, trying to spell it out the way he'd want Alisha to hear it. "Forget it. Matter of fact, let's forget the whole deal."

"Hey, wait a minute," Tompkins protested.

"Yes," Leitchen added. "You're mistaken about all this, Mr. Ovitz. Don't be a fool and spoil a perfectly good business relationship because of a woman."

"Shut up!"

Ovitz holstered his Browning and finished his drink, then flung the glass into the fireplace. While Tompkins and Leitchen were distracted by the outburst, Ovitz reached inside his coat and pulled out a small homing device the size of a dime. He moved quickly to Leitchen's suitcase, which lay open on a caddy inside a walk-in closet. He picked it up and swung it around, spilling its contents around the room. "I'll drill you full of lead and let the goddamn maid think you got offed by some burglar. What do you think of that, huh? You fucking bastard!"

"This is an outrage!" Leitchen railed.

"Hey, Cal, knock it off!" Tompkins protested.

Ovitz turned away from the other men long enough to wedge the homing device out of sight inside the suitcase, then flung it back into the closet and headed for the door, telling Tompkins, "You want to deal with this scumbag, fine. Count me out."

As his partner stormed out the room, Tompkins stood and glanced apologetically at Leitchen. "He's gone a little heavy on the sauce tonight, Tomi. Guy doesn't know what he's saying."

"I hope not," Leitchen said, the fear gone from his eyes and replaced by indignation. "I didn't take you into my confidence to be treated like this!"

"Let me talk some sense into him," Tompkins said as he started for the door.

"He's a madman!"

"No, he's just drunk... and maybe a little jealous. We'll get back to you tomorrow. You'll still be here?"

"Perhaps," Leitchen said coldly. "Perhaps not."

"Please, just stay put. I'll make it worth your while. I promise."

Leitchen hesitated, then picked up one of his rumpled shirts and stared at Tompkins. "Fine. But I demand an apology—from his lips!"

"I'll do what I can."

Tompkins closed the door and strode hurriedly down the hallway, catching up with Ovitz near the elevators. "Are you off your nut or what?"

"None of your damn business!"

"What? Hey, partner!" Tompkins retorted, following Ovitz into the elevator. "You fly off the handle and blow our best chance of unloading a few million dollars' worth of goods just because you think he's been plugging that Witt bitch, and you tell me it's none of my business?"

"I don't want to talk about it!" Ovitz pressed the button for the lobby and the elevator began to descend. They continued to argue all the way to the ground floor. When they exited from the elevators and headed out of the lobby, Ovitz detoured toward the bar, saying, "I'm gonna have a drink."

"You've had too much already."

"Get lost!"

"Fine," Tompkins said, struggling to keep his voice under control. "I'm going to stop by the office and run off an inventory list of what we have on hand."

"What for?"

"So we can smooth things over tomorrow, close a quick deal and get out of town for a while, all right?"

Ovitz waved Tompkins away. "Go ahead. Do what you want."

"And you stay away from Leitchen," Tompkins warned. "Give him the night to cool off."

Ovitz didn't answer. He turned his back on his partner and headed into the bar. As Tompkins shook his head and headed out the main entrance, Ovitz settled into a corner booth that gave him a full view of the lobby. When a waiter came by, he ordered coffee. He wanted to sober up, quick. If Leitchen was to leave the hotel, he wanted to be ready to follow. Something in his gut told him that Alisha Witt was in town, come to make sure Ovitz would prove himself worthy of her. He was going to follow Leitchen to Alisha, put a bullet through the Puerto Rican right in front of her, then declare himself ready to receive his due.

The waiter returned with a small carafe of coffee, filling a cup for Ovitz. He took a sip, then lit what he figured would be the first of many cigarettes. Staring out at the lobby, he saw a man emerge from the elevator. He had no way of knowing that it was Jack, Alisha Witt's chauffeur.

The man was carrying a small attaché case that continued a tape recorder and a suction microphone. Unbeknownst to Ovitz or the Puerto Rican, he'd been staying in the suite adjacent to Leitchen's since early that afternoon, and although he'd had to shut off the microphone during Ovitz's search of Leitchen's suite, Jack was sure he hadn't missed anything significant. The best of the rendezvous was on tape, and he felt sure his boss was in for an illuminating earful.

CHAPTER TWENTY-THREE

Leaving the Natchapo settlement, Jack Grimaldi was only able to follow tire tracks from the air for a few miles before losing them on an asphalt road. By changing tactics and flying the chopper in a gradually widening circle, however, he was able to pinpoint what seemed to be the nearest public phone, located outside a liquor store just beyond the reservation.

After setting down the chopper, he went with Schwarz and Blancanales to question the proprietor, who confirmed that he'd seen a man using the phone at roughly the same time the FBI had received the phone tip that had led to the arrest of Carney Jones. Equally significant, the owner recalled that the man had turned his back when he thought he was being watched, then quickly left after being on the phone less than fifteen seconds. The owner hadn't gotten a look at what kind of vehicle the man was driving, but when the three men left the store and questioned some of the Natchapos still loitering in the parking lot, they not only got a decent description of the caller but also learned that he'd been driving a panel truck belonging to some geological survey outfit.

As they returned to the chopper, Schwarz passed along their findings to Brognola, who in turn promised to contact the authorities and have an APB put out on the truck. Although on the surface it seemed as if they were at last on the verge of a major breakthrough, they knew that the bottom line was really unchanged. Barring the unlikely chance that the truck would be spotted and its driver apprehended, Bolan and Able Team were essentially back at square one.

And so it was decided that while Grimaldi continued aerial surveillance in the hope of spotting either the survey truck or the missing members of the Natchapo Armed Militia, the others would begin to look into the various outfits that Pat Inston and Randy Walker had been investigating prior to their murders. Splitting up so that they could cover more ground, Brognola and Kissinger went to stake out Mumdal Surveillance Systems, while Schwarz and Blancanales covered Woodward Electronics.

That left Bolan and Lyons with Tompkins-Ovitz Security, and within two minutes of entering the Perimeter Trust building, the two men hit pay dirt.

At the ground-floor guard station, Bolan flashed credentials at Ken, the man on duty, and explained that they were looking into the death of Randy Walker and wondered if he'd been in the building the previous night for a bodyguard class at the Tompkins-Ovitz suite.

"He sure was," Ken replied with a knowing smile. He had the look of someone sitting on privileged information and eager to make an impression with it. "And that ain't all."

"No?"

"No, sir," Ken said. Although there was no one else in the lobby, the guard lowered his voice, taking on a conspiratorial tone of voice. "Mr. Ovitz took me aside and asked me about Mr. Walker."

"Asked you what?"

"Asked me if Walker might have come by sometime when there wasn't a class going on. Like he was suspicious of the guy or something."

Bolan and Lyons exchanged glances, then the warrior asked Ken, "What's Ovitz look like? Is he tall, lean, gray eyes?"

Ken nodded. "That's him, all right. And he's a class-A prick, too, if you don't mind my saying so."

"Any chance he's in tonight?" Lyons asked.

Ken shook his head. "Not unless he's been here since before I came on, and that wouldn't be like him. His partner's here, though."

"Tompkins?"

"Yeah." Ken glanced down at his ledger. "Came in about a half hour ago, matter of fact."

Lyons headed for the elevators and quickly scanned the directory. "Seventh floor," he told Bolan.

The Executioner thanked Ken and followed Lyons into a waiting elevator. As the door hissed closed, both men went to their shoulder harnesses for their automatics.

"I think this could be it," Lyons said.

Neither spoke the rest of the way up. Getting off at the seventh floor, they moved down the hallway toward the Tompkins-Ovitz suite. A janitor was cleaning ashtrays near the drinking fountain and gasped at the sight of the armed men.

"Hey, peace, man!" he said, backing away and throwing his hands into the air.

"Federal agents," Lyons growled, producing his ID and gesturing at the nearby door. "Do you know if Marlowe Tompkins is in there?"

The janitor nodded.

Bolan held his hand out. "You have a master key, don't you?"

The janitor nodded again, fished a set of keys from his pocket and picked out the one Bolan wanted. "Here."

The warrior took the key and motioned to the elevators. "It'd be best if you got off the floor."

"Yes, sir."

Bolan and Lyons waited until the janitor was safely inside the elevator, then moved to the door. The Executioner slid the key in and slowly turned it. The lock gave off a noise like knuckles cracking. Then, shifting his grip to the doorknob, he whispered, "Let's do it."

MARLOWE TOMPKINS WASN'T foolish enough to have an inventory of illegal weapons logged as such in the company computers. For starters, the file containing the information was hidden and not subject to casual access. To pull the data out of the computer's hard disk required a special series of commands, and even then the readout that appeared on the screen made no mention whatsoever of M-1 carbines, missile components or any of the other munitions stored in the bowels of Holwell Mountain. Instead, the monitor displayed what seemed to be a list of baseball players and their performance statistics. Were anyone to wander into the room, Tompkins could have passed off the information as that of his own personal team in a rotisserie league. An avid baseball fan, he'd have had no trouble elaborating on this cover story.

Now, however, he had the entire suite to himself and was little concerned about the need for secrecy. Instead, he meticulously went about decoding the file, merging information from elsewhere in the computer's memories and changing the names of baseball players to those of weapons systems and batting statistics into inventory calculations.

In a little less than four minutes he had the most recent accounting of the weapons cache flashing across the screen, and after he adjusted the numbers to reflect the status of the stolen Air Force carbines, Tompkins cued up the printer and prompted the computer to spit out a hard copy of the inventory. Provided he could smooth things over with Tomi Leitchen in the morning, he'd hand over the list and lay the groundwork for what he hoped would be the biggest transaction since he and Ovitz had begun their clandestine enterprise.

It was while Tompkins was proofreading the printout that he heard the unlatching of the main door. He was down the hall, but his office door was open and he had a clear view of Bolan and Lyons slipping into the suite. Recognizing Bolan, Tompkins sprang away from the computer and reached for his gun. A shot tore into the office, exploding the computer screen and putting the machine out of commission.

Tompkins returned fire, forcing Lyons and Bolan to cover and buying himself enough time to scramble forward and close his office door. He locked it and sprang back as another blast of gunfire chewed through the wood. More concerned with fleeing than facing the enemy, Tompkins barreled across his office, throwing open a second door that led into the conference room where the bodyguard classes were held.

This was no simulated exercise, however, and he was determined to leave no margin for error. He closed the second door behind him and bolted it, then beelined to a credenza built into the wall. The piece of furniture was built on an unseen track, and when he quickly fumbled with a hidden switch, the credenza rolled to one side, revealing the secret entrance to the law offices one floor below.

Tompkins was slipping through the opening when the door crashed inward and Bolan's momentum carried him into the room. Tompkins got off a shot that just missed the warrior's face, then disappeared from view. The credenza began to slide back into place.

Bolan dived across the conference table and lashed out at the credenza with a karate kick that dislodged it from its runners before it could cover the opening.

The Executioner was wary of entering the crawl space, but after getting this close to Tompkins he wasn't about to risk letting the man get away. He grabbed a wastebasket and lowered it into the opening, and when there was no gunfire, he let the receptacle drop, then began to lower himself feetfirst after it. When Lyons appeared in the conference room, Bolan called out, "He went down a floor!"

"I'll try to head him off!" Lyons said.

Bolan dropped into darkness. The crawl space was cramped, less than three feet high and wide, leaving the warrior little room to maneuver. His legs were beginning to ache, and his injured foot started to go numb. He tuned out the discomfort, however, and proceeded. Less than five feet away the crawl space abruptly rounded a bend. Bolan saw light filtering up from a gaping hole where Tompkins had apparently dropped through a section of acoustic ceiling tile to the floor below.

As Bolan inched toward the opening, a shot rang out from below and echoed through the crawl space. The Executioner felt something sting his left shoulder and guessed it was either shrapnel or the ricocheting slug. In either case it was only a flesh wound. He wasn't about to tempt fate by drawing himself closer to the line of fire.

There was enough light seeping into the cavity for the warrior to see an offshoot just to his left. He backtracked and detoured, crawling on his hands and knees as stealthily as possible, constantly testing the surface just ahead of him until he felt another flimsy section of unreinforced ceiling. He had no idea what lay beneath the tile, but he hoped it would be something that would cushion his fall.

Lunging forward, Bolan's weight brought him crashing through the ceiling. The ten-foot drop ended with impact on a roll of inlaid carpet in the half-finished mail room. The warrior tumbled expertly and bounded to his feet. Between the numbness and the pain in his legs and feet he was wobbly when he drew a bead on Tompkins, who was fleeing through an arched doorway that led to the reception area. When Bolan pulled the trigger, what would have normally been a killshot only burrowed into Tompkins's thigh, dropping him to the floor.

"Stay down and toss your gun aside!" Bolan shouted as he advanced toward the doorway.

Tompkins had no intention of surrendering, however. Twisting to one side on the carpet, he swung his gun around. Before he could get another shot off, though, Bolan's Beretta spit three times. Any one of the shots would have been fatal, and the man was dead three times over as he slumped back to the floor, bleeding from the chest, throat and face.

Bolan emerged from the mail room and stood over the dead man. Out of the corner of his eye he had a view of the main hallway. He saw Lyons emerge from the elevator and head for the main door. Leaving the corpse, Bolan limped over and unlocked the door. Lyons glanced in and spied the body.

"He's not going anywhere. Let's check upstairs and see what he was printing out."

"I'm a step ahead of you," Lyons said, taking out the sheet of paper he'd grabbed from Tompkins's printer. "Take a look."

Bolan glanced at the inventory of weapons. His features darkened. "These are mostly Air Force munitions."

"Yeah," Lyons concurred. "And it seems to me he wouldn't have been running off a sheet like this unless he planned to use it."

"Right, and real soon, too." Bolan glanced down at the body. "Let's just hope that whoever he's dealing with can't figure out how to get their hands on the stuff before we do."

CHAPTER TWENTY-FOUR

Suldowyo National Forest had been named after Edwin Suldowyo, who'd surveyed much of Arizona during the nineteenth century on behalf of both the U.S. government and various railroad barons looking to expand their locomotive frontiers into the Southwest. Although the parkland had been given Suldowyo's name in recognition for his prowess as an explorer and naturalist, the man had also made a name for himself prior to these activities.

As a U.S. Army officer during the 1860s, Suldowyo had played a key role in putting down the retaliatory assaults by pockets of warring Natchapos opposing the encroachment of settlers onto their native land. Repeating a successful ploy masterminded by the forces of Colonel Kit Carson against the Navahos less than a year before, in December 1864, Suldowyo's troops had staged a no-holds-barred assault on Natchapo territory along the Little Colorado River near Flagstaff.

As it turned out, few Natchapos in this region had any history of clashing with the white man, and most of them fled at the Army's approach rather than fight. Nevertheless, Suldowyo's troops stuck to their battle plan and laid waste to anything and everything in their path. Hogans and foodstuffs were set ablaze, livestock was butchered, crops were trampled and groves of fruit trees were indiscriminately chopped down.

Homeless and dispirited, those Natchapos not apprehended during the initial assault soon surrendered and endured a forced march to the Fort Sumner holding camp, where the more than eight thousand Navahos displaced by Kit Carson's juggernaut were already languishing. Both groups were allowed to return to their respective homelands by the end of the decade, but for many the humiliation and degradation of their mistreatment cast a pall over their lives and that of their descendants.

The Natchapos, along with the Navahos and other neighboring tribes, had futilely protested the naming of Suldowyo National Forest after one of their most notorious oppressors, and when the surviving members of the Natchapo Armed Militia decided to take action in retaliation for the previous day's attacks against their slain comrades, the park area seemed an appropriate symbolic target, as well as a strategically desirable one.

It was now shortly before dawn. Night had brought the promise of rain. Thunder rumbled faintly in the distance, accompanied by tendrils of lightning that snaked down periodically from dark, swollen clouds massing out over the desert.

Timothy Gwynn spotted one particular flash of lightning and glanced down at his watch, counting off the seconds before it was followed by a peal of thunder. By his calculation, the storm was at least an hour away. If the winds didn't pick up, it might be even longer. He hoped the storm would shift north and bypass the park entirely, but he wasn't going to let the weather forestall his long-awaited chance to rise to the call of destiny.

Glancing over his shoulder, Gwynn signaled to the seventeen other NAM hard-liners. Under cover of the bleak predawn sky, they moved stealthily along the eastern rim of Bannon Canyon, a jagged gash in the earth that formed the boundary between the old Holwell Cavern film property and the national park. With them they carried the spoils of their raid on Ovitz and Tompkins's secret arsenal. Saturday-night specials and cheap revolvers had been discarded in favor of assault rifles and automatic pistols, and more than half the men wore grenade belts loaded with explosives. There were enough backup rounds of ammunition for the men to wage a protracted assault or defense of whatever ground they might choose to make their stand on.

The distant thunder sounded vaguely like mortar shells, stirring Gwynn and several other war veterans with memories of the last time they'd gone to battle, nearly a generation ago in Indochina. Unlike that war, however, this time the men felt a sense of purpose. If they were to lay down their lives today, at least they'd know why. Today they weren't just cannon fodder being sacrificed for the white man's fancy. Today they fought for their own cause.

Gwynn hadn't forgotten his Vietnam training, either, and he led his men down the steep face of the

canyon and across the boulder-strewn gorge with the
same earnest stealth with which he'd stalked Charlie
through the jungles of Southeast Asia. Here, though,
he felt more in command, more attuned to the land.
After all, he'd roamed this territory as a child, sometimes in play, sometimes hunting with his father and
older brothers. He knew how to interpret the play of
shadows across the rock, where to find pockets of land
where there was no breeze to alert prey of his approach, which pathways to avoid if one wanted to
avoid detection from surrounding mountain ridges.

At the far side of the gorge Gwynn called the men
into a huddle. A faint glimmer of morning light had
wormed its way through the gloom, and when Gwynn
unfolded a topographical map of the forest, the others
could see where he was pointing as he began to review
the battle plan one final time.

"Okay. Our primary objective is to take the information center," he told them. "They have a radio
there, and it's the easiest place to defend. But if we
have to, we can also take any one of these lookout posts
used by—"

"Hey, Juan!" a voice suddenly echoed from across
the gorge.

Gwynn glanced up and saw a ten-year-old boy
standing on a rock ledge halfway down the incline
they'd just traversed. It was the same youth who'd
stumbled upon the carnage at the hut the previous day.

"Shit," Gwynn muttered.

"Juan!" the boy cried out again, taking another step toward the canyon floor.

Gwynn turned to Juan Frasas, a short man with tattooed arms and short, graying hair. "Your brother?"

Frasas nodded angrily. "I'll take care of him."

"Good, 'cause if you don't, I will."

Frasas broke away from the group and raced across the gorge as Gwynn turned his attention back to the map. The boy cried out one more time, then fell silent as Frasas roughly cupped a callused hand over his mouth and shook him angrily. The boy wept at first, but finally he nodded and stayed put as Frasas rejoined the group.

"He's okay," he reported.

"He gonna keep his mouth shut?" Gwynn demanded.

"Yeah," Frasas assured him. "He doesn't know what's going on. I said we were going hunting, and he's supposed to wait for us in case we bag so many deer that we have to send for a truck."

"Well, he better not go blowing the whistle on us," Gwynn said, eyeing the child out of the corner of his eye.

"He won't." Frasas picked up the Uzi he'd set aside before tending to his brother. "Let's do it."

Gwynn nodded and stuffed the map back into his pocket. Thunder echoed through the canyon, and when he glanced back the way they'd come, Gwynn could see the young boy shiver slightly as he stared at the sky. His instincts told him that once the storm drew closer, the boy would flee the gorge and probably return to his hogan, sounding the alarm about the missing men. He couldn't risk that happening.

"Juan," he said, "you lead the way. Take Floyd and Chet."

Frasas nodded, signaling for the two youngest and most agile of the warriors to join him. They scrambled over a few boulders and through the mesquite, then were gone from sight. Gwynn looked at the others. "Everyone else break into bands of three and follow at ten-second intervals."

As the group splintered off, Gwynn took aside Lear Younghair, a tall, gangly Natchapo whose front teeth jutted out in a pronounced overbite. He had small, dark eyes that gave him a reptilian look.

"I want you to go back and take the boy to one of the caves so he'll be dry if it rains," Gwynn told Younghair. "Tie him up and gag him, then come and catch up with the rest of us, okay?"

Younghair looked back at the youth uncertainly. "Why me?"

"Just do it," Gwynn commanded. "He trusts you and won't put up a fuss until it's too late."

Younghair sighed and slipped a .357 Magnum into a hip holster, then headed back across the dry river. Gwynn fell in with two of the remaining Natchapos and proceeded to the base of the steep precipice. The rock facing was pocked with indentations and outcroppings that provided sufficient foot and handholds, and despite his missing fingers Gwynn was still able to pull himself up with an adroit skill that would have been the envy of the most seasoned climber.

Atop the cliff was a stone wall, but it was meant more to keep young children from tumbling into the gorge than to prevent outsiders from sneaking into the park. Clearing the barrier, Gwynn scrambled across a well-trodden dirt path and took cover beneath one of the tall pines that were the pride of the forest. Dry needles crunched under his weight as he crouched by the tree trunk, catching his breath. He could see the other teams fanning out in several directions, blending into the foliage.

Gwynn's team took a northern course and headed deeper into the woods. Although more sunlight had found its way through the cloud cover, little of it penetrated the thick canopy of pine branches. Thunder and the fallen needles muffled the men's steps as they made their way, avoiding established pathways. Several times they were startled by wildlife darting from cover, but they didn't encounter any park officials until they were less than a quarter mile from the information center. Gwynn dropped to his haunches at the edge of a clearing and signaled the men with him to do the same.

Up ahead a four-wheel-drive Jeep was parked next to a row of three latrines, and the Natchapos could hear someone whistling inside one of the wooden cubicles. Moments later a middle-aged rancher emerged, holding a scouring brush and a plastic bucket filled with soapy water. He was heading away from Gwynn toward the next latrine when he suddenly stopped whistling and looked around. Across the clearing Gwynn could see Frasas breaking from behind a picnic table and taking cover behind the Jeep, gun in hand.

"Hey!" the ranger called out. "Who is that?"

"Damn," Gwynn muttered under his breath. If the ranger forced Frasas's hand, Gwynn knew the other Indian wouldn't hesitate to fire his gun, and there'd be no mistaking the shot for thunder if someone else in the park service was within earshot.

Gwynn quickly reached down and unsnapped an ankle sheath. The snap drew the attention of the ranger, who whirled around as Gwynn stepped out into the open, flicking his knife, hilt first. The ranger winced, dropping the bucket as he glanced down at the knife that seemed to have suddenly sprouted from his chest. He coughed, and blood spilled out through his lips as he sank to his knees, then toppled over the fallen bucket.

As Frasas circled around the Jeep, Gwynn rushed to the fallen ranger, jerking the knife free and quickly unbuttoning the man's blood-drenched shirt.

"Hey, nice throw." Frasas crouched beside the dead man and helped himself to his watch. Gwynn reached out and cuffed the other man on the head, nearly bowling him over.

"We aren't here to loot!" Gwynn growled.

Frasas said nothing, but glared at Gwynn as he rubbed the side of his face. The storm was almost directly overhead now. Lightning flashed through the treetops; thunder cracked loudly on its heels. Large, cold drops of rain began to pound the dirt.

As he donned the ranger's shirt, Gwynn turned to the two other Natchapos who had followed him from the gorge. "You two, drag this guy off into the brush, then cover up the blood and join up with Juan."

"What about you?" one of them asked.

Gwynn picked up the fallen bucket, emptying a few remaining suds over the body of the slain ranger. As he dropped his MAC-10 into the bucket and headed for the Jeep, he told them, "Might as well make the best of this." He started the vehicle's engine. "Pass the word."

CHAPTER TWENTY-FIVE

Once Tompkins and Ovitz were identified as key pieces, it became easier for Bolan and Able Team to focus on the overall puzzle. They went at it through the night, and the long hours paid off. Things were at last beginning to fall into place.

While waiting for the authorities to arrive after Tompkins's death, Bolan and Lyons quickly searched the seventh-floor offices for Ovitz's and Tompkins's home addresses, then contacted the others with new assignments. Schwarz and Blancanales switched stakeouts, setting up a vigil at Ovitz's west side condominium, while Brognola and Kissinger detoured to Tompkins's home and began a search for further evidence detailing the covert activities of the two security analysts. Air Force Intelligence was alerted and began delving into all its associations with Tompkins-Ovitz Security Services, hoping to unearth the way they'd managed to siphon off munitions and classified secrets from various air bases throughout the state. Meanwhile, Grimaldi stayed in the air, continuing his search for the missing members of the Natchapo Armed Militia.

Back in Virginia, Aaron Kurtzman was roused from bed and sent wheeling to the communications room of

Stony Man headquarters, where he proceeded to delve into the deep waters of CIA personnel files in an attempt to further track the Agency careers of Ovitz and Tompkins. Having already established their relationship with Pat Inston, he was now looking for specific references to work related to the defense industry, munitions inventory or Native American Indians, as well as scanning for particular names, including Clark Reed, Ellis Hayes, Al and Zane Blyford, Tomi Leitchen and, of course, Alisha Witt.

During all this activity, Bolan and Lyons remained at the Perimeter Trust building, hoping to discover further information regarding the whereabouts of the cache of stolen weapons Ovitz and Tompkins supposedly had at their disposal. Although they had Tompkins's computer readout listing the various items, there was nothing on the sheet indicating where the hoard was kept. Figuring that the secret lay somewhere inside Tompkins's computer, Bolan hooked it up to a different monitor than the one he'd shot out. He gained access to a few secret files, but none of them specified a storage area.

Shortly after 3:00 a.m. Bolan and Lyons turned the suite over to Air Force Intelligence officers and slipped into one of the side offices for a couple of hours of much-needed sleep. However, both men were back up at dawn, far from well rested but ready to resume.

While Lyons used his communicator to touch base with the other members of the team, Bolan ventured down the hall and conferred with senior AFI agent

Alex Beauvais, a longtime friend of George Sax. Beauvais pointed out to Bolan that much of the equipment used for training exercises in the conference room was made up of stolen Air Force components. Elsewhere, the agents had managed to turn up a detailed client list of Tompkins-Ovitz Security.

"We figure at least five different places could be fronts for weapons storage," the agent told Bolan.

After he checked the list, Bolan said, "My gut feeling is it's either the old roller-rink complex or the film lot out by Holwell Caverns."

"Well, we're getting warrants drawn up, and we'll check them all out later this morning," Beauvais replied. "In the meantime we're going to stick around and question the help when it shows up."

"Good. You might want to run a thorough check on that legal outfit downstairs, too. I have a feeling Ovitz and Tompkins put in that secret entrance for something else besides a quick getaway."

"We're already on it," Beauvais said. "I can tell you up-front, though, that the Air Force does business with that law firm. So does T. S. Meyler."

"Yeah?"

Beauvais frowned at the expression on Bolan's face. "Why? Do you think he's involved in all this?"

"I'm not sure. I just remember Meyler having something to do with those Nightflasher goggles."

"That's right. One of his subsidiaries makes them."

"I want to check something out." Bolan grabbed a phone and put through a call to Daniel Blackpoint. His hunch proved correct. Blackpoint confirmed that his company was close to perfecting a different style of night-vision goggles that would make the Nightflashers obsolete.

After Bolan hung up and passed along the information, Beauvais said, "Then you think Ovitz and Tompkins were trying to sabotage Reed-Blackpoint on behalf of Meyler?"

Bolan shrugged. "Maybe. It's just a theory."

"We'll keep it in mind." A pocket pager beeped on Beauvais's waist. "Excuse me. I've got to make a quick call."

"That's okay. I want to go run this by my colleagues."

Bolan headed out and started down the main corridor. Glancing out the window, he saw that a storm was closing in. The sky was bleak, and off in the distance bolts of lightning shot down periodically from dark clouds. Despite the threat of rain, though, Tucson was gearing up for another day and traffic was thickening along the main streets and incoming highways. Bolan couldn't believe nearly seven hours had passed since he'd gunned down Tompkins. He made a note to give Barbara Price a quick call to apologize for not having made it back to the Roadrunner.

Lyons was on the communicator when Bolan entered. He looked flushed with excitement. "That's great, Chief. Have Grimaldi swing by and pick us up, then we'll head out there pronto. Over and out."

"What's up?" Bolan asked.

"Plenty." Lyons rose from the desk and led Bolan back out into the hall. "Schwarz checked the answering machine at Marlowe Tompkins's place and turned up a message from Tomi Leitchen. He's in town at a place called the Walk Inn and wanted to meet Tompkins and Ovitz."

"And?"

"Gadgets and the chief just got to the inn," Lyons said. "Tomi left, maybe five, ten minutes ago."

"Left to go where?"

"Well," Lyons said with a triumphant grin, "the bellhop says he had a limo pick him up. Had one of those vanity license plates—Saguaro. Chief ran a check on the registration and got an address of some country estate outside of town. We're going to pay a little visit."

A FEW TENTATIVE DROPS of rain splashed against the taxi windows as Barbara Price rode down the highway. She was exhausted, having been awakened from a fitful night's sleep by thunder shortly before dawn. She was still trying to come to terms with Randy Walker's death, and her anxiety was only compounded by the fact that Bolan hadn't returned to his room during the night. She'd taken small consolation in the fact that Able Team's van was missing from the parking lot, as well, suggesting that the men were still on assignment together. Given the extent of the violence surrounding the mission so far, she was glad that Bolan wasn't on his own as he had been so many times before. She couldn't bear the thought of losing him, too, not on top of everything else.

The thunder continued to play on her nerves. When a particularly loud clap rocked the air as the taxi left the highway, Price instinctively clutched the armrest and shuddered.

"You sure you wanna be going to the park on a day like this, lady?" the cabbie called out, glancing at the woman in the rearview mirror.

"I'll be fine," she insisted, drawing in a deep breath.

"You sure?"

"Yes, thank you."

"Suit yourself."

The driver made a right turn and headed down a two-lane road flanked on either side by tall pines. Two miles later he dropped off Price at the main entrance to Suldowyo National Forest. She stepped back as the man drove away. A solitary drop of rain landed on her cheek and rolled down her face as she headed for the ranger station.

The cabin door opened before Price could reach it. A middle-aged, silver-haired man wearing wire-rimmed glasses and a ranger's uniform glanced out at her.

"Mornin', miss. Not every day we see somebody take a taxi to— Holy Hanna! Barbara, is that you?"

She nodded, smiling stiffly. "Hi, Mr. Reuss."

"Well, I'll be."

Reuss, who was an old friend of both Price and Randy Walker, stepped forward and embraced her briefly, then pulled away, his smile giving way to a look of shared sorrow. "I heard about Randy on the news last night."

Price coughed slightly. "Is Mrs. Reuss still working here, too?"

Reuss nodded. "She heads up docent tours out at the information center. Come on, she'll want to meet you."

The ranger led Price to an old green pickup parked next to the station. They got in and headed off past the first of several camping areas scattered throughout the forest. Because of the weather half the lots were vacant and several families were hurriedly taking their tents down in hopes of checking out before the storm hit full force.

The sky grew darker, thunder continued to roll throughout the park and then rain sprinkled down lightly. Halfway to the information center, Price saw one of the ski lifts reaching up into the mountains as well as a lookout tower rising above the tree line on wooden uprights. The lift was out of service, but there was a ranger on duty in the tower, keeping an eye open for telltale signs of brushfire.

After a quarter mile the road cut back into the forest, then gave way to a clearing where a few other vehicles were parked in a huge lot meant to accommodate visitors during the height of the summer tourist crunch and ski season. Reuss parked and led Price up the walk to the information center, located just off the parking lot on a knoll overlooking the mountains.

Inside the center two teenager volunteers were stocking a pamphlet rack while an older woman rearranged a poster-board display illustrating various hiking routes at the park. When her husband got her attention, Bobbi Reuss was moved to tears by the sight of Barbara Price. The two women drew close for an emotional reunion.

Reuss circled around the counter to pour himself a cup of coffee. He had a clear view of the parking lot, and as he stirred sugar into his coffee, he noticed a Jeep crossing the parking lot and heading toward the information center. Picking up speed, the vehicle suddenly swerved onto a footpath and roared up to the front entrance of the center.

"What the hell's going on!" Reuss exclaimed when he saw Timothy Gwynn yank out a MAC-10 and charge up the steps. The older man cast aside his cup and bolted around the counter, intercepting Gwynn in the doorway. He tried to grab for the Natchapo's gun, but Gwynn was quicker and lashed out, smacking the ranger's jaw with the weapon's stock.

"Oh, my God, Mark!" Bobbi cried out as her husband crumpled to the floor.

"Stay put!" Gwynn warned, aiming the gun at her.

Price gently grabbed the older woman by the shoulder and held her back. Down on the floor Mark Reuss slowly sat up, rubbing his jaw, obviously in great pain.

Off near the pamphlet rack one of the teenagers inched away, extending his hand toward the microphone behind the counter. Gwynn whirled and aimed the MAC-10 at his face, yelling, "Touch that radio and you die."

The teenager froze in place, while the youth beside him had already begun to weep.

Sizing up the situation, Price guessed she was dealing with someone from the Natchapo Armed Militia. She was equally certain that the man would have no qualms about killing all of them at the slightest provocation. Forcing herself to be as calm as possible, she eyed Gwynn and asked, "What do you want?"

"Justice," Gwynn said. "And one way or another we're going to get it."

CHAPTER TWENTY-SIX

The small tape deck played back Tomi Leitchen's boasts of sexual prowess and manipulation. Alisha Witt idly dropped a cube of brown sugar into her coffee and slowly stirred it, watching it dissolve. Barefoot and dressed in a loose-fitting cotton robe, she had a vacant, unaffected look on her face, as if she weren't really listening to the tape. There was a wedge of toast on the plate before her. After taking a sip of coffee, she picked it up and nibbled the crust. Through a sliding glass door just off the dining room, she could see the black acreage of her country estate. Lightning streaked down around the water tower, and Witt smiled salaciously as she ran her tongue along her upper lip, tracking down a stray crumb of toast.

When the tape finished, she calmly switched the deck to Rewind, letting the tape run back to the beginning. As she listened one more time to the conversation between Leitchen, Ovitz and Tompkins at the Walk Inn, the woman pulled an emery board from the pocket of her robe and began doing her nails. She was working on her last pinkie when her valet appeared in the doorway. She turned off the tape deck and glanced up at him. "Yes, Gregory?"

"You wanted me to let you know when Jack returned with Mr. Leitchen."

"Thank you, Gregory. And thank you for breakfast."

"Yes, ma'am. Is there anything else?"

"Yes. Could you put the roof on the cart and bring it around back? I want to take Mr. Leitchen for a little ride."

"Yes, ma'am. I'll get right on it." He turned and left.

Witt quickly finished her nails and the last of her coffee, then retreated to her bedroom, where the valet had laid out her wardrobe for the day. Leaving the undergarments on the bed, she slipped on a satin blouse and black leather skirt, then pulled on a pair of knee-high riding boots. Pausing before a full-length mirror, she drew her hair back and tucked it under a red beret. She turned from side to side.

"Very nice," she told herself. As she raised one foot to the edge of the bed and leaned forward, she glanced back at the mirror, watching the skirt ride up her thigh to a point where it was clear she was wearing nothing beneath it.

"Okay, Tomi, my love," she purred on her way out the door, "let's see just how much I'm wrapped around your little finger."

CAL OVITZ SLOWED DOWN as he passed the entrance to the estate, watching the limo carry Tomi Leitchen up the winding drive toward the distant mansion, which was barely visible from the road. His professional gaze also quickly took in the security setup at the gate. In addition to a pair of remote cameras trained on the entrance, there was also one armed guard visible just inside the wall. And, of course, the steel-mesh gate was already swinging closed on its grooved track.

"So much for strolling in the easy way," Ovitz muttered to himself as he drove to the corner, then took a right turn and eased the Camaro to a stop behind a billboard touting a new housing development under construction a mile up the road.

Browning automatic cradled in his shoulder harness, Ovitz got out of his car and peered through the sprinkling rain at the east wall of the estate. Made of river rock and mortar, the wall was eight feet high and topped with spirals of razor wire—nothing he couldn't compromise with a strong length of rope and bolt cutters.

When another car headed down the road toward him, Ovitz opened the rear trunk lid and leaned in. He had various tools of the trade stocked there, including rope and cutters. Once the car passed, he coiled the rope around his shoulder and stuffed the cutters in the pocket of his coat. He moved to the wall and quickly scrambled upward, using mortar gaps for footing. He looped the rope around a section of the wire, avoiding the razor-edged barbs, then tied knots to form a makeshift harness to support his weight as he freed both hands for the bolt cutters. Another minute of work and Ovitz succeeded in opening the wire wide enough to pull himself through.

Dropping to the ground, he found himself on the estate property. Without hesitation he drew his gun and moved on, using the orchard for cover as he approached the mansion.

TOMI LEITCHEN WAS WAITING patiently in the downstairs living room, admiring a large nude painting of Alisha Witt posing in front of T. S. Meyler's tower window.

"You like?" the woman asked as she entered the room.

"Yes, very much so," Leitchen said with a smile, turning from the painting to take in her black boots and short skirt. "Almost as much as the real thing."

"Flatterer." Witt moved forward and kissed him lightly on the ear. "I have a surprise for you today."

"Oh?"

"Yes." Witt gestured out the window at the distant water tower. "It's up there at the top of the tower."

"What is?"

She smiled mischievously. "If I told you, it wouldn't be a secret."

"But the rain," Leitchen protested faintly. "It's starting to pour."

"I know." She grabbed a sweater and let the Puerto Rican hold it as she slipped her arms through the sleeves. "If we're lucky, maybe it'll let up while we're in the tower. The view from there is wonderful, and you've never lived until you've seen a rainbow in Arizona.''

She tilted her head back, offering him her inviting lips. They kissed briefly, and as she pulled away, Witt noticed the Puerto Rican stealing a glance down the front of her blouse. "Let's go, shall we?"

She led him outside, where Gregory had parked a three-wheeled cart topped with a lightweight shell of clear plastic. There was a padded bench to sit on. Witt slid across to the steering wheel, turning the engine on as Leitchen sat beside her.

"Always full of surprises, aren't you?" Leitchen said.

Alisha laughed lightly. "I try. You're not disappointed, are you?"

"Not so far."

"Good." As she rounded a turn and headed down a narrow asphalt path leading to the water tower, Witt let her legs part slightly, forcing the skirt to ride a few inches up her legs. Leitchen pretended not to notice, but she wasn't fooled. This was going to be easy.

"Hmm, you have a loyal staff," Leitchen muttered, glancing off to his right.

"What's that?"

Leitchen gestured back near the edge of the field of wildflowers. "All this rain and your gardener's still out picking weeds."

Witt glanced back, detecting a man crouched half-hidden in the foliage. Through the rain it was difficult to get a good look at him, and when he turned his back and headed away from them, she shrugged and drove on.

"Actually it's his day off. He likes to fish, though, so he's probably filching a few night crawlers for bait."

They rode silently for a while, then Witt casually asked, "So, Tomi, how was your meeting with Ovitz and Tompkins? Did you find out anything?"

"Not much, but I think Tompkins is going to come up with some kind of inventory of what they've stolen. That should be of some help, yes?"

"Very much so. Anything else? You asked them about killing me, didn't you?"

Leitchen nodded. "They said they'd think about it."

"Oh, did they?"

"I think if the price is right, they'd agree to it," the Puerto Rican confided. "So, as you suspected, they aren't to be trusted."

"I guess not." The woman sighed. And neither was he.

She drove past a pond and pulled to a stop in front of the brick tower. The Puerto Rican's hand drifted across the seat and rested on her right knee.

"I know this isn't the limousine," he whispered suggestively, "but, as you said, the rain is so romantic."

"Now, now..." Witt took Leitchen's hand from her leg and kissed it, then met his smile with one of her own. "You don't want to spoil my surprise, do you?"

"That would spoil it?"

She nodded, gesturing at the tower. "Inside."

He stepped out of the cart and stood in the rain as Witt wriggled past him and unlocked the tower door. The Puerto Rican followed her inside, closing the door behind him. As the woman turned on the light switch, revealing the water tank and spiral staircase, Leitchen frowned. "This is your surprise?"

"Not yet." She pointed upward. "At the top. I'll lead the way."

She started up the stairs, taking them two at a time so that when Leitchen followed he could see up her skirt.

"I'm liking this already."

Witt smiled down at him and laughed. "It only gets better, Tomi. You'll see."

As she led the man up the winding staircase, the storm continued to pour out its fury outside the walls, and between the clapping of thunder and the staccato drumming of the rain, there was no way for either of them to hear the approach of a low-flying helicopter.

"IT'S GETTING PRETTY ROUGH out there," Grimaldi said as he guided the helicopter through the pelting downpour.

"We're just about there," Lyons replied, peering down at the sprawling grounds. "Hey, isn't that a Camaro parked just outside the wall over there?"

Bolan glanced where Ironman was pointing. "Yeah. I can't make out the plates, but it's got to be Ovitz."

"All right," Lyons said. "It's about time some luck ran our way."

"Looks like he's an uninvited guest," Bolan commented as Grimaldi brought the chopper low enough for them to see the gap in the wall's razor wire. "Do a quick pass over the grounds. See if we can find a place to put down without bringing out the royal guard."

"Looks pretty quiet out by that water tower." Grimaldi banked to the right, taking them wide of the mansion, where Jack was out toweling off the limo under a carport. The chauffeur glanced up at them momentarily, then turned back to his work.

Passing over the horse pastures, Grimaldi set his sights on the riding trails that wandered up into the hills near the tower. Puddles of rain were forming along the dirt pathways, and Bolan was intrigued by the sight of fresh footprints in the mud. "If those are Ovitz's, he's headed away from the mansion."

Lyons had a pair of high-power binoculars, and he tracked the prints to the point where they left the hills and slipped down into the field of wildflowers. From there it was only a matter of following the wake of bent stems to figure out where Ovitz was headed.

"He's going for the water tower." Lyons pointed through the chopper's windshield at a figure stealing through the flora. "There."

"It's Ovitz, all right," Bolan confirmed.

"There's a clearing by that pond."

"Go for it." Bolan yanked his Beretta from his shoulder harness. "But come in low enough so you can drop me off on the way. I've got some business to settle with Ovitz."

"Come on, Mack—" Lyons was interrupted by the thump of a bullet ricocheting off the side of the chopper. He glanced down and saw that Ovitz had turned to fire at them.

"Lower!" Bolan shouted at Grimaldi, then aimed his Beretta out the opening and drove Ovitz to cover with a 3-shot blast. As the chopper swooped down to within ten feet of the ground, Bolan leaped out, landing on the soft earth near the edge of the pond. His bad leg gave off a fierce jolt on impact, but the warrior steeled himself against the pain and tumbled to one side, cushioning the fall. The Beretta remained firmly in his grip as he rose to a crouch.

Ovitz got off another shot, bouncing it off a huge boulder rising from the edge of the pond less than a foot away from Bolan. The Executioner swung around his automatic, and for a seemingly timeless second his gaze locked with that of the man who had tried to gun him down in the Reed-Blackpoint semi a few nights earlier. Both men fired simultaneously. Ovitz's shot zipped just under his adversary's gun hand. Bolan was more on the mark, and Ovitz keeled to one side as 9 mm parabellums burrowed between his ribs, ravaging vital organs. He was standing near the opposite edge of the pond, and when his legs gave out under him, he toppled into the water.

Bolan carefully circled around the pond, keeping his gun trained on Ovitz, who bobbed eerily in the shallows, clouding the water with his blood. The warrior waded in and dragged Ovitz ashore, easing him down on the wet grass. Their eyes met again, but there was only the faintest glimmer of life left in Ovitz's gaze.

"The good life," he moaned cryptically, staring past Bolan at the tower. With his last breath his face suddenly darkened and he sputtered, "Kill that bitch!"

AS SHE REACHED the upper platform beneath the studio, Alisha Witt sashayed to the railing overlooking the water tank, singing in a low, sultry voice, "He's a man who needs some teasin'. He's a man I'll soon be pleasin'..."

"Is that so?" Leitchen said as he cleared the last of the steps behind her and paused to catch his breath.

"That's right, lover boy," the woman cooed, leaning back against the railing. Reaching into her sweater pocket, she removed a slender leash connected to a leather collar studded with small steel spikes.

"What's that?" Leitchen asked, cocking an eyebrow.

Witt reached up behind her, fastening one end of the leash to something hidden in the shadows. Then, dangling the collar out in front of her, she whispered, "Down on all fours, Tomi."

"What?"

She smiled wickedly. "Sorry, but you're just so wild I need to put you on a leash."

"Oh?" Leitchen grinned back. "You mean like a dog?"

She raised her skirt. "Yes. Then you can bark and do me like a dog does it, Tomi. I like that."

Leitchen slowly stepped forward. "You do, huh?"

He chuckled lightly and dropped to his knees, then put both hands on the floor, as well. Looking up at Witt, he said, "Bow-wow."

"Oh, that's my good puppy." She took a step forward, crouching as she petted Leitchen's head and fitted the collar around his neck. He stared up her skirt and let his tongue dangle from his mouth as he began to pant.

"Oh, my puppy's hungry, is he?"

Leitchen nodded his head excitedly.

"I knew it." She buckled the collar, and as she stood up she began to unbutton her blouse. "And you're thirsty, too, I'll bet, huh?"

Leitchen grinned and cocked his head back, howling like a coyote. Witt laughed and took another step back to the railing. As she reached up into the shadows again, she said, "Let's give you a little drink, shall we? Then we'll see just how much you have me wrapped around your little finger."

Suddenly alarmed, Leitchen stopped barking. He was beginning to stand when Witt tugged hard on the overhead pulley. She'd attached Leitchen's leash to the concrete counterweight, and before the man had a chance to react, he felt himself being jerked forward. Witt stepped aside, and the leash's chain links clanged off the top of the railing. Leitchen was dragged forward by the plummeting weight. His face slammed into the railing with so much force that his nose shattered, spraying Witt with blood. In quick succession first the weight and then Leitchen plunged into the water below. Water splashed up onto the railing as Witt leaned over and looked down.

There was no trace of the Puerto Rican in the deep, dark water, but she could imagine the gunrunner dangling upside down at the bottom of the tank, probably in shock and disoriented, clawing futilely at the collar as his lungs burned for want of oxygen. Of course, he might have been lucky enough to have snapped his neck on the way over the railing, but she doubted it. More likely he'd die in slow agony, having time to reflect on the price one paid for trying to cross Alisha Witt.

"He's a man who needs some teasin'," she sang to herself as she buttoned her blouse and watched the water ripples slowly settle. "Specially when he's done some treason..."

Witt was suddenly startled at the sound of someone behind her. She whirled around and found herself staring at Mack Bolan and the bore of his Beretta.

"Another man over the railing," the warrior observed. "It's becoming your specialty, eh, Alisha?"

"Who are you?"

"Some people call me the Executioner."

"Oh, is that so?" She forced a seductive smile as she eased her hand down her side. "Some people call me the Dominatrix. Would you like to know why?"

"Not particularly. And keep your hand away from your sweater, okay?"

"Fine," the woman purred. "I'll let *you* take it off for me."

As she began to move toward Bolan, a shadow stretched across the floor, cast by a figure blocking the light coming down from the entrance to the upper studio.

"Alisha?" T. S. Meyler called out, starting down the lowered staircase.

Bolan glanced up, backing away at the same time. Meyler was silhouetted by the studio lights, and the warrior couldn't tell if he was armed. Witt took advantage of Bolan's distraction and reached into the pocket of her sweater. Bolan turned back to her, squeezing off two quick shots with his Beretta. The woman stumbled backward, firing an errant shot before dropping the small .22-caliber pistol she'd drawn from her sweater.

"Bastard," she snarled as she dropped to her knees.

Bolan moved forward, picking up the fallen pistol before Witt could reach it. She crumpled forward, landing facefirst on the cold floor of the platform.

"Alisha!" Meyler stumbled down the steps and lurched past Bolan to the woman's side. Dropping to his knees, he took her hand and rubbed it against his unshaven cheek. He was on the verge of tears. "No. You can't leave me, my pet. You can't leave me."

The Executioner slowly stepped back and holstered his weapon. Behind him Carl Lyons headed up the last flight of steps with his gun at the ready.

"You can put it away," Bolan told him quietly. "It's over."

"No, it isn't, Striker," Lyons told him as he reached the platform.

"What do you mean?"

"It's the Natchapos. They've taken over one of the parks."

Bolan instantly knew the bottom line. "Barbara," he murmured.

Lyons nodded. "She's a hostage."

CHAPTER TWENTY-SEVEN

The siege was in its second hour.

Rain was coming down in torrents at Suldowyo National Forest. The harsh gray sky lit up periodically with jagged scars of lightning. Barricades had been set up at the main entrance. A line of parked police vehicles, SWAT trucks and media vans spilled out along the shoulder of the access road. Campers had already been evacuated from inside the park, and County Sheriff's officers turned back new arrivals who hadn't yet heard of the hostage situation as well as the usual flock of rubberneckers drawn by the prospects of unfolding human tragedy. Drenched TV crews moved through the downpour with determination, trying to draw officials into interviews or otherwise come up with some promising footage that might land them on the evening news. One local station had nearly lost one of its traffic choppers when the pilot had disregarded police warnings and flown across the park, drawing fire from NAM snipers.

When Grimaldi arrived on-site, he set the chopper down on a clearing a few hundred yards from the park entrance. Bolan and Lyons disembarked with him, and they walked up the road, looking for the rest of Able Team.

"Looks like the goddamn circus has come to town," Lyons muttered as he walked between a County Sheriff's cruiser and a caterer's truck where customers were lined up for coffee and hot snacks.

"I guess that makes us one of the opening acts," Grimaldi said, zipping up a waterproof vest. Like the others, he'd changed into combat fatigues and wore a wide-brimmed hat that deflected the rain from his grease-marked face.

"Yep," Lyons said, patting the stun grenades clipped to his belt. "Send in the clowns."

Bolan was in no mood for levity. He remained silent as the men flashed identification at the deputies and were led to a makeshift command post set up inside the ranger station. Schwarz and Blancanales were already there, along with a couple of state troopers and Special Agent José Hesley of the FBI's antiterrorist unit, the man in charge of the hostage situation.

"Kissinger and the chief are out at that old film lot," Schwarz told Bolan after everyone had been introduced. "Near as we can figure, the Natchapos raided Ovitz and Tompkins's hideout for weapons, then trekked here to wreak a little vengeance."

"How bad is it?" Bolan asked.

"No fatalities that we know of," Hesley reported, "but they clearly mean business. Their leader's a guy named Gwynn."

"We know all about him," Grimaldi said.

"They have at least five, maybe eight hostages," Hesley added.

"And how many Natchapos are we talking about?" Lyons asked.

"They won't say other than hinting they've staked out a half-mile perimeter around the information center," Hesley replied. "We've only been able to count five men so far, but my guess is there's at least a dozen, maybe twenty."

"Demands?" Bolan said.

Hesley rolled his eyes and went over to a radio manned by a park officer named Doc. Doc handed Hesley a flyer, on the back of which was scrawled a seven-point list of demands. "They read off a whole grocery list for us. First off they want us to release all NAM members rounded up in yesterday's raid, along with a half-dozen others we've thrown in the can over the past year. Of course, they're calling them 'political prisoners.'"

"What else?"

The agent raided his shirt pocket for a half-chewed cigar. He clamped it between his teeth and rattled the flyer, then resumed listing the demands. "Second, they want official statements from the Air Force and the Justice Department accepting responsibility for both of yesterday's shoot-outs. The one at the salvage yard and the one at the old Baines mine."

"What!" Blancanales exclaimed. "That's ridiculous!"

The FBI agent ignored the outburst and continued. "Three, they want the Air Force to withdraw any and all claims to the disputed land tract in Suldowyo National Forest. Four, they want all present tribal councils as well as the Bureau of Indian Affairs to be abolished and for the individual tribes to institute self-government in a manner fitting with the wishes of their constituency. Five, in the settlement of all other existing land claims by the Natchapo Indian Nation against the U.S. government, they want, get this, five and a half *billion* dollars placed into a trust account, with NAM listed as custodians in perpetuity.''

''Sounds like one of them's a lawyer,'' Blancanales observed. ''I haven't heard this much legal jargon since I drew up my will.''

''Six,'' Hesley read on, ''they want the chief executive officers of all present corporations with mineral extraction operations taking place on or near Natchapo land to publicly apologize for the pillaging of sacred land and to accept personal responsibility for all incidences of cancer among Natchapos that can be attributed to said operations. And, lastly, they want immediate and unconditional amnesty for all participants in this little shindig they're putting on.''

He handed the slip of paper back to the radio operator as the others let the demands soak in. From the looks on their faces it was clear that none of them, including Bolan, felt that any of the demands were going to be met.

''And if they don't get what they want?'' Schwarz asked.

''Well, Gwynn claims that so far nobody's been hurt.'' Hesley glanced at his watch, then added, ''But if they don't have some sort of verifiable guarantee by noon, they say they're going to start killing off hostages. Slow death, Gwynn says, starting with the women. I wouldn't rule out torture, maybe a little maiming.''

Bolan took the news impassively. His eyes were on a map of the parkland posted on the wall. He was already formulating a course of action.

"Sounds like we've got one hell of a mess on our hands," Lyons growled.

"Exactly, gentlemen," Hesley said, "and I know for a fact that the President's on record saying he won't cut deals with terrorists, either here or abroad. So we don't have a lot of options. Negotiating's out."

"What measures have you taken so far besides closing off the park?" Bolan asked.

"We've got more than fifty men spread out awaiting orders," Hesley replied. "But Gwynn says if they spot anyone with guns, the deadline moves up and they start killing."

Bolan turned his attention from the wall map and eyed his cohorts, telling them simply, "We have our work cut out for us."

TIMOTHY GWYNN had called in three other Natchapos to help him hold down the information center. While Gwynn commandeered a post in front of the radio set, Don Kellan kept lookout at the front entrance and Lear Younghair was poised near the back, peering out the anything that moved. Jerry Salpen, Gwynn's jug-eared friend, stood guard over the prisoners, who'd been crowded together into a small room situated just off the information counter. In addition to Barbara Price, the Reusses and the two teenager volunteers, two more park workers had been collared and dragged inside for use as bargaining chips in Gwynn's desperate game.

Like the other prisoners, Price's hands had been tied behind her back, and her ankles were bound together and strapped to the legs of a huge desk taking up most of the side room. The bonds forced her to lean against the desk at an uncomfortable angle. Mark Reuss was tied next to her.

"How's your jaw?" she asked him.

"I'll live," Reuss whispered.

"Not if you keep shooting your mouth off," Salpen warned, aiming his Uzi at the ranger.

"We're just talking," Price reasoned with the man. "If it keeps us from freaking out, you should be glad."

"Guess again. I'd just as soon kill the whole lot of you as look at you, so if you want to push your luck, fine."

"Look," Price pleaded, "my friend Randy Walker was one of the people killed at the Baines mine. You look like you lost someone close to you, too."

"Yeah, that's right," the man said. "I lost a cousin in that raid at the salvage yard. Took a bullet in the brain."

"I'm sorry."

"At least he knew what hit him," Salpen added, throwing off the Uzi's safety. "Which is more than I'll be able to say for you if you make me use this."

"Please don't talk to him," one of the teenagers wailed. "I don't wanna die."

"Don't worry," Price said. "He doesn't look like a killer to me."

Salpen moved forward and placed the barrel of the compact gun against the woman's cheek. "Guess again, bitch."

She fell silent and glanced at a wall clock across the room. There was less than an hour before the first deadline would lapse. If Gwynn held to his word, one of them would be killed then.

"They aren't responding to your demands, are they?" Price taunted. "Time's running out, and pretty soon you'll have to make some hard decisions. Do you realize that?"

"Shut up!" Salpen warned her.

"As long as none of us gets hurt, you still have room to negotiate. But the minute they know one of us has been killed, they're going to come after you. Think about it."

"I told you to shut up!" Salpen lashed out with the back of his hand, slapping Price across the face. She took the blow without complaint, but smiled inwardly. She was making progress. Now if only she had enough time.

"WITH THE WIND letting up, this storm could last for hours," Lyons said as he and Bolan jogged down a muddy trail that ran along the perimeter of the park.

"Hopefully we can use it to our advantage," Bolan replied.

After leaving the command post, they'd split off from Grimaldi, Blancanales and Schwarz, who were circling around from the other direction. Both groups had the same objective—to find a way to get to the information center without alarming NAM gunmen into triggering a bloodbath. But in the event they encountered any gun-wielding Natchapo sentries out in the forest, the men had come prepared to defend themselves. In addition to both stun and fragmentation grenades, Lyons had his Colt Python and Bolan his Beretta.

"Well, the rain cuts down on their visibility, I'll say that much," Lyons muttered as he veered around a deep puddle in the middle of the trail. "Not to mention ours."

"Yeah," Bolan agreed, raising his voice above the loud rumble of thunder, "and we don't have to be quite as dainty on our feet with all this racket. But it's got to be wearing on their nerves, too, and that's not going to help things."

"Look, Mack, I know Barbara'll be okay. She's got a good head on her shoulders."

Bolan nodded, but without much conviction. Savvy could get one only so far when dealing with a terrorist situation. From all the Executioner had come to know about Timothy Gwynn and the other members of the Natchapo Armed Militia, he figured they were acting on impulse, fueled by a thirst to avenge a long string of injustices, both real and imagined. The list of demands they'd passed along to Hesley were as much provocations as anything else. The whole scenario being laid out was that of revolutionary martyrs baiting the enemy into battle so that they could go down in a blaze of glory, taking as many victims with them as possible. Bolan had seen it go down that way more times than he cared to remember.

A few hundred yards down the path, Lyons slowed to a stop and signaled for Bolan to do the same. Together they crouched behind the stump of a fallen tree. Up ahead a sniper was perched on the lower limb of a gnarled pine. Wearing a hooded camou poncho, the man blended in with the foliage and was peering in the opposite direction through the high-powered scope of his Marlin rifle.

"One of ours," Lyons whispered. Unclipping an FBI-issue walkie-talkie that Hesley had given to him back at the command post, Lyons keyed the mike and said, "Ground to Woodpecker. Two friendlies at ten o'clock."

The sniper, who was wearing a headset underneath his hood, glanced down the trail as Lyons and Bolan emerged from cover and approached him. After quick introductions, Lyons asked, "Any sign of them?"

"I've seen two and my partner's got a bead on three more," the rifleman reported, gesturing into the woods. "They're in about two hundred yards, spaced out about every fifty, sixty yards. They've got binoculars, so you're running a risk if you try cutting in anywhere around here."

Bolan moved close to the tree as he took out a topographical map and checked it against the sniper's field report. From the look of it, the militants had staked out a fairly impenetrable perimeter. There seemed to be only one possible weak link. As he pointed to the map, the warrior asked the sniper, "What about the gorge? Do they have that covered?"

"Just one man," the man replied. "They figure that with the rain nobody's gonna be trying to come that way."

"But that's the way they got in, right?"

The sniper nodded. "Probably. Wasn't raining then, though. Big difference."

Bolan glanced at Lyons as he rolled up the map and stuck it back inside his shirt. "Let's go."

Leaving the sniper to his surveillance, the two men continued down the trail. As soon as they came within view of the gorge, however, they broke off from the main hiking path, with Bolan leading the way. They proceeded through a belt of younger trees that provided less cover from the rain, then finally reached a clearing near the edge of the gorge. Most of the area was taken up by an electrical substation that provided the park with its power. The station looked out of place with its brick facade and huge transformers, surrounded by a formidable wire fence.

"According to the map there's a ledge just over the side of the cliff," Bolan said as they approached the fence. "If the rain hasn't slicked it down too much, we can cover a lot of ground without being seen."

"After you."

Both men holstered their weapons as they approached a section of fence that ran flush with the cliff's edge. Bolan went first. He leaned around the outermost corner of the fence and grabbed hold as he jumped forward. Swinging his feet around the corner, he groped for a toehold on the bottom section of the fence.

Lyons followed suit, and the two men inched their way along, refusing to look down at the precipitous drop to the bottom of the gorge. A few times they lost their footing for a second and grimaced from the pain of the wire biting into their fingers as they shifted their weight. Finally they reached a spot where the fence extended down another fifteen feet to a recessed, cave-like ledge that ran along the face of the cliff. The ledge was relatively dry, and the men paused to catch their breath and rub the soreness from their hands. Down below they could see the riverbed beginning to swell from the incessant rain.

Bolan used his communicator to see how the others were faring. Grimaldi reported that he'd split off from Schwarz and Blancanales and was just coming up on a fire tower commandeered by SWAT sharpshooters.

"They say they can pick off five, maybe six Natchapo sentries," Grimaldi told him. "All they need is a green light."

"Make sure they hold off for now." Bolan glanced at his watch. "We still have seventeen minutes before the deadline's up. Lyons and I are working on an end run."

"Good luck. I'm going to try to get a little closer myself. Over and out."

Bolan put away the communicator and started along the ledge. Lyons followed. It was slow going, with the ledge narrowing to less than a foot wide in places. Elsewhere, they had to inch their way through sheets of rainwater dripping like a beaded curtain from the cliff's edge. Novices would have fallen to their deaths several times over, but experience and determination gave the man an edge and soon they reached the point where the ledge abruptly ended. They were still more than twenty feet below the cliff's edge when Bolan pointed up at the glistening rock facing.

"Plenty of handholds," he observed, "but they look as slippery as hell."

"Well, I don't know about you," Lyons said, "but I'm not turning back now."

The Able Team warrior was about to head up when Bolan grabbed his shirtsleeve. "Wait a second," he said, pointing down into the gorge. "Take a look down there."

Lyons looked where Bolan was pointing and saw a boy, bound and gagged, lying just outside a cave near the riverbed. The youth was trying to move but seemed stuck in place, and the water level was rising around him.

"I'll get him," Lyons said. "You go on."

He eased out past the ledge, clawing at the rock and beginning the slow, torturous descent to the canyon floor. Bolan began the equally precarious climb to the top of the cliff. As he had on the fence, he lost his grip several times and nearly plummeted to the rocks below. Finally, however, he was able to pull himself up to the same rock wall the NAM warriors had climbed earlier that morning. He scaled the wall and dropped to the ground, then quickly drew his Beretta.

Twenty yards away a Natchapo sentry suddenly whirled around, bringing his AK-47 into firing position. Bolan worked his trigger twice, dropping the man before he was able to get off a shot. The Executioner stole forward and confirmed that the man was dead, then slung his assault rifle and went back to the wall, glancing down into the gorge.

Lyons had reached the youth and was untying his bonds. Bolan reached him on his walkie-talkie.

"It's the kid brother of one of the militants," Lyons reported. "He says there's eighteen of them, and they're all armed."

"How is he?"

"Scared. Might be suffering from exposure. I'm going to get him to high ground, then I'll be right up. You better start ahead without me."

Signing off, Bolan headed toward the woods. Looking at the ground, he was able to pick out several sets of footprints not yet washed away by the rain. He followed them into the forest, daring any other terrorist to stand between him and Barbara Price.

CHAPTER TWENTY-EIGHT

"Tough gig, huh?" Gadgets asked Blancanales as they crept through the woods.

Pol nodded. The storm was abating, but the pine boughs were still heavy with rainfall, and the man cursed under his breath when a few stray drops found their way down the collar of his fatigues. He was on edge, and getting wet wasn't helping matters.

The park had five different camping grounds, and when Schwarz and Blancanales came upon the largest, it was as if they'd stumbled upon some strange sort of modern-day ghost town. Although there were tents and mobile homes crowding the campsites, almost all of the cars were gone and there was no one about. Smoke rose from a few smoldering fires that had been only partially put out by the rain after the forced evacuation. The only activity besides the steady drizzle was the tussling of two raccoons that had ventured to one of the firepits to claim a huge charred trout left behind in a blackened skillet.

"I thought there was supposed to be a SWAT sniper posted here," Schwarz said, scanning the trees surrounding the campsite.

"Try the gab-box," Pol suggested, gesturing at the walkie-talkie clipped to Schwarz's waist.

"Always looking for the easy way out, huh?" Schwarz grinned as he took the receiver and keyed the microphone. "Ground to Woodpecker. Clearance M898. Do you read?"

There was no immediate response. As he waited for an answer, Gadgets detected motion out of the corner of his eye and suddenly lunged forward, shoving Blancanales.

"What—"

A gunshot sounded above the storm's retreating thunder. The window of an Airstream trailer directly behind Blancanales shattered as he and Schwarz hit the ground.

Gadgets rolled back to his feet and scrambled to the cover of a brick barbecue. Another bullet chewed at the mortar a few inches from his face. He ducked to the other side of the barbecue and peered out, raising his Colt Government Model .45. His assailant had just vanished behind another trailer.

"I'll circle around," Blancanales called out to his partner, heading in the other direction. Rounding the Airstream, he veered left and approached the nearest woods. A boot was poking out through ferns at the edge of the forest. On closer investigation he saw the crumpled form of a fallen SWAT officer. There was an arrow protruding from the base of the man's skull, and ants swarmed over his bloody neck. Not surprisingly there was no trace of the man's rifle. Pol suspected it was now in the hands of whoever had just taken a shot at him and Schwarz. On the more hopeful side, the sniper's walkie-talkie had been left behind, which meant there was still a chance the Natchapos at the information center hadn't been informed yet that their perimeter had been breached.

Glancing back at the campsite, Blancanales caught a glimpse of Gadgets racing between two tents fifty yards from the Airstream. On a hunch Pol rose to a firing position and kept his eyes trained on the far edge of the campsite. Moments later a Natchapo in fatigues bolted into view, fleeing the campsite for the forest. Pol tracked him with his .45, then squeezed off three rapid bursts.

The retreating man took two of the three shots in his midsection and toppled to the ground in pain, almost losing his grip on his stolen rifle. The militant managed, however, to drag it with him into the bush, and as Blancanales charged across the clearing, he was forced to dive to one side to avoid being nailed by return fire. He landed in a small pile of cinders that jabbed through his clothes and into his flesh. He tuned out the pain and flattened himself as much as possible behind the heap, using it for cover as he sprayed another six shots into the bush where he'd last seen his assailant.

The rain had let up almost completely by now, and the thunder was fainter each time it sounded in the distance. Pol's left knee was in a puddle, and he could feel the water seeping through his pants and up his leg, but he stayed put, not wanting to make himself any more of a target than he already was.

Schwarz, meanwhile, cautiously pulled himself up the ladder mounted on the back of a Winnebago parked at the edge of the campground. He crawled along the roof until he reached a point where he could see the Indian in the bush. The man wasn't moving, but Schwarz trained his gun on him, anyway, as he called out to Pol, "It's okay. I've got him covered."

Pol could see Schwarz from where he was lying. He stood up slowly. Some of the cinders were still clinging to his clothes. Gun in hand, he moved forward until he came upon the fallen terrorist, who was still clutching his rifle. His hand was off the trigger, however, and his eyes, though open, showed no signs of life. Blood drenched the side of his shirt where he'd taken two hits. Blancanales could see that at least one of the slugs had bored its way through the man's heart. He glanced back at the campsite and signaled Schwarz down from the Winnebago.

"Let's hope this is as bloody as it gets," Gadgets said as he joined his comrade.

Blancanales shook his head. "There's another body back by the trailhead. No, I think the bloodbath's just starting."

"NO!" TIMOTHY GWYNN shouted into the microphone. "No extensions! You have our demands, and you have ten minutes left to start answering them or the killing starts!"

As if to emphasize his threat, Gwynn held his submachine gun close to the microphone and rattled off a volley. Splinters of wood showered down as bullets riddled the ceiling.

"Stop it!" the teenage girl tied up next to Bobbi Reuss wailed hysterically.

Gwynn bolted out of his chair, and the hostages watched in horror as he aimed the gun and pumped half a dozen shots into her. She fell silent and slumped to one side, spurting blood onto the other prisoners.

"Anyone else want to shoot their mouths off?" Gwynn seethed, discarding his spent ammo clip and clamping a fresh one in its place. "Go ahead! Scream away!"

The captives said nothing. The surviving teenager was clearly in shock, staring in bewilderment at his slain friend. Bobbi Reuss glared at Gwynn and the other Natchapos, fighting an urge to denounce them.

Barbara Price was equally hard-pressed to keep herself under control. She'd been working at the ropes around her wrists for more than ten minutes, hoping she could somehow wriggle free and get to her purse, which contained a .38-caliber automatic Bolan had insisted she carry despite her protests. The Natchapos hadn't bothered to search her. Now, as she saw the sorry sight of the dead teenager, she realized she'd be able to overcome her reluctance to fire a gun—to kill. She also felt a pang of guilt. After all, she'd been the only one verbally baiting the renegades up until the past couple of minutes, hoping to distract them into making some blunder she could capitalize on.

"Oh, that was real bright, Cochise!" Don Kellan growled. "Kill some fucking girl! What do you think's gonna happen when they find out she's the first one we got rid of, huh?"

"They'll know we're serious."

"Yeah, and they'll also figure that we aren't going to spare anyone and they'll come at us with all they've got."

"No," Gwynn insisted.

"Trust me," Kellan said. "You blew it."

Gwynn faced off with the other Natchapo, and they continued to argue. With her concentration focused on the altercation, Price nearly let out a gasp of surprise when she felt something crawling up her arm. Reuss leaned close to her and whispered, "Don't look."

It was then that she realized Reuss had somehow managed to get his hands free and was in the process of untying her wrists, as well. She remained still and turned her gaze to her purse, lying on the floor less than five feet away. Even with her ankles still bound to the desk, she just might be able to reach it. But first she needed a distraction.

Suddenly they heard distant gunshots coming from one of the campsites. Gwynn and Kellan ceased arguing and looked out the window.

"They're coming," Kellan murmured.

"Bastards! I warned them!" Gwynn turned to Salpen. "Drag that dead girl outside and dump her where they can get a good look at her!"

Gwynn, Kellan and Younghair assumed battle stations near various windows, turning their backs on the prisoners. Salpen leaned his AK-47 against the wall and withdrew a knife, advancing to cut the ropes holding the slain girl. To get to the girl's ankles the Natchapo had to lean over Bobbi Reuss and balance himself by holding on to the edge of the desk with his free hand.

Mark Reuss saw his golden opportunity and seized it. Suddenly lashing out with his freed hands, he grabbed Salpen by the wrist, catching the Natchapo off guard and off balance. Reuss pulled the man close and they wrestled for control of the knife. Rage gave Reuss the edge, and he quickly succeeded in forcing the knife into the Indian's chest, killing him instantly.

During the scuffle, Price sprang into action, as well, throwing herself across the floor and unclasping her purse. By the time Lear Younghair turned to investigate the commotion, Price had out her automatic. Though she was flat on her stomach when she fired at Younghair, one shot was all she needed to bring the man down.

Don Kellan was an open target, too, and although he managed to blast a round into the floor near Price, he had no time to run for cover as she swung her automatic his way and shot again, wounding him in the leg.

Reuss, meanwhile, shoved Salpen aside and grabbed the AK-47. He was no marksman by any means, but the assault rifle's rapid-firing capabilities made up for the meager quality of his aim. Two of twelve blasts found their target, ripping through Kellan's midsection and doubling him over.

That left Gwynn.

Taken by surprise by the rear attack, the leader fired blindly at the prisoners, wounding Bobbi Reuss in the shoulder before he fled out the front door, just avoiding a blast from Price's automatic.

As she heard Gwynn starting up the same Jeep that had brought him to the information center, Price quickly sat up and tore at the knots binding her ankles to the desk. Across from her Reuss used his knife to cut his ankles free, then rushed to his wife's side.

"Are you okay?" he asked.

Bobbi nodded meekly as her husband pressed his hand against her bleeding shoulder. Price took the knife from him and cut loose another ranger, telling him, "Get the others free, then get on the radio and explain what's happened."

"What about you?" the ranger asked.

Price grabbed the AK-47 and headed for the door. "I'm going to get that cowardly bastard if it's the last thing I ever do!"

WITHIN SECONDS after Special Agent Hesley received the radio call from the information center, he passed word to the SWAT snipers that the hostages were no longer in immediate danger. The park's public address system was put into use, telling the Natchapo Armed Militia that it was over and giving them one last chance to surrender.

Certain that the authorities were bluffing, several of the Natchapos guarding the perimeter around the parking lot fired warning shots into the woods. They were answered by an almost uninterrupted fusillade that lasted close to three minutes. Then, one by one, the surviving militants threw down their weapons and moved from cover, hands either in the air or on their heads.

Except for Timothy Gwynn.

Spooked by the sudden change of events, Gwynn drove wildly down the forest paths, both hands on the steering wheel, foot pressing the accelerator to the floorboard. His mind was racing as fast as the Jeep. He was already thinking ahead beyond his escape. He wasn't beaten yet. He'd flee and hide out until he could gather another following. He knew his mistake. He'd gone too fast, tried to grab too much too soon. It wouldn't happen again. Next time he'd take it slowly. Build converts, build an arsenal, plot every move in detail...

Coming up on a sharp turn, Gwynn was forced to let up on the accelerator or risk crashing into a boulder half the size of the Jeep. As he slowed and cranked on the steering wheel, a figure suddenly lunged out from the brush and leaped forward, just managing to grab hold of the tailgate and pull himself aboard.

Gwynn barely managed to negotiate the turn and almost succeeded in shaking Mack Bolan off the vehicle. The Executioner held firm, though, planting both feet on the rear bumper and aiming his Beretta at Gwynn.

"Stop the Jeep!" he shouted.

The man responded by jerking the steering wheel back and forth, swerving sharply from side to side so that Bolan was unable to draw a steady aim. He sped along the same pathway he'd taken to reach the information center, and soon he was coming up on the clearing near the gorge.

"Stop!" Bolan warned a second time.

Gwynn refused, picking up more speed. He freed one hand from the steering wheel and grabbed his submachine gun. He was about to fire over his shoulder when Bolan emptied his Beretta. Gwynn's head snapped to one side as two shots slammed into his skull. Dead at the wheel, the man lost control of the vehicle. The Jeep bounced off a trash receptacle mounted to a concrete upright and went into a sweeping skid. Bolan pushed free and tumbled roughly across the dirt before coming to a rest. He looked up and saw the Jeep spin out toward the edge of the cliff, throwing Gwynn clear as it struck the stone wall and somersaulted.

Bolan slowly rose to his feet and limped to the break in the wall. Peering down, he saw the ravaged Jeep lying in a heap at the bottom of the gorge. Gwynn lay nearby, his body contorted on the rocks. Lyons was down there, too, less than a quarter of the way up the sheer rock facing. He looked up at Bolan and shouted,

"Hey, this is hard enough without you throwing garbage at me!"

The Executioner cracked a grin and stepped back from the wall. Overhead, the clouds were beginning to break, and a dazzling shaft of light poured down from the heavens, creating a rainbow out over the gorge. Bolan heard a sound behind him and turned, bringing his Beretta into firing position. He quickly saw that he wouldn't be needing it, however.

Barbara Price moved out into the clearing, lowering the AK-47. Her stride widened as she approached Bolan, and then she cast the gun aside and ran into his embrace. "Oh, Mack," she whispered, holding him tightly.

"It's okay," he told her, stroking her hair. "It's going to be okay."

From the publishers of AGENTS, an action-driven new miniseries focusing on the war against drugs.

CODE ZERO

D. A. HODGMAN

**Welcome to Deathlands,
where you don't have to
die to go to hell.**

JAMES AXLER
DEATHLANDS®
Chill Factor

Trekking through the ruins of a nuclear-devastated America, Ryan
Cawdor and his nomadic band of warrior-survivalists search for
the secrets of the past that might promise a future.

To rescue his young son enslaved in the frigid North, Ryan must
first face one of his oldest enemies—and play out the deadly fi-
nale to their private war.

**A BID FOR ULTIMATE POWER PITS NOMAD
AGAINST A RUTHLESS TECHNOMESSIAH.**

NOMAD

DAVID ALEXANDER

Code Name: Nomad—an elite operative trained to
fight the ultimate technological war game. Waging
high-stakes battles against technoterrorism, Nomad
is a new breed of commando.

The year is 2030. The battle is over satellite-har-
nessed energy. The enemy is the supercomputer con-
trolling the satellite network. This time, the game is
real—and the prize is life on earth.
